RAVENOUS GHOSTS

Kealan Patrick Burke

ISBN: 148112837X
ISBN-13: 978-1481128377

In Memory of Jack Cady
1932 - 2004
Great writer, great friend

BOOKS by KEALAN PATRICK BURKE

THE TIMMY QUINN SERIES

The Turtle Boy
The Hides
Vessels
Peregrine's Tale
Stage Whispers
Nemesis

NOVELS

Kin
Master of the Moors
Currency of Souls

NOVELLAS

Thirty Miles South of Dry County
You In?
Midlisters
Seldom Seen in August
Saturday Night at Eddie's
Underneath

COLLECTIONS

The Number 121 to Pennsylvania & Others
Theater Macabre
Dead Leaves: 8 Tales of the Witching Season
Dead of Winter
Digital Hell

"The Room Beneath The Stairs" originally appeared in *Wicked Hollow #2* April 2002

"Editor's Choice" originally appeared online at *The Palace of Reason* May 2002

"Cold Skin" originally appeared in *Gothic.Net* September 2002

"Someone To Carve The Pumpkins" originally appeared at *Horrorfind* September 2002

"Familiar Faces" originally appeared in *Wicked Hollow #4* ed. John Hodges (October 2002)

"From Hamlin To Harperville" originally appeared in the PDF promotional anthology *In Search of Monsters* October 2002

"Sparrow Man" originally appeared in *Vicious Shivers*, ed. Cullen Bunn

"The Barbed Lady Wants for Nothing" originally appeared at Horror World

TABLE OF CONTENTS

INTRODUCTION
Jack Cady

'Nightmare' is a much-overused word in the Horror genre: thus, when true nightmares emerge one fumbles for an adequate combination of words to allow 'nightmare' its full meaning. One such combination is surely *Ravenous Ghosts*. These stories by Kealan Patrick Burke are, most certainly, short and jolting nightmares. I don't ever want to dream this kind of stuff, nor would anyone else mildly sane, I think; including Burke.

And, since no one, including Burke, actually wants to dream such stuff, the thoughtful reader has to ask where it's coming from. Obviously it's coming from an imagination, and a context. The imagination is Burke's, the context is the horror genre, and at that point one falters. That's not enough explanation, because the stories rise above the genre in the most unusual fashion. They actually have to do with actions, and consequences.

How different this is from what usually happens in the horror genre. I am sick, from the back-of-my-eyes to six-inches-under-my-toes of stories about stuff that 'just happens'. I am, for example, deadly tired of unexplained monsters appearing in shopping centers, where no one has really done anything to deserve confronting a monster. I am bored with vampires searching for the sacred bloodline of the Virgin Mary, simply because they are meanies. I am, quite frankly, 'up-to-here' with most of the genre, since it attains to nothing greater than warmed-up Hollywood. Or, to put it in concrete terms, the genre is rife with cheap shots. Or, to put it in even more concrete terms, the message is not that Evil exists, but that b.s. exists.

Since no nightmare is ever a cheap shot, but rather a message from the subconscious, these stories command interest (from both writer and reader). They deal with consequences. They even deal with conscience.

I especially liked *From Hamlin To Harperville* where the Pied Piper of Hamlin seeks redemption and makes a grim choice. He has, you see, been out-and-about in the world, and has learned about children. He knows that he once, metaphorically, visited a wrong address, and, no matter what the cost, is not about to go back.

Or, perhaps, I like *Haven* best, because it takes on a knowledge of the existence of Evil. Evil steps out of history, as if unburdened by history, and a fearful past becomes the present as well as the probable future. Evil, in *Haven* is not a casual look at darkening horror; it is horror.

In *The Barbed Lady Wants For Nothing* an awful and immediate future appears in the pages of a comic book. It would not have appeared had the reader not been engaged in robbery. In *Editor's Choice* a man pays a dreadful price for the sin of pride, i.e. listening only to his ego; thus failing to learn anything. In *Not While I'm Around* a woman loses her husband, loses hope, and loses a way of life because of denial.

Stories such as these come not only from imagination and context, but from the subconscious of a writer whose interests are not content with an easy road. They are in the tradition of true horror, the kind where, if you search for the unforgivable sin as in *Ethan Brand*, or commit murder as in *The Black Cat*, retribution follows.

There is, as in Poe if not Hawthorne, an Old World touch to these stories. They come from a modern and educated mind with origins in a mythic background. Burke was born and raised in Ireland. The context of these stories is not so much American or Irish, as expressive of Occidental history and experience. There is nothing Eastern, here; no balancing of good and evil. Instead, there's an awareness of the Dark: of that which lies in the subconscious of the western mind. Poe understood horror in that context. So, obviously, does Burke.

Jack Cady

December 2002

THE DROWNING ROOM

"Summer sun, gonna get me another one
Of those fine-assed women
And a belly full of rum."

"Amen, brother," Jake Quaid told the radio and tapped a steel-toed foot on the accelerator in time with the music. A surreptitious check in the rearview showed nothing but red-tinted darkness behind the Pontiac. The highway was deader than a one-legged mutt at a dogfight, and that suited Jake just fine.

Especially tonight.

As a light speckling of rain breathed across the windshield, Jake fished a cigarette out of the pack wedged between the seats. He inspected the large splash of maroon on the passenger seat and chuckled.

The hooker.

She'd been a pretty little blonde thing with lips that could suck the egg out of a chicken but when he'd tried to get a little more adventurous with her she'd thrown a fit. He'd ended up losing his cool and rammed her face against the door until he heard a crack and she dropped like a sack of meat.

He hadn't meant to kill her.

After all, those stories about guys dying in fights because of a single punch to the nose were just that – stories, right? He'd figured he'd leave her banged up as a lesson not to fuck with Jake Q. Quaid again. When the son of an oil baron asked for something it was best to give it or end up looking like Quasimodo in drag for a few weeks.

He hadn't meant to kill her. No sir. That most certainly hadn't been the plan at all.

As he flipped his Zippo and lighted the cigarette, he shook his head at the senselessness of it all. Killing the whore might have been the end of him, had they not been in an area where no one in their right mind walked after dark. After a second reserved for stark, unbridled panic, he had simply stuffed a few rocks in her mouth and purse and tossed her into the Olentangy River. He soon relaxed enough to laugh about it. After all, who would miss a whore?

Out of the darkness and the worsening rain, the neon lights of a motel danced and wobbled into view. Jake squinted through the smoke at the words:

COBB'S MOTEL: VACANCIES

before they blinked out and he was past them. A low huddle of buildings crept into view beyond a small rise on the right of the road, periodically lit by the pink and blue glow of the sign then once again shrouded in darkness save for intermittent pools of yellow light.

A motel.

Jake scratched his chin. Stubble whispered against his blood-encrusted fingernails.

He *could* stay the night at the motel and get some much-needed rest before continuing on to Virginia in the morning. But that would mean slowing down and if there was anyone on his tail – which he sincerely doubted – then it would give them plenty chance to catch up.

On the other hand, the place looked like a real shithole and probably had countless escape routes courtesy of the many felons that had temporary called it home in the past. And if not, he was an imposing kind of guy and could promise a world of hurt to anyone who looked like a squealer.

In the end though, what decided it for him was the thought of food. He was starving and the image of a steak, rare with some mashed potatoes on the side set his belly flopping like a nailed fish.

With a grin, he wrenched the wheel to the right, cutting across the highway and launching the Pontiac down the uneven dirt road that meandered along the cluster of low gray buildings.

The rain drummed on the roof as he pulled into the parking lot, which he shared with a rust-eaten yellow Volkswagen Bug and a ragtop speedster of some indeterminate breed. He sat for a moment listening to the rain and watching what he took to be the main building. A lone shadow bobbed beyond the grimy glass.

There were perhaps a dozen 'cabins' scattered willy-nilly around the main building, which really looked no different from the cabins apart from the small neon sign out front. That, and the open door. As Jake readied himself to run the short distance to the office, he bet himself twenty bucks they would have a little cutesy bell above the door that would chime his arrival. *Easy twenty*.

With a grin, he flung open the Pontiac door and ran, slightly hunched, into the rain, his good boots splashing in deep muddy puddles that more than once threatened to send him sprawling. Cold water trickled down his neck.

Fucking boots will be mussed up, he thought as he reached the slight overhang at the front of the office. At his feet, a threadbare welcome mat declared: "GOOD HEARTS FLOAT, EVIL HEARTS DROWN."

Yeah, he thought with a smirk, deliberately sidestepping the mat so the majority of the mud from his boots would end up on the manager's floor, *everyone drowns in this fucking rain, baby*.

As he opened the door into the relative warmth of the office, a small silver bell above his head *tinged!* Jake grinned.

"Help you?"

The guy behind the chipped Formica counter was ancient. Bald and more wrinkled than anyone Jake had ever seen. His eyes were close set and milky and after a moment spent waving his hand in front of the old guy's face, Jake realized he was blind. The hands splayed out on either side of the registration book were like ordnance survey maps of the Rockies. Jake approached, still smiling and clopped his boot heels on the bare wood floor until thick globs of mud sloughed off.

"Yeah, I'm looking for a bed. Possibly some food. You do food here?"

The old man smiled, his blank eyes wandering the room. His lips were so badly wrinkled they resembled tiny pink combs. "We have a woman, name's Gertie. She does the cookin' round here. I can't cook for squat."

"That so? Well, could Gertie fix me somethin' to eat?"

"Sure she could!" the old man enthused. "If'n she was here."

Jake nodded, reluctantly relinquishing all hope of being fed.

"I guess if you was real starved I could fix you a sammitch."

Jake dropped his gaze to the man's fingernails. They were dark green. "Naw, forget it. How much you want for a room?"

"Now that we *do* have," the manager said and chuckled as he fumbled beneath the desk and produced a small silver key connected to a ridiculously oversized and rusted metal hoop. "You by yourself?"

"Yeah."

"Just one night?"

"Yeah."

"Well, normally a room'd run you forty bucks, but we all outta the good 'uns this evening, so I'm gonna have to put you in Number One. It ain't the best we got. Gets a bit leaky now and then, so I'll only ask you for twenty if'n you still want it."

"Outta good ones? There's only two cars in the lot."

"Not everybody drives, mister."

Jake frowned. "My gonna be able to sleep in this room?"

"Oh yes, sir. Long as you don't mind a bit o' water."

"How much water?"

"Some. Gertie calls it The Drowning Room."

"Aw for Chrissakes. Here," Jake said, tugging out his wallet and tossing a twenty on the counter. Then, as he watched the old man fumbling for the note, he quickly produced a five and traded it for the twenty. The old man's wandering hands finally settled on the note, felt it, gave Jake an unreadable look, then nodded. "That'll do her," he said. "Just sign your name down on one of them free lines if you don't mind."

He slid the key over the register and Jake took it, then quickly scribbled "F. U. Smiley" before stepping back from the counter. "Vending machines?"

"Sir?"

"I said have you got any vending machines? You know, big steel motherfuckers with slots and candy bars, sometimes even an apple?"

"No call for that kind of language here, mister," the manager said, though he was still smiling as if Jake had told him his wanger had to be a record breaker.

"You didn't answer my question."

"No sir, no vender machines here. Much too expensive and they'd only get themselves all busted with the kind of people we gets in here at times."

Jake scoffed, inwardly chastising his decision to stop here. So far all it had gotten him was irritated, and short a five. He slipped the huge metal ring over his wrist and headed for the door.

"Yours is just around the corner. Number One. Can't miss it."

* * *

In the strained light from the office, the cabin looked the same as all the others – cheap, disused and sagging, something a suicidal carpenter might build between outhouses. The roof was a peaked jumble of jigsaw shingle, some of which were missing. A small square block of incongruous red brick sat atop the mess masquerading as a chimney.

The building was small, a single white-framed window with rotting sills in front.

A hobo'd turn this shit down, Jake thought, disgusted as he threw open the door and hurried inside. The rain hissed into ever-swelling puddles in the parking lot. The sky above the motel murmured the depressing promise of an imminent storm.

Jake slammed the door on the rising wind and flipped on the light.

The room was, as he'd expected, a pigsty.

Here, a small single bed, leaning slightly toward him and wearing sheets knotted with what looked like dried vomit but which was more likely some cheap kind of fabric.

There, a crumpled rug lay half under the bed like a mangled tongue.

Beside the bed was a nightstand; an old rotary phone perched atop it.

The walls looked creased with age, much like the manager and just as appealing.

A sink, bearded with mold.

A toilet, stained and foul.

Fuck it. Jake shrugged out of his denim jacket and flopped down onto the bed. The mattress shrieked, springs stabbing his back, but he decided to ignore it. He was exhausted and with a few hours of shuteye he would be back on the road and far away from the mistake he'd made in Harperville. *Stupid woman*, he thought. *If she'd only done what I asked.*

The wind rattled the window beneath its skin of rain as he sank lower and lower into the dark cradle of sleep.

* * *

Something woke him.

A sound.

Annoyed, he checked his watch and saw that though it felt like he'd only been asleep a few minutes, two hours had passed. He wiped the sand of sleep out of his eyes and sat up with a groan he wasn't sure had come from his mouth or the bed.

He waited, trying to discern what it was that had woken him, and then the wind pounded against the door so hard he almost hit the roof.

"Jeez-*us*," he whispered as a fresh spray of rain hammered against the window.

As he forced himself up from the bed, a sudden ice cold needle pricked the back of his neck and he shivered, looked up and saw the next drop of water readying itself to fall from the crack in the ceiling.

He moved, and another drop splattered against his forehead. Frowning, he wiped away the water and studied the cream-colored ceiling. It was spider-webbed with fissures, some large, some near gaping. All of them leaking.

"Sonofabitch." Clearly, the old fart hadn't been exaggerating. If anything, he'd been dumbing down the fact that the room had more holes than a sieve.

Jake reached for his jacket, driven by the rude awakening, exhaustion and the stress of the day into a mood that demanded some busted heads.

In an instant he was out the door and shivering, his breath pluming before his face.

When he reached the office it was empty.

"Hey, old timer!" he called, peering over the counter into the narrow stretch of darkness he assumed led to the manager's sleeping quarters. "Hey, rise and shine buddy, we got some shit to square away!"

There was no answer. Only the rain and the hollow roar of the wind buffeting the office. Jake gave a rueful grin and rounded the counter, clenching and unclenching his fists as he stormed down the hallway.

The old bastard won't see this *coming,* he thought and laughed aloud at the joke. But when he reached the other side of the office, into what was—as he'd suspected—the old man's living quarters, he found nothing but a cot with springs erupting from the sides, an old portable television with a busted tube stacked atop some wooden boxes and a chair short a leg.

Cursing, the adrenaline already draining out of him, he turned to leave but paused when he saw in the gloom a white rectangle pinned to the wall above the cot. Closer inspection revealed it to be a newspaper clipping. The light was too poor to make it out, so Jake took his Zippo from his pocket and sparked it into life. He brought the flame closer to the cutting and saw a grainy black and white photograph of a body, draped in a white sheet and surrounded by somber uniformed men. The headline read:

WOMAN FOUND DROWNED IN MOTEL ROOM

Jake straightened and rummaged around in his pocket until he found a cigarette. He screwed it between his lips and lighted it, puffing as much smoke as he could into the room as a signature that he'd been here.

"Fucking motels," he said out loud, wondering what kind of a freak kept newspaper clippings of murders on his bedroom wall. He studied the clipping a moment longer, found little of interest then trudged back to his room.

* * *

He stood on the threshold, the door open, the wind nudging him forward like an impatient passenger waiting to board a train.

Water.

Holy fuck!

There were six, maybe seven streams of water pouring freely from the ceiling, bits of plaster flaking away as he watched, widening the holes. One spilled directly onto his pillow, another onto the rug.

Jake moved away from the door and shut it, locking the maelstrom outside. Then he stood, head cocked, watching the streams of water gushing from the ceiling as if they held some kind of magical wonder.

No.

It wasn't wonder.

It was rage.

The sink spat dirty brown water from both its faucets, drawing Jake's attention to where it stood, a pale shape in the gloom. He took a step toward it and the toilet gurgled.

Jake smiled. "Oh this is really something now, ain't it? Whoo-wee! Wait till I get my hands on that goddamn porch monkey, just fucking wait! Steal my goddamn five dollars. Stick me in a hole."

A crack above his head and he quickly sidestepped, expecting another torrent of water down on his head. It didn't come, but when he looked toward the wall behind the bed and saw that it was now a waterfall, thick rivulets cascading over the shoddy wallpaper he laughed and slapped his knee. "They got me!"

The Drowning Room.

"Oh they got me good..."

His smile dropped abruptly, evaporated by the heat of his fury. This was the final straw in a day full of broken camel backs. It was done. Over. His father had always told him to pick his fights. This seemed like as good a fight as any.

Teeth clenched, muscles quivering, he spun on his heel and grabbed the door handle. It rattled in his grip but the door stayed firmly closed.

"What the—"

He tugged. Nothing.

Locked.

Behind him a crunch and smack as another chunk of plaster dropped to the floor. The sound of splashing water grew louder as the streams of water became rivers.

Jake, livid, backed away and kicked out at the door.

It held.

He kicked again.

And again, it held.

"Oh you sorry sons*abitches*!" he roared and gave it one final kick. The vibration traveled up his leg to settle with fiery claws in his knee. He winced and looked down. The water sloshed around his heels.

The room was filling up.

The Drowning Room.

He turned and looked toward the sink, where dark brown brackish water had clogged the plughole and was now spilling over onto the floor.

All right, Jake told himself. *Nothing to worry about. Just water. Break the window and we're gone-ski.*

"Yeah," he said aloud. "And then we'll show 'em a few tricks of our own won't we?"

Thunder rumbled over the cabin.

Jake hurried to the window and tugged the curtains aside, a cry of victory already swelling in his throat.

The old man stood outside the window looking in.

Startled, Jake backed up a step before he remembered himself and quickly slipped off his jacket.

The old man wasn't smiling now. His milky white eyes simply stared.

Jake wrapped the jacket around his fist and moved closer to the glass.

"Won't do you a damn bit of good to break the window, mister," the manager yelled at him.

"That so? Well if it's all the same to you I think I'll try anyway."

As he prepared to send his fist through the glass, there came a tearing noise, a stuttering rip behind him and he turned in time to see a quarter section of the ceiling come crashing down, breaking apart on the sink and toilet. A surge of water flooded into the room from the hole above, bringing the level of flooding up to Jake's knees.

Christ. Where is it all coming from? This can't be just rainwater. And why isn't it draining out through the floorboards?

"People like you belong in the Drowning Room, mister. People like you and that girl."

"What girl?"

"I think you know," the manager said and still did not smile.

"Oh you mean the girl in the newspaper on your wall? The girl

you drowned in here?"

"I didn't kill nobody. Never have never will. The room does that. Room picks who needs teachin'."

Jake rammed his fist against the window and was stunned when it bounced back, the window wobbling from the impact but remaining fully intact.

"Unbreakable," the old man said. "Bad area of town. Keeps the rain out."

And the rain in, Jake added, trying his best not to panic. He looked around the room, all too well aware that the steady flow from the ceiling had brought the water level almost up to his waist in a matter of seconds. He had to get out, and fast.

"So what is it I'm being punished for?" he asked, curious to see if the mad old geezer knew. But when he looked back, the manager was gone, the parking lot lit by intermittent bursts of clean blue light, making silver threads of the rain.

The sky roared and crackled, the rain coming down in a staccato rhythm against what was left of the roof.

Jake closed his eyes for a moment. More words of wisdom from his father drifted through the haze of panic: *I never raised no losers, Jake. There's an answer to anything worth knowing.*

"Think dammit."

The water was ice cold now and lapping at his belt buckle. He tried the door again, throwing himself against it with as much impetus as the water would allow. This time the wood didn't even budge and Jake earned nothing but a sore arm for his efforts.

The storm was right over the motel now, right over *him*, the air alive with electricity.

He tried the door.

He tried the window.

He beat at the walls until his knuckles were raw.

He dove beneath the water and clawed at the boards.

And when he rose from the chill water and stood, it reached his chest.

And as he grit his teeth to hold back the whimpered prayer that crawled across his tongue, he felt the water rise, felt it freezing him, taking him, and he wondered if this was God's doing – justice for murdering the whore.

Yeah. Had to be.

"I didn't mean it dammit! It was an accident. I didn't mean to kill the bitch, okay? All *right?* Is that what you're waiting to hear?"

A rumble from the Heavens, a searing flash of lightning that turned the world blue and the water heaved, carrying him toward the door.

His father's face, good ol' daddy, who liked strong men in more ways than was healthy for his marriage, flashed before him, his jowls jiggling, beady eyes fixed on his son as he kneaded the crotch of his pants. *S'easy to die, Jake. Too easy. And no one knows when that day will come for us, so it's best to keep living loud while your feet are still beneath you.*

He sailed the wave of dark water, the tears flowing freely now as he mourned the life he'd never had, never wanted until the threat of death surrounded him.

...while your feet are still beneath you...

He seethed with feeble rage at the thought of his old man, the hereditary sickness he blamed him for. All the ridiculous choices he'd made once free of him.

The thunder split the heavens. Jake moaned. The window filled with oily dark.

...your feet are still beneath you...

He reached the door, arms out to brace himself.

And his eyes widened with realization.

...your feet...

— *are touching* the floor! He was no longer being held aloft by the water and as he slapped his palms against the wood, he felt an almost debilitating surge of relief at the sight of those black waves sinking lower and lower, draining away through some unseen hole in the floor.

Afraid to move for fear doing so would set it off again, he watched the debris from the ceiling spin in lazy circles as a vortex began in the center of the floor and whipped the miniature tide into a black dervish. A sucking sound, loud enough to make him clamp his hands over his ears, and he closed his eyes.

Waited. And listened to his heart thudding in his ears.

The cold water slid down his legs like the hands of a dead lover and when he opened his eyes again, nothing but sodden debris remained, the bed a wet sack, the rug gone.

Jake allowed himself to breathe, and then to smile.

And then to laugh.

"HA-HA! Fuck *you*, old man, I…"

He stopped as something registered in his peripheral vision.

There was something written on the door, carved in the wood. He tried to remember if it had been there before and decided it hadn't.

How much more fucked up can this get?

The words were tidy, etched with care in the grain.

WHAT HAVE YOU LEARNED?

Jake, struggling to suppress a grin, and with a quick glance over his shoulder to ensure the water really had disappeared, clamped a hand to his soaking chest and affected a sincere expression.

"My lesson," he said as the thunder gave an upset rumble. "I've learned my lesson."

This time there was no lightning.

I've learned that sometimes murder is justified, he thought, as he envisioned what he would do to the old prick that ran the joint.

He allowed the grin free rein when the handle turned freely and the door swung open.

And was smiling, still smiling around the guttural scream that tore free of his mouth as the titanic black wave waiting outside came crashing down upon him.

FAMILIAR FACES

Grant looked at the clock on the dashboard and sighed.

Almost midnight.

He had hoped to be home by now but the conference had gone on a lot longer than scheduled. Worse still, he'd driven two hundred miles to learn nothing new except it was a bad idea to drive two hundred miles for a conference. His boss had been all smiles and friendly shoulder thumps, raising his eyebrows as the cream of the commercial advertising crop entered the room, carrying sleek briefcases and disarming smiles. While his boss had exuded enthusiasm, Grant had found the representatives from AmeriCom smug and condescending. By the torpid applause that greeted their demonstrations, he figured he was not alone in this opinion.

As the hood of the car devoured the blacktop, he rubbed his eyes with a thumb and forefinger and yawned loudly. Like a bad dream, home seemed dimensions away and getting no closer.

He thumbed on the radio and listened to confused static before the bright neon light of a gas station sailed over the horizon through the darkness, beckoning to him with its promise of company like a brightly lit island to a shipwrecked sailor. He took the turn-off and pulled up to the first pump on the way in. Through the security glass set at the far right end of the low squat building opposite the pumps sat the attendant, busy reading a magazine and nodding his head to some distant tune.

Grant filled the car, stretched his aching muscles, and made his way over to the window. He had to tap on the glass to get the attendant's attention, but when finally the guy looked up, Grant was struck with a peculiar sense of déjà vu.

"Hey, sorry about that," the attendant said cheerfully and fixed him with dark, glittering eyes. "The gossip columns in these things are awesome. Makes me feel a whole lot better about any strange habits I might have, y'know?" His laughter sounded like cogs grinding together.

Grant couldn't shake the feeling of familiarity, not with the situation itself, but of the boy's face. Where had he seen him before?

"Do I know you?" he asked, studying his face more closely as the guy leaned forward to retrieve Grant's money card from beneath the protective window.

The attendant frowned and smiled at him as he conducted the transaction. "I don't think so. Are you from around here?"

"No. Ohio."

"I have cousins in Ohio. Columbus. The Greenwoods?"

Grant nodded. "That's probably it. Small world isn't it?"

The attendant nodded and slid the card back to him. "And getting smaller."

Grant considered asking him what he meant by that but decided he was too exhausted to hear the explanation. He thanked the attendant and went back to his car.

As he drove away, he looked in the rearview mirror and saw the guy finger wave at him before the road pulled the station out of view.

The odd feeling of recognition persisted, nagging at his brain like a piece of meat snagged in his teeth.

He was certain he had met the guy before. But where? And when?

You're tired, his mind told him and he had to concede that this was probably the case. He turned up the radio and blinked invisible grains of sand from tired eyes.

Static hissed like an enraged basilisk and he stabbed the off button, squirming in his seat and wishing he were home. Frances had said she'd wait up for him but that had been before the conference had run two hours over schedule, thanks in no small part to those AmeriCom jerks, who had instead of apologizing for the delay, blabbered on and on about 'crowded skies and private jets'.

He resolved to call Frances from the next payphone he met, even if it meant waking her. She wouldn't mind and he needed to hear her voice if for no other reason than to help him shrug off the uneasy feeling sticking to his skin since leaving the gas station.

The image of the attendant waving at him came rushing back and he floored the accelerator, suddenly anxious to put as much distance between himself and the gas station as possible.

The clock read 12:23. At this speed he would make it home in less than an hour unless something stopped him.

And that something manifested itself as a sudden wail behind him. Startled, he looked in the rearview mirror and groaned. Splashes of red and blue lit up the car's interior as a police cruiser inched closer to his fender.

"Damn it," he moaned, and pulled over.

The clock told him ten minutes had passed before the state trooper tapped on his window.

"Morning, sir."

"Good morning, officer."

The trooper looked uncharacteristically friendly despite his imposing height. A miniature network of laugh lines radiated out from beneath his dark glasses and his mouth looked like he seldom wore it angrily.

Dark glasses at night?

"License and registration please, sir."

Grant handed it over. "Was I speeding?"

"'Fraid so. This is a fifty mile an hour zone right here."

"How fast was I going?"

"Sixty-five."

"Oh . . . sorry."

"Just a moment please," the trooper said calmly and walked back to his car. Grant muttered a curse and watched the trooper returning to the cruiser in the mirror on the driver door.

If he was lucky he'd get a ticket, but who knew how tough the cops were out in the sticks. He'd heard stories but now was not the time to give them credence. He was unsettled enough already. Drumming his fingers on the steering wheel and whispering a prayer, he watched the trooper consulting with his partner.

And his eyes widened.

The guy from the gas station.

At least he *looked* like the same guy. Through the windshield of the cop car, Grant couldn't be sure. The man's face was lit only by the green light from the computer display in the cruiser's dashboard. His doubt was overruled by another jolt of déjà vu, this time almost physically painful as it prickled its way across his scalp and down the back of his neck.

After what seemed like hours, the trooper standing outside the car nodded once and walked casually back to Grant's vehicle.

"I'm going to have to write you a ticket, Mr. Wendell."

Grant licked his lips. "I understand. Can I ask you a question?"

The trooper nodded.

Grant cleared his throat. "Who is your partner?"

"Excuse me?"

"The man sitting in your vehicle? Who is he?"

The trooper looked from Grant to the cruiser and back. "That's Trooper Williams. Why do you ask? You know him?"

"I-maybe. Tell me, does he also work at the gas station a few miles back?"

The trooper stared at him for a few moments then made Grant flinch when he burst out laughing. "Hey!" he called back to his partner. "Hey, Danny. C'mere. This guy thinks he knows you. Says you work back at the gas station!"

Grant accepted his paperwork from the chuckling cop. "It's all right really. I just thought I recognized him from somewhere, that's all. Can I go?"

"Uh...you can pay your fine now or send a check to the address on the back. Hey, Danny. Something you're not telling me, bud?" the cop said, his voice brittle with mirth and Grant felt irrational fear surging through him as in the mirror he watched the other trooper step silently from the cruiser.

He's not laughing, Grant thought, his fingers clawing toward the keys dangling in the ignition. "Can I go?"

The question was drowned out by the cop's guffaws as he motioned for his partner to hurry. "Cop by night, pump-jockey by day, huh, Danny?"

"Sir, can I go?" Grant swallowed. The trooper from the car closed on them.

"Just a second, I may need you as a witness if my boy here is moonlighting for Texaco," quipped the trooper, and he backed away to give his partner room to peer in through Grant's window.

Oh shit. He's going to kill us both! Grant thought with sudden, striking clarity as he felt the air shift between him and the window. The other trooper was still laughing.

"Can I . . . " Grant began as a uniform moved into view and a thick-fingered hand clamped down on the door. He started the ignition and hit the accelerator before the face could float down into the window. The other trooper yelled a half-hearted protest, his voice still infected with mirth. Grant drove away as fast as he could without breaking the speed limit again.

What the hell is going on?

In the mirror, he saw one of the troopers shaking his head and walking back to the cruiser. The leisurely pace suggested Grant was not going to be pursued, and for this he was thankful. Not because it might mean another ticket or time in jail, but because it would mean he'd have to face the other one. The attendant who was dressed as a state trooper, or the trooper who'd pretended to be an attendant.

It made Grant's head hurt to think about it. *I'm tired that's all. Been a long day.*

Struggling to regulate his breathing, he tried the radio again. A shriek and he turned it off.

What's wrong with the radio?

What's wrong with me?

Surely it was possible that exhaustion was creating this nightmare, that two cops were now laughing at him and back further a gas station attendant was still flipping through his magazine. Was this how it felt before someone had a nervous breakdown? Was paranoia a symptom of something far worse ahead?

"I'm not crazy," he said aloud and lowered his high beams as a truck coming against him crested the hill. "I'm just tired." He wondered if it would be safer just to check into a Motel 6 for the night rather than risk driving home when his mind had apparently already vetoed the idea.

With his gaze flicking from the road to the odometer to the rearview mirror, he almost sideswiped the eighteen-wheeler coming in the opposite direction. He swung the wheel to the right and gasped as in the blur of motion, a familiar face leered at him from the cab of the truck as it blared its horn and sped by in a cloud of dust.

Grant pulled the car to a halt and gripped the steering wheel with both hands, knuckles white and teeth clenched.

This time he'd been wearing a red baseball hat and his hair had been long but there was no doubt in his mind who had been driving the truck. The face, though he'd only glimpsed it for a split-second, was mocking him, attempting to push him over the edge of reason. It was toying with him.

I'm not crazy, he *is*. The thought offered him little comfort. A story he'd read once where a man was stalked cross-country by a faceless truck-driver in a massive black rig came to mind and he chided himself for being ridiculous. Things like that never happened in real life, especially not in his carefully compartmentalized world.

He restarted the car and drove over the hill, eyes wide and searching for a payphone. *I'll call Francis. She'll tell me I'm being a fool.*

Careful to adhere to the speed limit, he continued on over the dark and endless highway, trying his best to ignore the staring white faces pressed against the windows of passing cars. Trying his best not to feel *watched.* He dared not meet their eyes as they swept past his little metal box for fear of what he might see in them. Murderous rage? Wicked glee? Sympathy? Hate? Accusation?

A pale blob in the distance crawled from the side of the road and stretched itself out as if to grab hold of his car. He whimpered and prepared to mow it down should it be so bold. But as the shape loomed nearer he saw it was nothing more sinister than a hitchhiker, thumb outstretched to snag a ride.

It did not occur to Grant to stop for the hitcher. He was, after all, a young man and, on this highway at least, young men had a habit of wearing the same faces. In the corner of his eye he saw the hitchhiker wave his arms but then he was past him, the man swallowed by darkness.

The relief faded a few miles later when he saw the same hitchhiker.

And then another one.

And another. And another, all sharing the exact same faces. Enraged to the point of violence, Grant swallowed his fear and stamped on the brakes, sending the car into a fishtail that left the front of the vehicle pointing back the way he came. He jumped from the car and stalked toward the hitchhiker, fists clenched, face scarlet.

"What do you want from me, you son-of-a-bitch?"

The hitchhiker said nothing and when Grant got close enough to take a swing at him he saw why.

It was a mannequin.

A very life-like mannequin with flesh-colored skin and a pose perfectly suited to a teenager brimming with attitude. The face stared indifferently at Grant as he frowned and looked it up and down.

Mannequins spread out along the road? What kind of insanity was this?

Yours, his mind hissed and Grant began walking backwards to his car. "Funny."

He swung the car around and continued on, his eyes registering the mannequins dotted along the road, craning his head to look at them even as they turned to look at *him*.

Soon they went unnoticed as Grant's eyes glazed over, the road growing darker, slipping beneath the car like a velvet carpet.

I have to get home. He was nearing hysteria, could feel its hands prodding his back, testing his resilience before it pushed him headlong into the abyss.

I have to. The realization that the attendant was now sitting next to him in the car and drooling fine silvery threads from a mouth that took up the entire lower half of his face gave him no pause.

I have . . . The familiar face from the gas station had been a face he'd recognized at the conference, he knew now with sudden clarity. The face had even then been watching, staring, gloating, worn by a man in a dark suit and light blue silk tie, a man feigning interest in statistics and market reports.

The leader of the AmeriCom group.

He kept us late so I'd be on the road after dark. So they could get me.

In the periphery of his vision, the mannequins were whipping past the car as he shoved his foot down on the accelerator, waving their plastic arms at him, their grins wide and oozing darkness darker than the night, drooling ink and shrieking.

He snapped his head to the right and the attendant was gone.

Frances.

Payphone.

I need . . .

A weight was removed from his chest at the sight of another gas station ahead of him, another neon-lit oasis in the madness of the night. His relief faded quickly however when he saw the crowd milling aimlessly around the parking lot. There were hundreds of them, weaving and staggering, moving with no apparent purpose.

"No," Grant breathed and a hush fell over the crowd as they turned as one to look at him. His heart stopped. "No."

All their faces were the same.

They began to move towards his car like B-movie zombies.

All their faces were familiar.

Their mouths stretched wide into black crescent moons that oozed black nothingness.

All their faces were *his* face.

"No!" he roared and the rear wheels spun as he stamped on the gas.

A thousand figures wearing his likeness staggered closer. It was an obscene sight, an image that transcended nightmare.

He released the brake and the engine cut out with a fading whine.

"What?" Panicked, he looked around the car as if the answer to his predicament lay somewhere nearby.

The crowd surrounded the vehicle. He was watching himself through a million other eyes. A million of *his* eyes.

His breathing ragged, he looked out through the windshield at them, waiting for whatever fate they had in store for him. But they simply stood in a crude circle around the car, watching. And that was much, much worse.

As darkness began to run, pour, ooze from their eyes, a terrible certainty came over Grant.

It no longer mattered if he made it home. There would be no one there he'd want to see.

Frances...

He opened the door, the cool breeze turning the perspiration to ice on his skin.

His wife would not be the woman he'd married.

The mannequins turned their heads to watch his approach, their grins widening.

Frances, forgive me.

He entered their circle, their excitement palpable, coursing through the air around him like glass hornets.

Someone would be waiting at home . . .

I'm sorry.

But no one familiar.

THE BARBED LADY WANTS FOR NOTHING

"The hell kind of name is that for a bookstore?"

I shook my head, only because I didn't want to get into an argument with Kane about the proprietor's choice of title. He was the kind of guy that loved to lose his temper because it served as a distraction, kept him from looking too closely at the shambles his life had become.

Although I never told him as much, I could relate. In fact, I didn't know anyone who couldn't. The world had gone to hell.

Rain ran down my neck in icy streams while Kane huffed and snorted his derision up at the green neon gorgon leering at us from the sign. I nudged him into moving. "C'mon, he'll be closing soon."

Above our heads, the glowing green letters read:

'THE BARBED LADY WANTS FOR NOTHING'

I agreed with Kane that it was an odd name for a store but not one that specialized in rare and out-of-print science fiction novels. I remembered a time when this place had been my utopia.

The small golden bell above the door announced our arrival to the only ears inside the bookshop, those of the venerable Arthur Glimmsbury.

"Egads, a customer. No wait, two customers! Is it Christmas already?" he quipped as we both shuddered off the rain and glided toward him.

He stood behind a waist-high mahogany c   influ
fingers splayed out atop the surface like claws,   "
crimson. He grinned from ear to ear, allowing us   you'
reflections in his silver teeth. Tufts of hair curled   own
pate like frozen smoke, held in place by some lub   shru
were blissfully unfamiliar.   the

Kane grunted and nudged me forward. I sigl   Kan
Arthur for years and though the name had changed   F
my childhood, the bookstore had always been hei   "
of dust and age and mildewing secrets. A quaint c   '
by the barreling, destructive train of time.   feat

I had never considered the old man with the rub   '
his face was a part of the neighborhood that had s   in t
the fine, strapping young criminal that I became
unpleasant of characteristics had brought me back t   pea
the bookstore with the name Kane didn't like, to rok   liste

"So what pleases you on this dismal evening?" A   '
silvery smile and winked, his wrinkled lid making   pla
sound as it slid over the scarlet gem in his eye soc   Ka
Kane snickered.   bej

The rain hissed against the pavement outside, on   bla
by the large plate glass windows. Kane's boots cla
hardwood floor in a Morse code of impatience.

"We're here for your money, Arthur. All of it."   bo

If he'd had an eyebrow, it would have risen wher   wa
of flesh now wrinkled in surprise. Or was it amusemei   kel

"I see. Won't you check out my new comic line f
to rescue some truly ancient copies of *Ray Gunn* and
are some more recent copies of Salamander Nigl   vig
remember they sold out when that bizarre religion cam   ha

"Hey, did you hear what he *said*, old man?"   ve
pushing me aside and slamming his tattooed knuckle
counter. "We didn't come here for comic books. We w
and if you intend to see tomorrow, you'd better ha   pa
where the credits are at, capisce?"   du

This time it was definitely amusement peppering
cheeks.   al

"*Salamander Nights* really took off though, didn't it   in
have thought a comic book would have had such   th

nce on such troubled times? You really should—"

Io, *you* really should clean the wax out of your ears and do what
e told or I'm gonna have to show you a few antiques of my
' Kane said patting the bulge in his raincoat. The old man
ged and the movement allowed me to see the sparkling light in
vall behind him. Understanding flowed over me and I tapped
· on the shoulder.

e spun, teeth clenched. "What?"

ook behind him."

Yeah, what? I—" He trailed off and rage contorted his gaunt
res. "He's a goddamn hologram?"

Looks like it, but he must be projecting himself from somewhere
e store."

ane scoffed. "No wonder he was so ballsy. Well this is just
hy. 'Straight in, straight out' you said. I'm a bigger fool for
ing to you."

That could indeed be the case. It really does pay off to know the
e you intend to rob," Glimmsbury commented. Without a word,
e whipped out his revolver and pumped three bursts into the
weled Holo light in the wall. It fizzed and crackled and coughed
k smoke as Glimmsbury shriveled out of existence.

Ve broke up and began searching the store.

Vhile Kane made as big a mess as possible, knocking over
kshelves and overturning baskets full of cheesy paperbacks, I
dered down the aisles where I knew from past visits the old man
t the ancient comic books.

'Where the hell is he?" Kane roared. "Is there a back room?"

'Yeah, but make sure you lock the front door or we'll have
lantes all over us before we get a chance to look." Bad enough we
the cops to contend with, now neighborhoods were amassing
table armies to keep us from doing what we had to.

He cursed and a moment later, a lock snapped closed.

I found myself in an aisle, six shelves high on both sides and
ked full of old comic books preserved like mummies in their
tproof shrouds.

Images of spacemen in laughably inept attire battling multi-headed
ns on barren dusty planets and sexy, scantily clad beauties caught
the act of shrieking as untold horrors bore down on them, filled
shelves. I smiled despite myself, remembering a childhood not

always tainted by corruption and the many nights in my room reading *Ray Gunn* long after I was supposed to be sleeping. It was a warm memory that I shelved with the promise that it wouldn't stay there forever.

On the center shelf, just above eye-level were all twelve copies of *Salamander Nights*. They were priceless I knew, the dozen copies having sold out immediately on release by fans eager to escape the generic retreads being shoved in their faces in an attempt to restore commercial thinking and family values. *Salamander Nights* had been a rage, a pop phenomenon destined to fade into obscurity but not without leaving a few lives touched by the experience.

Sadly, mine hadn't been one of them.

"What the hell are you doing back there?" Kane said and I looked to my left at his scarecrow-like silhouette at the top of the aisle. "Catching up on your reading?"

"I'll be there in a minute," I said, my eyes alighting on something on the shelf nearest the floor. "Go check out the back room."

"Hey, less ordering, buddy. I don't work for you."

I shrugged. "Whatever. You want the money or not?"

He spat and stalked off muttering obscenities.

But at that moment, his attitude was lost on me. I dropped to my haunches and stared in bewilderment at the comic that had caught my attention. Water pooled around my feet as I reached out and gently picked it up.

"This isn't right," I whispered.

The comic book had a color and ink drawing of the very bookstore in which I now stood clutching the comic book on the cover. The sign above the drawing read: THE BARBED LADY WANTS FOR NOTHING, complete with lovingly rendered green neon gorgon.

The name of the comic was *Salamander Nights: Issue #13*.

"Aha! Gotcha!" Kane yelled in triumph as the sound of screeching metal reached me through the shelves. "I found a door!"

I didn't answer. Couldn't. Compelled by a curiosity long abandoned, I had opened the comic book and was now staring at another picture of the bookstore, smaller and less detailed but with no doubt as to what it represented. I felt my heart turn to cold crystal, sending shards of glass shooting into my throat.

Outside the store stood two men.

A speech bubble hung between them.

Written in small, barely legible lettering inside the bubble was: "The hell kind of name is that for a bookstore?"

The thumping continued as Kane struggled to get the door open.

I flicked through the pages, my eyes stinging with sudden panic at the barely glimpsed images populating the pages.

It was a chronicle of this night, every detail, every nuance and every ounce of dialogue captured, our story set in gloomy colors for the world to see.

Or for *me* to see.

A trick. It had to be. I ran my fingers over the pages, testing it, hoping the ink would run beneath my damp fingers. Such a simple thing could have convinced me that this was an elaborate hoax perpetrated by Glimmsbury but the moisture on my fingertips did nothing but darken the images.

I heard the metal door shriek and clatter, followed by another triumphant holler from Kane. "I got it open! You comin?"

"Just a second," I called to him, hoping the unease hadn't been evident in my voice. Kane would have a field day with any sign of weakness.

"Fine," he answered. "But I get a bigger cut for doing all the grunt work."

I turned the page and there I was, down on my haunches, brooding over a comic book. It was starting to make my head hurt.

The next panel showed Kane battering the door, teeth clenched, with his thick-soled boots leaving muddy rainwater dripping down the blue metal. He had been drawn as the villain, a stereotype, the bad guy who gets his comeuppance in the end by less than pleasant means. Five o' clock shadow shaded his comic book self's jaw, his eyes dark as night as he focused on the task at hand.

The next panel showed him grinning at the open door. A speech bubble snaked from between his yellow teeth.

"It's dark back here," the real-world Kane said and I followed his progress inside by turning the page. I read my lines like an actor at an audition: "So find a light."

I flipped the page and terror stuck like a chicken bone in my throat. I jumped to my feet, almost slipping in the puddle that had gathered while I read. The last page.

"Oh Jesus. Kane!" I cried out, my eyes hopping from panel to panel, from one horrifying image to the next. Amid them all was Glimmsbury, red jeweled eyes sparkling in the gloom, looking like he'd always looked, benign and patient. But this image showed something in his face I had never seen before: Malice.

"Kane!"

"What, what? The hell you screeching for?"

"Get away from the door."

"What?"

I read my lines, the dizzyingly surreal quality of the scene perfect for the comic book in my hands, but utterly horrifying outside it. "I said—" My caricature stopped in mid-sentence.

Four panels from the end. This panel devoted entirely to darkness except for the speech bubble representing Kane's sudden terror. "Hey. What's—"

"Kane, get out of there!" I screamed, wanting to run from the store, wanting to run to help Kane but afraid of the thing the comic book told me was in there with him; refusing to believe this bundle of recycled paper could be right about anything and yet it was. I was watching it unfold.

My shadowed caricature showed my face stretched by fear. Ghostly bubbles over my head told me I could flee, that I could live with the guilt of leaving Kane to die just as I had lived with guilt all my life.

Third panel from the end.

"Oh God!" Kane screamed and I flinched at the sound even though I had known it was coming. I looked back down at the comic book, suddenly and horrifyingly aware that only a series of shelves stood between that door and me.

The shadows in the back room parted like a curtain and Kane became the wearer of that oft-used defensive pose, so popular for comics of this type.

"Kane!"

The second last panel showed a slim pair of light green arms reaching for the stricken victim from somewhere offstage, thorn-like protuberances studding its skin, black tattoos threading their way over the flesh like vines. Over where the darkness concealed its face, the artist had speckled in amber sparks to convey a multitude of hungry eyes. A cheap way of doing it, but oh so very effective now.

And I had full sound effects to accompany the pictures.

I dropped the comic. It fluttered into the puddle on the floor like a dead bird. I ran the length of the aisle and wrestled with the door, forgot the lock, remembered the lock, opened the door and burst out of the store with a scream to drown out those at my heels.

I ran, and ran, propelled by that last scene in a comic book no-one knew existed, that perhaps didn't exist except for two men who'd picked the wrong store to rob.

The last panel.

That hideous image of the store's namesake...

Not nearly so absurd looking in the flesh.

HAVEN

"It's your mother. I'm afraid she's passed away."

Yes, yes. Old news. Never once has he stopped to think about how odd it is that he is so certain. The knowledge was just *there*, shortly before the phone rang, manifesting itself as an ability to breathe unrestricted, to straighten his shoulders and not meet the resistance of her eternal gaze, to dust off a genuine smile and use it without feeling it ephemeral.

Gone, and the days that follow are among the most wonderful he's ever had. Scarcely had he dared to imagine the release could be so full, so overwhelming, allowing him to tread with lightened step and floating heart. He encounters strangers and rather than showing them the top of his head in a cowl of cowardice and shame, he beams at them and bids them the sentiments in accordance with the age of the day. That these greetings are seldom reciprocated bothers him little, for his resolve is growing ever more formidable now that he has only one shadow trailing behind him.

Gone, and the nights exude peace, the mattress accepting his tired bones like clay in the hands of a potter. His dreams are golden, exorcized of the heavy cloying darkness that was the signature of life with Mother. There is no doubt that he loved her, but she molded him into a creature of indifference, isolating him in his own little box of shadow where there was never room for any kind of feeling.

He suspects what little grief he feels at her passing stems from his being accustomed to her constant presence rather than any true emotion on his part. This suspicion in turn ignites guilt, but guilt is something he has learned to master and, aided by his newfound happiness, it is soon beaten into submission.

The celebration of her death is a tawdry affair and Tom finds himself at the hub of a ring of people he doesn't know, or care to. The minister is a patrician man at least twenty years his senior, all practiced smiles and Bible passages as he leads them in a chorus of emotionless verse that rises like startled ravens above the gloomy fall graveyard. The air smells of cold earth and dying leaves.

Tom weathers the condolences, secretly wondering what it is about death that leads people to the assumption that they can immediately insinuate themselves into the lives of the grieving. If anything, he finds a note of condescension in those voices, powered by the look of *there but for the grace of God* in their eyes. It sickens him and reinforces his need to leave as soon as this stunted procession of sympathy is over.

When the last bleak face has moved away, he stuffs his hands into the pockets of his dark overcoat and rounds the church, the sympathizer's last words to him carried on ill-formed tendrils of autumn wind, falling just short of his desire to hear them.

Grumbling, he slips through the wrought-iron church gate, the spire of St. Andrew's like a chiding finger at his back, reminding him who might be watching his disregard for all things sacred. The image weighs on his shoulders like the memory of the woman he has left behind him in the ground. A woman he scarcely knows.

* * *

He has come home to the house on Marrow Lane.

As expected, his mother complains about the length of his hair, how much weight he has lost and asks him why he has bothered to come visit her after so long an absence. Her frequent wincing and moaning about her incessant headaches render his excuses meaningless.

"They steal my sleep and it's getting harder to keep anything down."

"You need to eat to keep your strength up," he replies, feeling achingly redundant and thinking: Who is this woman?

Her dramatics are almost certainly a cry for attention, a trait not unknown to her and worsened by age. He delivers the customary platitudes and takes his leave of her, ushered out on a cloud of protest only silenced by the thick oak door of the house.

* * *

Now, standing before that very same door, running a trimmed fingernail over the cracks and ridges in the wood grain, he ponders the irony of her death.

An aneurysm. If it's any consolation, I doubt she felt a thing. It would have been very sudden.

I see.

Had she been complaining about headaches or dizziness lately?

No. At least, not to me…

Realizing he might have been able to save her had he taken her histrionics seriously brings to mind a far darker question: *Had you known, would you have done anything?*

Brushing the thought aside, he opens the door of the two-story memory vault he used to call home. As he steps into the hall his senses hone in on the smallest, the slightest

(Tommy, is that you?)

of sounds. He waits, the dust settling around him in the chorus of quiet, ears attuned to the soundtrack of the old house. Eventually he straightens, exhales heavily and continues down the hall until he comes to the living room.

From the doorway, he sees the familiar sight of the old 10" television set in the corner opposite. A miniscule and fog-shrouded representation of himself is all that's showing on the vapid eye of the screen as he enters the room.

The beige carpet knots itself beneath his shoes and he resolves to have it torn up as soon as he moves in proper. He suspects that foul, vomit-colored layer of shag is older than himself and he has hated it for as long as he can remember.

The same goes for the sofa, a bloated brown semblance of intestines passing itself off as Naugahyde. The upholstery is ripped, yellow foam winking lewdly at him from elliptical eye-sockets. *Gone,* he thinks, relishing the thought of being rid of these particular harbingers of memory.

His double shadow bids him look up and he nods at the imitation gold chandelier, missing two of its four bulbs, then down to the once white wallpaper, curling from the mildewed plaster beneath...*Gone.*

The photographs, sepia-toned and black and white depictions of stern-faced young men cradling even sterner looking women in their burly arms, people he has never met but who he assumes are his relatives...*Gone.*

Gone, gone, gone. All of it. Anything not immediately pertaining to *his* life will be dumped and with an abandon impervious to the wheedling pleas of sentimentality. It is after all, *his* castle now.

Grinning, he makes his way down the hall to the kitchen.

This room seems smaller than he remembers it and he wonders if it has shrunk in on itself after years of absorbing the auras of subconscious misery from the inhabitants of this place.

The lemon-hued walls seem to sag as he wanders around the room. He sniffs at the leaky radiator with the small plastic bowl beneath the tap to catch the water and shakes his head at the grease-smeared range, the picture on the wall above it speckled with spots so that the faces of the two watercolor children look positively leprous. A foul smell drifts to his nose from the trash compactor beneath the sink. He decides to investigate that some other time.

Against the far wall stands a simple pine table with three chairs and it is here his gaze stalls as the bloated corpse of memory rises to the surface of his mind.

You're a dreamer Tommy, you'll always be a dreamer and a man who spends too much time in his own head never gets a goddamn thing done.

Don't talk to him like that.

I don't remember anyone asking your opinion, Agnes. It's a sweet life for both of you, living in your daydreams while I'm out busting my ass to put food on the table.

Tom stems the flow of recollection, feels it swell against his resistance. The surface of the table is pitted with scratch marks and tiny holes where knives have been used to make a point. Coffee rings on the left—his mother's side of the table—stare up at him like blinded eyes. On the right, paler circles where his father lost himself in the liquid utopia of liquor.

And in the middle where Tom used to sit there is nothing.

He can almost see himself now—a young boy, eyes permanently narrowed in anticipation of a blow that could come at any time, skin sallow, devoid of the youthful glow typical of a child his age, sitting in a chair that only emphasizes his diminutive frame, his parents flanking him like birds of prey, always watching and waiting as if they expect something profound to trickle from his small tight-lipped mouth. But Tommy remains silent as much as possible. It is safer.

Shrugging off the memory, Tom shuffles over to the range and the bulbous white kettle, the base blackened by time and negligence, the handle loose, screws rattling. He opens it and angles it toward the naked bulb behind him. To his surprise it appears moderately clean. Nevertheless, he rinses it until he is sure nothing untoward will end up in his cup, fills it and lights the gas ring beneath, the thought of piping hot coffee staving off the unpleasant chill reminiscence has brought in tow.

Suddenly the blue flame beneath the kettle sputters as the kitchen door drifts open. He turns as it groans wide, allowing him to see down the length of the hallway.

Damn it.

The front door is standing open. He figures he must have forgotten to close it when he came in so drawn was he by the familiar. He stomps down the hall, grabs the door handle and is pushing it closed when a faint shuffling gives him pause. He listens, glances at his wristwatch: almost eight. Not an odd time for people to be out wandering, surely?

Peering around the edge of the door and out onto the cracked pavement reveals nothing except the lazy onset of twilight; the air is heavy, stars twitch into life in the vermillion canvas that hangs above Marrow Lane. A neighborhood dog yips and growls, yips and whines like a violin with ill-tuned strings. Someone yells: "shut that damn dog the hell up," and is ignored.

Tom frowns and shivers at the autumn chill insinuating its way through the fabric of his coat. Just as he is about to shut the door, he catches sight of an old woman standing by the streetlight a few feet down from his house, her hair a wild halo of sodium fire. She is dressed in nothing more than a housecoat and slippers and appears to be staring right at him, sending an unwelcome spark of unease through him and he backs away from the door, starts to ease it closed.

The old lady moves.

He pauses, one eye peeking through the inch-wide space between door and jamb, watching though now he feels as if he has donned a coat of snakes, his skin crawling as the shadow-faced woman moves along the sidewalk with short, stiff steps, the orb of fuzzy darkness hiding eyes that may or may not be fixed on him. She shuffles closer still and he realizes this is the sound he heard earlier. *Shhhnick! Shhhnick! Shhhnick!*

He wants to close the door, an action that will leave his sudden inexplicable fear outside with the old woman, but he is powerless to do anything but watch.

She reaches the mailbox—a simple black tin semi-cylinder staked in Tom's garden but jutting out over the pavement—and stops, cocks her head and brings a gnarled hand toward it.

Is she pilfering the mail or what? He wonders, his unease no less potent as the idea of confronting her is rapidly abandoned.

He hears the soft scraping sound of the mailbox door being opened and watches in disbelief as the old lady stoops down and peers inside. After a moment in which he imagines he can feel the victory radiating in icy waves from her skeletal frame, her hand emerges clutching a small white rectangle. Clutching the letter to her chest, she swivels on her heels and shuffles back up the street, passing through the orange glow from the streetlight much quicker than she had on her way to steal the mail.

I should have done something. He watches the shadows swallow her. *That letter might have been important.*

The kettle shrieks and jars the thought from his head.

* * *

Later that evening, he stands at the threshold to a time capsule, held in place by a feeling of unreality that almost makes him dizzy.

Over the last few years his visits to this house have been infrequent and he has never stayed, had in fact come armed with a plethora of excuses should such a thing be suggested. As a result, he has never come upstairs and seen his old room.

He is shocked to find it is exactly the same, from the crimson toy chest at the foot of the bed to the Mickey Mouse wallpaper. His old teddy bear Rufus, now missing an eye, sits atop a once white pillow, arms splayed in frozen greeting. The carpet whispers as he advances further into the sanctuary of his childhood, head pounding, eyes wide with the strain of trying to absorb the sudden rush of familiarity.

A small oak desk, rescued from the local dump and restored to nothing like its former glory by Tom's father in one of his rare charitable moods, stands solemnly before the small white-framed arched window overlooking the neighboring rooftops.

Through one of the four panes, a thin crack like mercury lightning streaks an eternal path in the glass from top to bottom. Beyond that, the darkness rolls over the silent neighborhood, dampening the sounds of life and nodding its ethereal assent to the night creatures and the hunters waiting for their time to shine.

Tom shakes his head, looks down at the pockmarked surface of the desk and remembers... *Just as his father jabs the kitchen table with his knife or fork or the stub of his carpenter's pencil, so Tommy waits until he is alone and punctuates his own confused anger with the corner of a ruler, or pen, or...*

"Did I hate him?" Tom asks the empty room. "Did I hate them both and not know it?"

He kneels down before the desk as if it is the armrest in a confessional, his knees quickly growing sore on the threadbare carpet. He studies the indecipherable doodles and unfinished scribbles printed on the table. Only one is clear and etched with an angry hand into the wood:

HAVEN

This one he understands, even if he can't quite remember carving it.

In here, in this room, he had been permitted to believe the misery wasn't endless, that someday his father would arrive home wearing a smile in place of his ever-present scowl and smelling of wood and sawdust instead of whiskey. In here, solitude had provided the perfect movie screen for the illusions his hope projected and as long as he stayed here, nothing could break the spell imagination wove around him. Here was peace, love and happiness. Out there, over the moat and a million miles away, were misery, hate and pain.

Tom lifts his head and looks out at an encroaching darkness unique to the season. He pictures the dying leaves caught in a maelstrom, spinning round in a mindless vortex like lost souls and he realizes nothing has changed.

As he gets to his feet, he sees himself again, youthful body hunched over the desk, hiding the bruises on his face, weeping as he mourns the death of another fantasy at the vicious hands of reality.

He decides then that he will not stay here tonight. Even though he has long since dismissed the idea that adolescent fantasies can soften the edges of life, he doesn't want to sleep in a place where that very belief died.

This room is haunted, but not by ghosts. He can sense his childhood self here, the child that has stayed in this room, poring over the marks on the table, still hating the Mickey Mouse wallpaper, still trying to figure out why his daddy beats him while his mother watches with tears in her eyes. He is still angry and probably still dreaming of a better life he will never get.

"But my life did get better," Tom tells the silent room, surprised by the lack of conviction in his voice. The taste of stale coffee clings to the back of his throat as he swallows and turns to leave.

Stop lying to yourself. This was the only safe place.

The voice in his head is devoid of malice but filled with determination. He ignores it for it is just another unwanted memory and one he has the luxury of dismissing.

With a rattling sigh he slowly makes his way back downstairs and wonders if it might be better to put the house up for sale, to let someone oblivious to the horrid memories make it their home, someone immune to the tapestries of pain fashioned from the dust itself and the sting of sharp tongues still lingering in the air.

He thought it would be different coming back here, that his mother had been the only remaining anchor to a past too dreadful to contemplate. A foolish assumption.

If anything, her presence had allowed him to think only of her part in the shadow play that had been his childhood. With her gone, the curtains were thrust open, every room a set upon which the dramas of a miserable youth waited for an audience.

But the fact remains that he has no place else to go.

He supposes a few weeks here won't hurt, just until he comes up with something better. Perhaps an extended vacation, to clear his head and relax for the first time in as long as he can remember.

He stops at the bottom of the stairs; sure he hasn't heard what his brain is telling him he has. A few moments of listening yield nothing to confirm there has been any noise and the tension begins to ebb from his muscles. Then it comes, softly, seeping under the door like floodwater: *Shhhnick! Shhhnick! Shhhnick!* He doesn't move; waits instead for what he is now certain will follow.

A brief scratching like nails on a garage door.

Or an old mailbox being opened.

This is crazy.

It takes a great deal of effort for him to swallow the knot of inexplicable fear that has lodged in his throat but he is suddenly tired of being afraid, can't remember the last time he hasn't been, and a surge of uncharacteristic resolve brings him to the door, makes him wrench it open, propels him down the garden path and delivers him to the mailbox and the old lady standing before it.

She is peering once again into the bulbous darkness inside.

"Excuse me," he says, his voice brittle in the cool air.

She ignores him, apparently too intent on her felonious task, but this close he can see that she is a lot older than he first thought, the myriad lines in her sallow face retaining the shadows as if they are an intrinsic part of her. The black pools of her eyes are curved at the behest of a toothless smile as she retrieves her second prize of the night from his mailbox.

It occurs to him that he has seen her somewhere before but is not altogether surprised. Marrow Lane is a small neighborhood.

"Excuse me but what do you think you're doing?" He wants to tap her on the shoulder, to grab her elbow or anything that might bring her focus round to him, but for some reason he senses that touching her would be a dreadful mistake.

She is holding the small white envelope up to the streetlight and he has almost conceded, is in fact formulating a parting caveat when she suddenly turns and says: "You always had a great imagination, Tommy" before once again shuffling off into the shadows, leaving him helpless to do anything but watch.

"Wait, who are you?" he cries after her and she looks back over her shoulder at him, her face a creamy blur in the darkness but then even the shuffling ceases and the sounds of night rush back in.

Only the soughing of the wind answers him.

Frowning, he goes back inside.

How did she know my name?

* * *

In the hallway, Rufus sits against the wall.

Tom stands paralyzed, the door clicking shut behind him, muting the wind.

"Hello?" he asks the hallway and thinks that if the teddy bear turns his head in response he will most certainly drop dead of a heart attack. While the old lady was bizarre, she certainly wasn't beyond rational explanation. This however, is dancing on the boundaries of sanity.

He clearly remembers seeing the toy seated on the bed in his old room. He hadn't moved it, would recall if he had. How then, has it ended up down here?

Horrible images of the teddy bear carefully navigating the stairs while he was outside flash behind his eyes and he scoffs, a little too casually and feels his hackles rise.

"To hell with it." He rushes forward and scoops up the stuffed toy, then marches up the stairs, the loud clumping of his boots deliberate and reassuring. If someone else is here, they will know he is coming and that he isn't happy.

He reaches the landing and takes a deep breath, steels himself for whatever he might find in his old bedroom. With his heart chiseling its way through his ribcage, he stalks into the room. And comes to a dead halt.

A little boy, sallow-faced and sheet-white, has replaced Rufus on the bed; an ugly bruise purpling his left eye and most of his cheek. He is dressed in Mickey Mouse pajamas, *Tom's* old pajamas and as Tom watches, the boy raises his hands to receive the bear. Despite the surrealistic feel reality has draped over its shoulders, Tom tosses the bear to the child and tells himself to remain calm.

"Who are you?"

The boy looks at the bear as if he's addressing not Tom, but the toy. "You know who I am. Who do I remind you of?"

In truth, this is a question Tom has been hoping the boy doesn't ask, because the answer is something he is not prepared to face so he says: "I don't know."

The child looks amused and Tom feels his nerves fraying at the edges, unraveling. "How did you get in here?" he asks.

"I'm the one who makes stuff up, not you. So stop pretending you

"We'll see."
His eyes are on the door.
"I missed you," says the boy.
Tom tries to ignore the creaking of the stairs.

THE BINDING

Bill Cates awoke restrained. Muscles aching, he allowed panic to surge inside him and the hair on his neck to prickle with cold fear before he sighed and let the tension run from his throbbing arms.

Feet and wrists bound, he rolled his eyes around, wincing at the starbursts of pain at the base of his neck where the skin felt like stretched leather.

He tried to move his neck to relax the muscles but couldn't, felt resistance.

When had she bound him?

The panic ignited again but he choked it down. If she had bound him this tightly then she hadn't gone far, hadn't left him in such a dangerous state where at any moment he could pass out from the lack of blood circulating to his brain. Because now he was sure she had cinched a rope around his throat too, not tight enough to strangle him but enough so that his head sat atop the loops of cord as if severed.

Only his eyes would move and he used them to take in the room in which he'd allowed her to make him a captive in pursuit of the utmost sexual pleasures. Paintings. Strange depictions of tortured creatures, all in various stages of transformation, all displayed in vibrant living color, were propped up against all four walls. It seemed she spent her free time painting monsters and binding men.

He looked straight ahead. Something was different. Something that hadn't been there the night before. He didn't remember much but he remembered the darkness, no light filtering through from anywhere.

A window.

Impossible.

And yet it had to be possible because he was looking at it—a small square window looking out onto a gleaming sunlit hallway better suited to a college or government building where cleanliness was a priority seldom neglected and not a crumbling tenement building in...well, wherever he was. At the far end of the hallway, a set of glass double doors filtered the sunlight onto the tiled floor. A ground floor.

Why would someone put a window at the end of a hallway? Especially if it looks nowhere but into a shabby apartment on the top fl—

Wait a minute. She had taken him to her apartment on the top floor. He remembered because he'd been out of breath and sweating like a baked hog by the time they'd navigated the endless stairwells to get there. Why then, he wondered, was he now looking through a window that showed a hallway leading to doors that in turn led out onto what appeared to be a ground floor courtyard?

He stopped his bewilderment in mid-mutter and listened. *Voices.* He tried to cock his head but was forced to strain mentally toward the sound instead.

Yes, definitely voices but from where he couldn't tell. The loft appeared reluctant to proffer any clues and he slumped inwardly, constantly aware of the rope biting into his wrists and ankles, growing annoyed and hoping at the same time there would be no marks. Marks would be noticed.

This enforced paralysis began to anger him and he tried to lean forward. Nothing happened. His brain had apparently been labeled a pariah by the rest of his body and the only sensations allotted him were gnawing fear and increasing discomfort.

Where the hell is she?

He tried to close his eyes and his heart lurched.

I can't close my eyes.

The calm he'd forced himself to muster dropped like a theater curtain torn from the rails and he tried to open his mouth to set free the scream trapped in his throat. His mouth wouldn't open.

Oh God.

Remember her. Start by remembering her, he thought, his mind spinning so fast he was almost able to convince himself it was really his body circling the room, somehow released from the vicious constraints.

What good would it do to remember her? Would recalling her name send her running to his aid?

It should damn it.

But you can't scream his mind countered and ice flooded through his veins at the spoken and yet not spoken truth of this waking nightmare.

She drugged me. The bitch put something in my drink.

Yes, that was it. Had to be. What other rational explanation was there? He was paralyzed, unable to move anything but his eyes. But then, why bind him?

Of course, she would have had to seduce me into this so that the drug had a chance to work.

A bar. He'd been in a bar after a meeting with the insurance folks. One of their workers in the plant was threatening to sue after a routine check had shown his lungs were clogged with asbestos particles. It was a potentially lethal situation business wise and Bill had been drafted in to tackle the situation, to offer a significant amount of money to keep everybody happy and more importantly, keep it out of court. Five figures they could afford to part with for the sake of maintaining their good name; seven or eight was out of the question.

The meeting had gone well, though afterward he wasn't entirely convinced that they were going to escape the guillotine. Still, he'd done his part and done it well and when the blonde chocolate-skinned woman at the bar had started giving him the glad eye, he decided he had earned the reward.

Fresh anger bloomed in his chest, his hands begging to clench but frozen, a denial that further inflamed him.

A whore. I've been fleeced by a goddamn whore.

Rage poured into his eyes and suddenly the urge to blink it away became a need and the need became desperation. And that led to torture as the inability to blink began to make his eyes boil.

She had brought him back to her apartment, whispering promises of acts he was sure his wife had never even heard of. After the grueling ascent to her place (she told him the elevator was broken), she had led him inside. Told him to take a seat. This is where memory failed him.

Now he prayed to God to stop the madness and felt an itch wind its way like an army of fire ants over his wrists. His teeth tried to clench, eyes flitting madly from one dank corner of the sunlight-shunning loft to another. Finally, aflame with agony, he looked straight ahead, through the small window and the shimmering hallway, looking less impossible now and more like the path to salvation, held cruelly out of reach for men who awoke to find themselves bound and frozen.

Oh Jesus.

And then someone swept into the doorway. He paused and watched, feeling sweat inside his skin looking for an exit that wasn't there.

It was a woman, wearing an ankle-length black coat, her auburn hair dancing in the breeze before the door hissed shut behind her and left it drop to her shoulders. As she strode purposefully down the corridor, a plastic name badge flashed in the sunlight, the light hitting him straight in the eyes. His mind compensated for his mouth's uselessness and shrieked, echoing hollowly through the canals that were his nerves, setting his soul ablaze and wracking his body with shudders that rippled through his innards and broke well before the surface of his frozen flesh.

Inside, he wept, knowing no tears were spilling from his eyes because that would have taken away the burning and it was obvious to him now that no reprieve was forthcoming.

She'd left him here to die or go mad. Or both.

But then he remembered the woman in the hallway, his eyes swiveling toward the window again. She was coming right towards him. Surely she'd see him if she came close enough?

He listened to the clip-clop of her high heels on the tile, imagined her peering in at him and gasping, running to fetch someone to break the window, or to come round and kick in the door of the bitch's apartment, untying him...

The spit had long since dried in his throat but he tried regardless. Nothing, of course. He began to whisper promises that if he somehow escaped this he would never again cheat on his wife. It wasn't worth it; adultery was becoming a lethal practice.

The woman drew nearer the window and now he saw how tall she was.

She'll see me, he thought, allowing rays of his own personal sunshine to chase the shadows off his brain. *She'll call someone and they'll get me out of this goddamn chair. I'll be in pain for days but anything will be better than...*

The woman was so close now that he could see how pretty she was and how wrong he'd been in assuming she was tall.

She wasn't tall, she was enormous. Impossibly so and the closer to the window she came, the more anxious he became until anxiety dissipated under the sheer weight of horror that descended upon him, teeth bared.

Her face filled the window. Or rather, her eyes did.

He felt like a bug, someone in the front row of the theater, a doll in a dollhouse, a little boy looking at the doctor's magnified eye, an insect... He felt like prey. Anything caught beneath an eye that big must surely be the victim, be it insanity or the supernatural wielding the upper hand.

His whole being erupted in a trembling panic but never moved; wouldn't move. Everything he was faltered in the face of what must surely be a god or a giant or a product of incredible trickery. It made a mockery of his hope, an idiot of his sanity.

This is wrong. Something is dreadfully wrong.

The face moved back from the window, the expression on that porcelain countenance one of disgust, of confusion as if unable to understand how he had ended up in—

"This painting..." a booming voice said suddenly, sending pulses of sound vibrating through his body and his heart ceased fuelling his torture for a moment as the loft thrummed along with the speaking giant. "...It's hideous. Why would anyone want to hang such a thing on the wall of a public building? If this is what's passing as art these days then it's no wonder the world has gone to hell."

Another voice, another giant chuckled. It felt like hands clapping against his ears. His guts roiled.

Who are these...things?

"I thought a picture of a man bound would have appealed to you, Detective Chambers," roared this new voice.

Detective? A picture? What are they talking about?

"Funny. You have breakfast yet?"

"Not unless you count coffee. I've been down to Flaherty's Tavern on Third. The barman says he remembers the guy leaving with a dark woman, blonde hair, dressed kind of funny."

Bill's brain pulsed with agony, ears near-bursting as the glass rattled between him and the giants.

No, they're not giants. It's a television screen. I'm watching a television screen that bitch set up to scare me.

The room began to vibrate again as the man's thundering voice continued. "Kind of funny?"

"Yeah, her clothes were stained with paint but the barman couldn't swear on it. Says it might have been part of her costume. Good-looking broad, weird eyes; says she wore some odd gold symbols around her neck too, one like a crooked pentagram, the other of a bound man."

They both looked in at Bill, who summoned the last vestiges of strength from where they had pooled somewhere in the depths of his pain-ravaged body and tried to scream. Silence filled his throat, sweeping aside the tears, ushering them away to wherever his voice had gone and in the end he sat still, motionless. Watching.

The floor continued to hum.

"Like *this* guy."

"Yeah."

"Looks like he wants to scream."

"Gives me the creeps."

"I guess. See how the eyes follow you around the room?"

"Yeah. Like those pictures of Jesus."

He watched them, waited to wake up. Waited for salvation he had no choice but to believe would come, whether by cruel of kind means...

"So our boy was diddling around behind his wife's back. Maybe he ran off with the voodoo lady?"

"It's a possibility. I'm hoping some of his co-workers here will be willing to enlighten us on what our Mr. Cates got up to after hours."

"All right. Let's go check it out."

The window cleared.

Bill watched, waited and screamed in silence from inside his frame.

THE WRONG POCKET

This one was going to be a breeze. Stan sensed as much and penguins would fly before his instincts were proved wrong.

The guy with the purple coat stuck out like a diamond in a turd – as Greta was known to say – and thus, caught the eye of the thief as soon as he entered the train station.

Fat cat, Stan thought, busy pretending to read the schedule mounted on the wall beside the restrooms while the ghost of the purple man crossed the plexiglass. *Tonight my dear we eat at the Golden Sword.*

For weeks now his wife had been nagging him to make a score they could actually live on for more than a week. Greta was quick to goad him into working but just as quick to blow his take on expensive clothes and jewelry, a habit that annoyed the hell out of him. All it would take to bring the end of everything would be a suspicious cop acting on a tip-off and calling to their house. He pictured Greta opening the door, wearing more chains than a moored boat, the cop slowly reaching for his own less fashionable set of bracelets...

Stan shook his head and cast a glance over his shoulder.

The purple man was heading towards the men's room, his eyes fixed on the floor ahead of him as if fascinated by people's choice in footwear.

Stan pondered his next move but Greta's voice shrilled in his head, making him wince. "Wait until boarding, you idiot. You're less likely to be spotted in a crowd and he's not going to feel you lift his wallet with fifty or sixty people crushing against him."

She was right of course, as always but how he hated to admit that.

His wife frequently used his lack of education against him whenever they argued and he would more often than not be forced to back down, as if the mere reminder was enough to lower his actual IQ, rendering him incapable of an adequate response.

Still, he loved her and as long as her decisions bore fruit and he got to spend half the money, then he could live with her claim of intellectual superiority.

The purple man emerged from the restroom, adjusting his belt with a meaty ring-studded hand.

This guy looks like a gangster from a Dick Tracy comic, Stan thought, his mouth curling into a smile.

Indeed the purple man did seem better suited to a comic book. A three-piece suit concealed a massive bulk, presided over by an ill-tempered face mashed between meaty jowls. The guy's pencil-thin moustache looked phony, drawn on for dramatic effect. A purple fedora with a yellow feather-band capped off the walking beetroot and Stan was caught between amusement and nervousness as he fell into step behind him. Some obscure cologne wafted into his face and he winced. It smelled like burnt leather.

"Remember not too close. People can feel it when someone is treading on their shadow," Greta's disembodied voice advised.

I know. Give me a little credit.

However, as he kept his head low in a manner much the same as the purple guy, he noticed something odd.

Even if he chose to take his wife's advice literally, there was no shadow to tread upon. He raised his face and looked at the bank of lights over the platform entrance. They were shining directly towards them. Stan looked over his shoulder at the tiled floor behind him. His own shadow followed obediently.

When he turned back, certain he'd made a mistake, the purple guy was nowhere to be seen.

Goddamn it!

He made no attempt to hide his frustration and when he stalked past a cop, muttering about missing shadows and how the purple man had moved fast for a fat guy, the uniform didn't even register. Luckily for Stan, the cop spared him only the briefest of curious glances before going back to watching for real criminals.

There were several arched walkways leading to the various platforms. Stan danced with indecision for a moment before opting for the nearest one to him, the platform where any minute now the train to New Orleans might whisk away his chance at a successful score.

Struggling to retain his composure—because now this was no longer just another job but one he was convinced would yield unprecedented rewards—Stan weaved his way among the morose passengers, sidestepping trundling suitcases and enormous backpacks and searching for the slightest hint of purple.

Just as his heart began to lose some of its buoyancy, he spotted him.

Standing on the platform like a man who has all the time in the world, the purple guy rolled on the balls of his feet and whistled soundlessly. Wisps of dark hair poked out from beneath his hat and caressed his ear like the legs of beetles. He seemed oblivious to the gathering crowd of passengers who, unlike him, seemed impatient to be aboard the train and moving.

Stan moved behind the ever-growing crowd and waited for the jostling to begin as the train doors flapped open. Through the heaving mass of sweaty bodies, he caught a glimpse of the purple guy's back pocket and beamed. A thick lump stretched the pocket to the point of bursting, the lip of a leather wallet pouting over the purple line.

Stan could already see himself at home with an excited Greta, patiently counting out the hundred dollar bills as his wife paced relentlessly around the room and his nerves.

Perhaps, if they were lucky enough, they could afford a vacation courtesy of Mr. Purple and his straining wallet. The thought was enough to make his mouth water.

The jostling began, a subtle rubbing of bodies as people began trying to squeeze themselves together. Ignoring the stabbing elbows and stamping feet, Stan slithered through the crowd and ended up right where he wanted to be.

He had almost forgotten the smell, but now that the purple man was this close, the odor of scorched hide almost choked him. He clamped his mouth shut, drew breath through his nose and concentrated on the bulge in the back of the man's pants.

Okay, nice and slow.

Mr. Purple was making it easy and not squirming uncomfortably like some of them did. Stan pressed his back against the crowd and shoved a little. Paused. Held his breath. The crowd shoved back. Perfect. By way of a tide effect (Greta's name for the ebb and flow of a crowd), he found himself forced up against the fat man's back.

In a flash, he let out a grunt, apologized to the fat man –who bore the inconvenience of Stan's forced proximity without so much as a sigh—and melted ever so slowly back into the crowd until he was out the other side, slicked with sweat and barely able to control his elation.

Gripped like the Holy Grail in his left hand, was the purple guy's wallet.

Whispering self-praise, Stan hurried through the station to the exit.

* * *

It was an unspoken rule between Stan and Greta that the score not be assessed until he got home. Although the primary reason for this was that his wife wanted to share in the joy or as the case may be, disappointment with him, there was always the danger some eagle-eyed citizen would report him to the police after spying him digging through a wallet quite obviously not his own.

Now, with the small but swollen dark brown leather wallet lying on the coffee table, Greta took a seat across from him and nodded. "Do it."

Stan bit his lip and watch as her smile grew by the second.

Taking a deep breath, he reached over and flipped open the wallet. It lay between them like a crippled bird, the contents of the lining still a mystery. There were no credit cards or family photographs in the clear plastic window and this made Stan a little uneasy. Could it have been a ruse? Was the guy accustomed to carrying around an empty wallet?

No. Although the inside of the wallet was bare, it remained fat, indicating that something was inside the folds.

"How much are you guessing is in there?" Greta asked, another ritual of theirs.

He shrugged. "I'm hoping the guy was on his way to buy a car and wanted to pay cash."

Greta giggled and motioned for him to hurry.

He sucked in a breath and grabbed the wallet. The frown was beginning even before he spread apart the imitation velvet folds and saw what was inside.

Greta's smile dropped as surely as if he'd slapped her and in a way he had. Slapped her with another week of fast food.

The wallet was empty.

As they watched in abject misery, the wallet deflated with a sigh, the air above it wobbling as if it had exhaled heat.

"What the hell was that?" Stan asked, letting the wallet fall to the table and still staring at where the bizarre shift in the air had been.

Greta stood up and looked down at him, disgust wrenching her face into ugliness. "Sweat from the guy's ass. Who gives a damn? That's another job down the toilet, another day playing Fagin when you could have been out looking for some real work."

Stan said nothing. This unfortunately, was also standard whenever the score was less than fifty dollars, or worse, nothing but air, and he knew he would be better just letting her vent. It wasn't as if she meant any of it anyway.

"How long more are you gonna keep this up?"

He shook his head and turned away to avoid the coals her beautiful sapphire eyes had become.

A peculiar smell had risen from somewhere within the room and Stan sniffed while Greta continued her spiel. "This, Stan is what happens when you don't abide by the rules. Mistakes are made and people get caught. What the hell would I do if you ended up in prison? I'd have to take up the job myself. God knows I'd probably be better at it than you. Are you listening to me?"

He wasn't and when she followed his gaze, she saw why. "Stan? What's that smell?"

A pool of shadow had formed in the corner of the room, between the ceiling and the wall farthest from them. It looked like a three-fingered hand, as if a child were using a torch to make strange animal shapes on the wall. But there were no children here, just Stan, his wife and the shadow.

They watched, paralyzed with horror as the shadow lengthened and ran like oil down the light blue surface of the wall.

"Stan?" The fear in Greta's voice did nothing to allay his own but as much as he wanted to, he could not move.

"Stan? What…" It was separating now, dividing itself into what could only be described as puddles if puddles had suddenly decided to ignore the natural laws of gravity.

They began to widen and reconnect.

"Stan?"

"I don't know Greta but stay where you are."

The shadow turned.

"Oh God," Greta collapsed back into her seat. "Oh God, what is it?"

Although Stan had an answer, it wasn't one he thought he could force past his lips for fear it would drive him insane if he acknowledged it.

The shadow had taken the shape of a man.

Stan shook his head. He felt like someone in the audience at a shadow theater, the wall of his living room the screen behind which an actor waited for his cue.

"Stan, what's happening?"

It stood motionless, featureless, and yet Stan had the feeling it was staring directly at him. He swallowed.

The doorbell rang.

"Don't answer it," Greta begged and crammed her knuckles into her mouth.

The shadow of the man on the wall nodded once and though there was nothing about this scene that made sense to Stan, he knew what had to be done.

"I have to, honey," he told Greta and made his way toward the front door.

"Why? Why do you have to?"

He started to answer and then thought better of it. How could he possibly put into words what had happened, what he'd done?

He saw himself following the purple man in the train station, curious as to why he cast no shadow but too preoccupied to give it much thought. He thought about the smell…

And as he opened the door to a gust of blistering heat that singed his eyebrows, he finally knew exactly what he had stolen.

And from whom he had stolen it.

SPARROW MAN

It's a Thursday. Down by Tanner's pond.

I'm sitting there minding my own business and thinking about nothing in particular, when this old man sidles up to me with a strange, crooked smile on his skeletal face.

I do my best to ignore him, but he is so close I can smell him. Stale beer and cigarettes. I recognize the smell from my father.

He starts to rock back and forth on the heels of his pointy-toed shoes like he's doing nothing more than waiting for a bus and follows the trajectory of the bread crusts I'm throwing with his beady black eyes.

I know by the way he keeps sneaking glances at me that he probably has something unsavory on that wrinkled old mind of his, so I stop throwing the bread and angle my head so I can see him clearly. "You a pervert or something?" I ask him.

He looks at me like I've just smacked him across the face. I almost laugh, but manage to hold it back at the last second. I might be acting brave, but my father hasn't raised me to be a complete idiot. His face pales, an incredible sight since he was the color of death to begin with and now he looks more like a hollowed out corpse. It takes him a second to regain his composure and then his smile widens. It looks forced.

"Son, I don't mean to bring harm to you. I'm just an old man out for a walk, that's all."

I go back to throwing bread and watching the ducks fight each other for the scraps. Wings flutter furiously, water sprays into transient rainbows and the old man shuffles uncomfortably. Feathers have been ruffled. I hawk up a booger and shoot it at a point on the ground between him and me. He flinches.

"Didn't your father tell you how rude that is?"

"My father taught me how to do it. He says there isn't any need for stuff hanging around inside you if you can just as easily spit it out."

The old man says nothing.

I say nothing.

The birds drift closer to the grassy bank, eyeing me with short sharp snaps of their heads. Overhead, white snatches of cloud hang in the air like nailed cotton. There is no breeze.

"Do you smoke?" the old man asks. I look at the silver case he holds out to me in one fragile looking hand and back to the water.

"I never take smokes from strangers."

In the corner of my eye I see him shrug and hear the fizzle and flare of a cupped match. A contented smoky sigh and then I am once again the object of his attention.

"You go to school?" he asks and I spare him a quick glance. I realize my supply of bread crusts has dwindled to nothing more than a few brown crescents, like a giant's dirty nail clippings. I have been throwing them fast to avoid looking at the old man and now I am almost out.

"Why do you ask so many questions?"

"Just making conversation."

"I didn't come here for conversation. I doubt anyone comes down here for conversation."

He takes a deep drag on his cigarette and I feel his eyes on the nape of my neck, resting there like cold stones. I want to shudder but don't. Instead I look down at my hands, one crust left in each.

"Almost out of bread there, son," he says and I am irritated that he has noticed.

"Why don't you go bother someone else?"

"There's no-one else here," he answers after a moment and flicks his cigarette into the pond, right into the center of the feeding birds.

I toss the last two crusts into the water. "Well, I'm not much of a talker."

"We've all got our stories, boy. Scoot over there and let me rest these weary legs of mine, wouldya?"

I give him a long hard look that I hope tells him he's messing with the wrong kid if indeed that is his intention. He begins to massage his leg and winces for dramatic effect so I shift myself onto the very edge of the bench, one leg off to the side ready to propel me out of there should the need arise. He sits.

He's wearing a long navy overcoat, buttoned up the center almost to his throat. I wonder how he isn't roasting to death in it. It is early August after all and I'm sweating in a tee shirt and jeans. But, that's his business and I'm not too curious about what might or might not be under there.

"I use to come down here when I was your age," he says wistfully and I pray this isn't going to be one of those merry jaunts down memory lane. "Feed the ducks, skip stones, just like you."

"Fascinating," I tell him and scan the park for the tenth time since we sat down. I find it odd that on a day as warm as this, we're the only ones here.

He reaches into his pocket and I move further away so that now the edge of the seat is wedged firmly into the crack of my ass. He shakes his head and withdraws the silver cigarette case. "I don't bite," he says and offers me a small smile. "But I commend your caution. Places like this aren't as safe as they used to be. Not with the way people are these days."

Lighting his cigarette, his eyes move to the sky.

Something small and brown flashes past his head and thumps to the ground. We both turn to look though I have to strain harder to see around him without getting too close.

"Wouldya look at that," he mutters, not sounding surprised at all.

It's a sparrow. The bird is lying flat on its back, legs curled up to its breast as if it died looking for a perch.

"You're lucky it didn't hit you on the head," I tell him and quickly move away as he swivels back to face me, an amused smile on his face.

"That I am. Poor thing must have been old."

For some reason the idea of a bird dying of old age makes a laugh swell in my throat but I force it away. "Yeah. Maybe he was a smoker."

I expect him to find this funny but instead he fixes me with those horrible black marble eyes and shakes his head. "It's a 'she'."

I don't get this immediately and my face obviously tells him so because he points a long thin finger in the direction of the dead bird. "The sparrow. It's a 'she', not a 'he'."

I give him a moment to crack a smile or otherwise indicate that he 's kidding. He doesn't.

"Right, mister. How do you know that? The boys got big dicks or something?"

He does smile then but there is no humor in it. "I just know," he says quietly. "What's your name, kid?"

"Why do you want to know?"

"Just being courteous, that's all. I figure since we're talking, we should introduce ourselves. I'm Janus."

"As in Joplin?"

"Not exactly, but close enough. And you are…?"

"Leaving," I finish for him and get to my feet.

"What's the rush? You must know by now I don't intend to hurt you? We're alone, wouldn't I already have done something if that were my intention?"

I look over my shoulder at him as I start to walk away. "How the hell do I know? No offense mister, but you give me the creeps and I have better things to do on a day like today than sit around with creepy old men."

He makes no move to stop me, for which I am only marginally relieved.

What does make me stop is the sight of another dead bird lying in the short grass a few feet away from where I've been sitting. I stare at it for a moment before moving on; thinking that maybe some kid hidden in the bushes around the park is having fun with a BB gun when I find another one. And then another. For some reason, my curiosity makes me turn to see if the old man has noticed the little brown lumps lying in the grass like feathered dog turds.

He's standing right behind me. I give out a startled yelp, restraining the immediate impulse to strike out at him and stagger backwards. "What are you doing?"

He ignores the question and drops to his haunches beside the dead sparrow, a somber look on his face.

The sky breathes down on us then, making the few remaining strands of silver hair on the old man's head dance in the new breeze. I watch, fascinated as Janus clamps the cigarette between his teeth and cups his hands together as if he's about to collect water from a stream. Instead, he uses them as a shovel to scoop the dead bird up and with a faint smile, puts it into the pocket of his overcoat.

"What...?" I start to ask but fall silent as he walks a few steps forward and repeats the process with the other dead sparrow.

He's filling his pockets with dead birds, I think to myself, now sure that the old man is out of his mind.

The bizarre ritual continues a while longer as Janus zigzags across the grass, stooping to collect the birds I haven't gone far enough to see. Eventually he stops and returns to where I stand open-mouthed and wide-eyed. He offers me a grin I'm sure he means to be reassuring—it isn't—and returns to the park bench.

Don't go back, my mind insists, *he's nuts. Next thing you know he'll be scooping you up and trying to shove you in his pocket.*

Before I can argue, my legs are moving towards the bench. This time it is I who stay standing, frowning at the strange old man who now looks almost serene.

"I'm guessing you didn't pick those birds up to help out the litter warden?"

His eyes are fixed on something over my head. "No."

"Then what was all that about?"

"Sit and I'll tell you."

His voice has become flat and emotionless but I don't sense a threat anymore and so, eager to learn his motives, I do as he asks.

"You remind me of me when I was young and naïve. Things were much simpler then."

Mental yawn. I have heard this same line about a thousand times from both my grandfather and my father, who are both it seems, desperate for a chance to relive the past. I sometimes wonder what changes they would make if given the opportunity and if I would be one of those changes.

"Nowadays it's all greed, death, drugs and deceit. I don't know if I could ever have survived as a child in this."

"In what?"

"The world the way it is now." He pokes my shoulder with a finger and winks. "You seem to be managing okay though, eh Kieran?"

I freeze, a trapdoor opening in the pit of my stomach, allowing the butterflies to fly in.

"How do you know my name?"

Thump!

I want to look but know what I'll see if I do. Sparrows. They're dropping all around us, but suddenly that doesn't seem so bizarre right now.

"Would you believe I read minds? Or that I work for a carnival that's about to pass through town and clairvoyance is my particular talent?"

The tone of his voice tells me that none of this is the truth.

"Or would you rather I tell you I'm a supernatural being who could wipe you out of existence with a flick of my finger?"

A splash from the pond; it might have been the ducks. Are they to die too? If so, how will he retrieve them? The mental picture of Janus trying to stuff a duck into his pocket would have been funny if not overruled by the creeping sense of dread that ripples beneath my skin.

I steal a glance. The ducks are still there, alive and well but now they are gathered around a small brown object floating in the water.

"Perhaps I'm a demon sent to spread chaos throughout the earth?"

My eyes meet his and those black orbs are filled with such an intense look that I am forced to drop my gaze.

"You live in an age where television, books and computer games sell monsters to the imagination of children in staggering doses. There is not a doubt in my mind that I could convince you I am one of those monsters. But I won't."

His words are punctuated by the sound of birds dropping from the sky and hitting the earth. Surrounded by this impossible phenomenon, I know he's right. If he tells me he's the devil himself, I might just believe it.

"Then who are you?"

A bird dive-bombs my shoulder and rolls into my lap. I grimace and swipe him off into Janus's waiting hand. He casts a scornful glance at me before pocketing it.

The sky becomes the work of a time-lapse photographer; clouds suddenly flicker and grow larger and darker than they had been only moments before. Silver light blinks through holes in the ever-spreading canvas of gray above our heads.

When I look back down, Janus's face is hovering mere inches

from my own. The desire to move away is immediate, powerful and impossible. His eyes hold me in place.

"You'll go home," he says tonelessly. "You'll talk nonsense with your family and argue with your sister. You'll pet the dog and eat dinner. You'll brush your teeth, urinate and go to bed. Your daddy will stay up two hours later than you so that he can finish the bottle of whiskey your no-good uncle Isaac brought him last week. Then he too will urinate, forget to brush his teeth and go to bed. An hour later, I will visit your house and leave a sparrow outside."

I can't tell you why but my skin is tingling, as if I've just stuck my finger in a plug socket. The old man's eyes seem to churn, the clouds above our heads somehow finding a home in those narrow orbs.

"I don't understand," I tell him with a voice that illustrates my fear perfectly.

"The sparrow is a symbol of death where I come from. Tonight, a sparrow will be left outside the houses of the sinful in Harperville and tomorrow, they will be no more."

I want desperately to believe that I am listening to the ravings of a madman. But if he is insane, then so am I because I believe him and I doubt anything benign is making the birds fall from the sky all around us.

Janus turns and looks back at the pond. The ducks are gone and now I can see several of those little lumps bobbing on the water.

"Whoever touches the sparrow will die," he continues. "Whoever moves it will die instantly and awake to find themselves where they belong."

"Where's that?" I stammer, feeling my lower lip start to tremble. "Hell?"

"That is not my concern," he replies. "Or yours."

"Why are you telling me all this? Why are you here? Why now?"

He seems irritated by the barrage of questions and sighs, the brown clumps pattering on all sides of him.

"You bring back memories, boy. Innocence untainted, naivety undamaged. All the things I used to be, back in the day. There are times when I regret not holding onto such things. If I had, the path I travel now might have been a lot different. For a brief while, you have allowed me to remember and for this simple gift, I am giving you a warning."

He levels me with a liquid gaze. "The bird is not for you. Stay away from it and leave it work for the one who has earned it."

Wild panic erupts inside me. "But...who is it for?"

"That, I can't tell you."

"You have to tell me. You-you can't just tell me something like that and leave!"

"No."

"Fuck you and 'no', I want you to tell me. You're going to take someone away from me and I want to know who it is or..."

He grins. "Or what?"

I slump, defeated and next to tears for the first time in years. For this, I hate him. For all his dark promises, I want to kill him right here and now, regardless of the consequences. Anything to make what he has predicted a lie.

A simple day in the park has turned into a tour of hell.

"You can't do this," I croak.

"I'm afraid I can. There is no vendetta against your town, Kieran. This has happened before. Indeed you can read about such things if you look in the right places and although I have not always been the harbinger, the sparrows have been the signature of many a downfall."

"But why *my* family? They're not evil. They've never harmed anyone!"

"Haven't they?" he asks, his raised eyebrows mocking the certainty I thought I'd had. "There are lots of things you have yet to know. Until you do, you cannot begin to understand the significance of this day."

The tears come freely then, trickling down my cheeks as I weep and grieve for deaths that have yet to come.

"You have to tell me. Who's going to die?"

"I can't."

"You have to!"

"No I don't. I've told you enough already."

"Then I'm going to stop it."

"You can't."

"I'll try."

"You'll fail."

I stare at him then, my eyes silently begging him to tell me it's all just a sick joke. For that, I could forgive him. For taking away someone I love, never. He continues to stare at the burnished steel surface of the pond, watching the splashes until they stop. Wiping my nose against the back of my hand, I look up.

The sparrows are no longer falling.

"Why?" I mutter, half-expecting the deluge of dead birds to recommence.

Janus stands. "Thirty of them have fallen. Thirty souls will be taken."

I join him in standing, my fingers twitching as I hold my hands out, not knowing what it is that I want to do or say, but desperate to stop him leaving. "Wait!"

He turns his back on me and begins to collect the birds. I notice then that as he shoves them into his coat the pockets stay flat as if empty.

"What if I touch the bird first? You said I'm not wicked, so what happens then?"

He straightens, his knees popping loudly and turns back to face me. "Would you really want to take that chance?"

"Yes," I blurt, not entirely sure if it's the truth.

"Wouldn't you rather see that sister you hate so much getting her just desserts?"

"No."

He smiles that crooked smile and nods. "We'll see."

With that, he turns his attention back to the birds again, whistling tunelessly as he does so. I watch him for a moment, terrified and helpless.

And then I run, as fast as my legs can carry me, no longer able to watch him collecting his weapons.

I burst in the door at home, almost giving my father a heart attack. The glass in his hand spits whiskey onto the table and he curses loudly. "Kieran. What in the name of God are you doing?"

He seems embarrassed that I have caught him drinking but I don't care about that now. Instead, I take a moment to catch my breath and then tell him in a commanding tone I would never have dreamed to use in other circumstances for fear of punishment: "There'll be a dead bird outside the house in the morning. Whatever you do, don't touch it."

He stares dumbly at me for a second, his blinking slow and I realize he's drunk. "What are you talking about?"

"Didn't you hear them hitting against the roof? It was raining birds!"

He laughs loudly and waves me away with a calloused hand.

"You have to listen to me, Dad!" I step closer to him.

"I am listening to you but all I'm hearing is some shit about rain and birds that's making me wonder if you've been smoking something you shouldn'ta been."

He fingers the tumbler of whiskey and looks from me into its amber depths, eager to return to his drinking. His guilt is dwindling, being replaced by the impatience so much a part of him these days. I am keeping him from his business and it won't be long before he tells me so. I stand frustrated, searching for some way to penetrate the indifferent murk shrouding him. His eyebrows draw further down the longer I watch however, so I go to my room, my heart pounding in my ears.

As I gaze out the window, the clouds begin to separate once more, allowing the sunlight to dominate the sky as they had before I met the Sparrow Man.

I am alone, cursed with a horrid, dark awareness that twists my guts into knots. Who will it be? My father, my sister?

Sometime later I hear the front door open and a high-pitched voice filters up the stairs. Sheryl is home. Her job at the local Wal-Mart keeps her away from me most of the time, but when she's home, I am her verbal and often physical punch bag. It has been that way for as long as I can remember. All the pictures that grace the hallway walls of us smiling and hugging were taken before we grew wise to each other and usually the idea of hugging her makes me physically ill.

But I know I could stomach it now as I kneel on my bed with my elbows on the windowsill and wonder how she will die if she is the one to touch the sparrow.

"Where's the dillweed?" I hear her call as she mounts the stairs. Ordinarily, this would provoke an equally spiteful and creative response from me, but today the rules have been changed.

"In here," I yell and the door creaks open.

"Howdy, butt-face."

I turn around and her smug smile fades just a notch. "You sick?" she asks.

"No, why?"

"You look sick."

"No. Come in. I need to ask you something."

She frowns, already deciding that she isn't interested but pushes the door closed behind her and walks over to the bed where she stands, arms folded. "What? You want to borrow my underwear?"

It occurs to me then, as I sit on the bed and look up at her, that devoid of the mean streak she could almost be pretty. As it is, she is developing a deep wrinkle between her eyebrows from frowning so much and she's trying too hard to make herself a blonde when her natural auburn is a lot nicer. "No. I really need to ask you to do something and I need you to take me seriously."

She rolls her heavily mascara-ed eyes. "What? Want me to set you up with a boyfriend?"

"Look, just shut up a minute will you? This is important. Make fun all you want later, but for now I need you to listen."

I don't want to say it, but know it's the only way I can get her attention. "If you don't, someone could die."

Sheryl blanches. "What are you talking about?"

"I told Dad already but he's too drunk to care."

"Told Dad what?"

"About the bird."

"What bird?"

And then I tell her everything. The park, the birds, Janus and the mission he claimed to be on to rid the town of evildoers. It sounds ridiculous to my own ears so I guess I shouldn't have held out much hope of Sheryl buying it.

"Are you smoking something?" she says, laughing. "Do you really expect me to believe this shit? Raining birds? Do you really think no one would have heard about that if it had really happened? That kind of thing is world news!"

She leans close as if to whisper something but punches me hard on the arm instead.

"Ow!"

"That's for being such a little retard," she sneers and spins around. "You're lucky Dad's wasted or he'd probably smack the shit out of you for lying to him."

I pound the mattress in frustration as she opens the door to leave. "And try growing up just a tad, wouldya? I've hawked snot that was more mature than you."

She leaves me alone to ponder the horror I can sense drifting ever closer towards our house. An image of my father opening the front door and kicking the dead sparrow off the step comes to me and I feel the tears rushing up my throat.

What if I touch the bird first? You said I'm not wicked, so what happens then?

Would you really want to take that chance?

I decide I do want to take the chance, not out of any sense of duty or heroism but because this is all so wrong. This is not how things are supposed to happen. People can't just drop a bird at your door and rob you of your life. A dead bird is a dead bird and not a symbol of anything.

I know what I have to do.

* * *

Almost all of Janus's predictions come to pass. Before dinner I go out and sit down on the step with Gabber, our Labrador who seems uncharacteristically agitated, as if he too knows that something terrible is gathering on the horizon.

Over a meal of broiled fish and cold vegetables, Sheryl gives me grief and I end up telling Dad that I know she's having sex with that pimple-studded guy named Felix who sometimes calls round. Unsurprisingly, she goes nuclear and threatens to kill me but Dad lets a spittle-winged roar out of him and we are quiet, with nothing but murderous looks to exchange.

Sheryl storms off to her room and I do the same, but not before giving my father a hug he reluctantly accepts and then I leave him muttering to himself by the fire.

Just out of spite, I don't brush my teeth.

After a while I hear my father stumble into his room and slam the door.

When he starts to snore, I ease open my door and creep down the stairs, wincing every time one of the old steps groan. And then I am outside.

The day has been humid but the night has sucked the heat from the air as I take my post on the step, glad I have worn a thick sweater. Gabber lies beside me, his head between his paws, eyes opening every now and again, ears pricking up as he listens to something I can't hear. I grow cold and hug myself, clicking on the torch I brought down to dissuade the shadows.

I sit like that for hours, unmoving. A boy and his dog, watching for death.

Despite my courage and determination however, I fall asleep.

And then just as suddenly I'm awake, wracked with violent tremors, the dog barking at the fence that surrounds our garden, a squashed red orb rising in the morning sky…

…And on the ground before me is a dead sparrow.

I scramble to my feet and snap at the dog to shut up as I back away from the bird.

"He was here," I mumble to myself, scarcely sure I believe it. I try to rub warmth back into my arms.

The sparrow is splayed out on its back, legs hooked into claws, eyes open and staring at nothing.

The dog is tethered to a pine tree to the left of the house by a rope that extends as far as the front door, just out of reach of Janus's gift and for this I am thankful.

The knot around the tree is strong.

The collar on Gabber however, isn't.

There is a loud *ping!* And I am knocked off my feet by the weight of the dog pushing past me. Before I can gather myself, the dog has snapped the bird up into his mouth and is racing out the gate.

I scream at him until I am hoarse and the house has woken, unaware that I am crying until I find myself looking into my father's bloodshot eyes as he shakes me.

"Gabber's going to die," I sob, my father's hands on my shoulders as he leads me back into the kitchen.

"No he's not. He'll come back," he assures me, with not the slightest ounce of conviction in his voice.

I feel no better after a cup of strong coffee but at least the tears have stopped pushing against my eyes.

My father, dressed in a thick blue robe, his dark hair tousled, studies me carefully as we both sip the black brew. "How long were you out there?"

I shrug. "A while."

"Why for God's sake?"

"I didn't want you or Sheryl to touch that bird."

"What bird?"

"The one Gabber ran off with in his mouth."

"Why?"

"Because..." A mild sense of relief accompanies the realization that seeps into my chest. I love Gabber as much as any boy loves a dog, but by being the first to touch the bird, he has saved my father and sister and probably me. Our dumb Labrador has saved us all.

"Never mind. We won't be seeing Gabber again, that's all."

My father stares at me, confused, hung over and no doubt wondering what is going on in his son's funny little head. I offer him a smile that feels crooked but he returns it and pours me another coffee.

A while later, I take a hot shower to wash away the chill and the guilt that eventual creep into my head. Could I have saved the dog too? Could I have saved all of us, instead of letting Gabber sacrifice himself?

After getting dressed, I decide to go find the dog. I dread the thought of seeing him dying or dead, curled up in some strange place, hit by a car or worse but I smother the thought and tell my father where I'm going.

"Do you want me to come too?" he asks, surprising me. It has been a long time since we have gone anywhere together.

"Sure," I reply with a smile, "I'll wait outside."

"Okay. I'll go get dressed and tell Sheryl where we're off to."

I open the front door and wonder when the screams of anguish will begin. It is early yet. How many houses will awaken to find their loved ones dead on their front lawns? Will this become a national tragedy? Will the media soon overrun the town? The morbidity of the idea chills me but not nearly as much as the scream that sounds above my head.

Startled, I look up at Sheryl's open window, directly above the front door.

My father is screaming in pain and abject horror.

The terror and confusion that fills me then is debilitating. I shake my head in denial. No, Gabber took the bird. The dog was going to die, not...

A single brown feather drifts down from Sheryl's window ledge and the chilling truth hits me.

Janus never said he would leave the bird on the front step, I had assumed that on my own. Outside the house had meant anywhere.

Including Sheryl's second floor window ledge.

In my mind's eye I see her opening her window in a sleepy daze, not noticing the little brown dead thing on the other side of the glass, not hearing it scrape along the stone and falling to the ground outside the front door.

Whoever moves it will die instantly and they will awake to find themselves where they belong.

Where they belong…

As I fall to my knees to the accompaniment of my father's hoarse cries, I think I know where Sheryl is now.

I am going to be living there for a while myself.

THE ROOM BENEATH THE STAIRS

Andy hated being forced to visit his grandmother.

As he watched his parents drive away in their battered Taurus, he once again found himself beneath the ivy-choked architrave that led into her terribly small and tangled garden. It made him wish his brother was still alive to do it but this in turn made him feel guilty. Before Steven had died, the task of representing parents who really couldn't be bothered to visit the old woman had been his charge.

Andy had only been to Gramma West's house a handful of times but it had been enough.

Even with his family around, he had felt threatened by something lurking in the permanent shadows of the old lady's home but those unseen watchers seemed patient to wait until he came by himself.

And now he was.

He quickly made his way up the narrow bramble-bordered path and wished he were somewhere else. Intimidating houses were not the place for a twelve-year-old boy on sunny Saturday mornings. He'd much rather be playing with Jimmy, the boy next door, or watching *Transformers* on the Cartoon Network.

Dewdrops glistened and dangled from black thorns like poison from the fangs of serpents. His discomfort seemed to draw the stares of invisible things. He felt a thousand hungry eyes on him, aroused by the scent of adolescent panic, hiding behind blankets of ivy and watching, waiting.

Lifting the bronze knocker he thumped three times and waiting a short forever before the door whooshed open and a florid rosy-cheeked face peered around the opening.

"Hey, Gramma."

The old lady swung into full view and made a face that suggested she might cry.

"Andy! Oh, how good of you to come see your Gramma!"

Her considerable frame heaved forward and swallowed Andy in an embrace tight enough to make him gasp. Just as he was beginning to formulate a polite protest, she released him and gestured for him to enter the house.

"Come, come!"

Beaming at him, she vanished inside with an agility that belied her eighty-three years.

Andy took a deep breath and stepped over the threshold into the gloomy hallway.

He followed his grandmother into the kitchen but not before casting a wary eye at the heavy oak door beneath the stairs. A thin shard of hazy amber light seeped through a crack in the wood as if someone was shining a torch through from the other side.

He recalled the last time he'd been here; the scraping noise that had come from inside the room. Despite his fear, he had approached the door with the intention of flinging it wide to gaze upon the horror it undoubtedly contained, but had scarcely touched the knob when Gramma West appeared behind him. He had almost suffered a heart attack when her pale hand fell on his shoulder.

"Hey, Gramma?" he asked as he entered the kitchen, pleasantly surprised by the thick aroma of freshly baked apple pies that greeted him.

"Yes, dear?"

"What's behind that door beneath the stairs?"

He half-expected her to tense and turn to look at him, the still piping hot pie slipping from her oven mitt, a guilty look on her bespectacled face.

"Oh, the devil is locked behind that door, Andy. He keeps me fit and healthy and I feed him little boys who are foolish enough to ask questions," she didn't say.

Instead, she raised her eyebrows and offered him a cheerful smile that made her cheeks puff up to twice their normal size.

"Oh, that was your grandfather's workroom. He was always a bit upset that we had no back garden or cellar for him to build a tool shed, so he used the room beneath the stairs. It's plenty big. Surprisingly so."

She opened the oven door and as Andy took a seat at the large pine table in the center of the room, he asked: "Can I see it?"

She wheezed as she bent over to slide two more pies into the oven.

"There's nothing to see in there, Andy. Just junk. I haven't given it the cleaning I've been promising myself I would. Can't bear to face it to be honest. Too many memories of your grandfather."

She took a seat opposite Andy, who was now picturing trans-dimensional portals hidden beneath stairwells.

"Some day when I get around to fixing it up, you can investigate to your heart's content."

Andy nodded. Her attempt at appeasing his curiosity had only further inflamed it, however, and he resolved to make another attempt to peek inside the room before he left.

"So how are things at home?" Gramma asked, poking the bridge of her glasses back into place.

He told her everything his parents had told him to tell her. Mostly lies. His home life since Steven's death had rapidly decayed and now their once benign unit had become a somber vigil to a stolen child. His parents went about their daily routine like hollow vessels, acting only on memories gleaned from happier times.

His grandmother's eyes told him she knew most of what he said had been from a script approved by his parents and that it was okay.

"I expect they'll end up spoiling you yet, Andy. Parents who've lost a child tend to lavish affection on the remaining one once the initial impact of grief subsides."

Andy nodded and drummed his fingers on the table. He was already bored and uncomfortable talking about his life with a woman practically a stranger to him.

"I suppose," he replied.

She clapped her hands together. "So how 'bout some pie?"

"Sure."

As they ate, Andy noticed the old woman staring at him with an intensity that made him squirm. He tried to reason she was simply glad to see him, but couldn't bring himself to believe it.

"You look a lot like your grandfather, you know," she said at last, breaking the silence forming like a pane of ice between them.

Andy raised his eyebrows in response, his mouth full of baked apples. He had been stuffing himself almost greedily as an excuse not to talk to her.

She looked at him with dark green eyes filled with remembrance.

"When he was young, I mean. Same chin, same ears. You even eat the same way as Ben."

Andy blushed, juice leaking from the corner of his mouth.

"You have the same hands too—a craftsman's hands. Elegant in a rough sort of way."

The boy dropped his gaze to his long, thin fingers. He quite liked her description of them. He had always just thought of them as…well, as hands. Now they were something much more. Now he had *craftsman's* hands. He smiled.

"There was nothing your grandfather couldn't make with his hands. When we were younger and moved into that terrible rattrap on Haybury Street, he made it into a little palace. The landlord refused to charge us rent for the next few months after he saw what Ben had done with the place. I imagine he was quite pleased when he thought of how much he could charge for it after we moved out."

Her eyes glazed over and Andy continued to eat, aware she wasn't actually looking at him anymore but using him as a focal point for her trip down memory lane.

"He built cabinets, tables, and chairs. Anything we needed and couldn't afford, he went out and chopped down a few trees from his father's place and made himself. By the time he was finished, the house looked nothing like it had when we first moved in."

She smiled, revealing polished dentures, and put her hand atop Andy's. The boy resisted the urge to pull away and secretly chided himself for being so cruel. Although he didn't know her and her house made him uneasy, she was still his grandmother. Plus, the pie was terrific.

"Another thing about Ben was that he was a pleasant character and made friends easily, whereas I was perfectly happy to stay at home, cooking and cleaning. I doubt there are very many women left these days who'd be so content with that!"

She chuckled and Andy grinned awkwardly, the humor lost on him.

"He began to do work for his friends, a favor here, a favor there, until word began to spread about the quality of his work. Soon the jobs were pouring in and so was the money. We went from being a struggling couple, held together by love and not much else, to a relatively well-to-do couple that could afford things we'd only dreamed about in the past.

"We moved out of Haybury and into this fine house, with plenty of money left over to think about starting a family. And so, we did. The day your father was born changed everything for us."

She stroked Andy's hand with her forefinger, a rueful smile on her face. The boy found his interest piqued despite himself and he abandoned his study of the cobwebs in the far corner of the room.

"We knew raising a child would not be easy and as Ben was up to his neck in work he'd been contracted to do, I was left with the task of bringing up your father. However, there were times when my husband would find himself summoned from his much needed slumber to deal with the wails of a hungry baby. Even when the child was distressed and filled the house with screams, Ben's hands would soothe it back to sleep. There was nothing he couldn't do. More pie?"

Andy was confused for a second by the change of subject and, when he realized what she was asking, shook his head and thanked her.

She nodded and continued to stroke his hand. Her skin was soft and supple on his.

"This went on for a year or so. If I was so tired that I wouldn't wake immediately, Ben would go to the baby and feed him, change his diaper, or stroke him back to sleep. I should have known at the time that he would not be able to continue like that without it having some kind of adverse effect on him."

"Adverse?" Andy interrupted, now so engrossed in the tale he didn't want any of it to pass him by.

"Bad. I knew it would end in disaster. We never argued. Well, not enough to worry about anyway. So when he began to grow irritable, I put it down to the long workdays and the inconvenience of having to tend to the baby whenever I deserted my post."

She took her hand away and clasped them together beneath her chin.

The sunlight that filtered in through the kitchen window to Andy's left made her eyes glisten and he found himself hoping she wouldn't weep. Such an outburst of emotion from his grandmother would leave him embarrassed and helpless.

"But it eventually came to a point where I was beginning to question whether or not he loved me anymore. His bouts of irritation turned to anger too fast for me not to be concerned. His hours grew longer and longer until seeing him home at all became a rare treat. He told me he'd been given a lot of work at the Fallon Mansion where that weird old guy Howie Phillips lived. For much of the time, your father kept me distracted, but lying alone in bed at night I had plenty of time to worry.

"When I confronted him about his hours, he would fly into a rage as if he thought I was accusing him of something. The arguments would end with my questions unanswered and my heart more wounded than ever. As for Ben, he would storm off and lock himself into the room beneath the stairs, where he would continue to work long into the night. As you can imagine, the clamor of his labors upset the child and I would be left dealing with a cranky baby the next day. I grew miserable and lonely."

When Andy spoke, his voice was tiny. "What did you do?"

Her eyes seemed to brighten at his obvious interest and she grinned slightly. "The only thing I could. I walked in on him in the room beneath the stairs and locked the door behind me, blocking any attempt he might have made to escape me."

Andy's eyes widened. A needle of fear pricked the back of his neck. "You didn't…"

Gramma West looked shocked. "Oh Dear Lord, no! I would never have done anything to hurt him. You must understand, Andy, that despite the fact he seemed to have lost all love for me, I still cared for him as much as always. The thought of losing him was unbearable and because he wouldn't speak to me, I imagined all sorts of unpleasant things he might be doing while not in my company.

"That night, he was outraged at my invasion of his sanctuary and tried to throw me out. I stood my ground, more out of shock than defiance. I could hardly believe what my eyes were showing me. But when he noticed that I had seen the fruit of his labors, he seemed to slump, and for the first time in months he spoke to me like the Ben I remembered, the man I loved."

Andy found himself leaning forward slightly, eager to hear what his grandfather had hidden in the room he, himself, was so curious to see.

"He had been in the middle of carving something. A figurine. From what I could see of it, it looked to be a rendition of a woman. It would go perfectly well with the thousands of others piled around him. Some of them were scattered about his feet, others stacked against the walls so high they squeezed beneath the slope of the stairs. All of them were carved from a light wood, maple perhaps, but not all of them were the same.

"As I scanned them in disbelief that he should be forsaking his family for such a repetitive hobby, I noticed that, amid the stacks of wooden men and children, there were monsters. Here was a representation of a woman with her hands to her face, screaming. There, an ill-formed, man-shaped thing with lovingly carved tentacles sprouting from its chest.

"Some were cowering wolf-like creatures with mouths full of jagged teeth and wild eyes. Others were so vile it hurt my eyes to look at them. And in the center of them all with a work-in-progress clutched tightly in his fist, stood my husband.

"He told me I should have stayed away from things that were none of my concern. This made me laugh out loud, Andy, it really did. I told him he was my concern and that I had only come to his little room to find out what was keeping him from his family, what was so important to him that he preferred their company to ours."

She sighed and fingered a curl of silver hair, her eyes boring through the kitchen table and Andy found himself wondering if his grandfather had made it.

"He had fallen in love with his own ability to create. And still, I tried to rationalize what I was seeing. Perhaps he had fallen into debt and been forced or consigned to produce thousands of odd little figurines in return. Perhaps it was just a large order he had received from someone, someone like Phillips. I thought these things and tried to tell myself that it had to be something that innocent. Only the look of shame and fear in my husband's eyes convinced me otherwise. That, and the sinking feeling in my bosom that whatever had taken hold of Ben wouldn't ever let him go.

"Eventually he told me everything."

She let her eyes drift around the room, settling on the window as she spoke.

"He told me it was his hands. He told me that the very things he relied upon to keep his family content were now responsible for trying to take them away. I didn't understand and I told him so. He sat down and hung his head, looking defeated and exhausted, and I went to him. When he flinched at my touch, I almost cried, deciding in that instant that I would fight his demons for him if it came to a point where he was unable to do so himself.

"His love for his work had died almost without him noticing, but he had snapped to attention one night in the middle of carving one of the figurines and realized that he had been in a daze, a trance of some sort and had made almost three-hundred of the ghastly things in an hour. He was up to his ankles in wood shavings with no recollection of ever carving them. He said that some of the statues were imitations of the child and me. Others, he didn't know quite what they were, but they were all things he had seen in dreams...or nightmares.

"He was being driven by some unwanted compulsion, what he called 'an outside influence,' to carve these things, and it scared him half to death whenever he came back to himself and found he had made a hundred more. Would it continue to make him work until they filled the house, the streets, the town?

"He had no answers for his own questions and I could not answer for him. I was just as scared by his revelations but not for the same reasons.

"I was beginning to doubt his sanity, you see. I thought that perhaps he had overworked himself into a fever and the threads of his composure were beginning to unravel. I felt guilty not believing him, but who would?

"His story continued in the same vein. He was not in control of his hands. A higher power was using him as a tool to make these ugly wooden statues. He did not know why but suspected its motives were not entirely wholesome. He begged me for help and as I held him in my arms in that small little room beneath the stairs where my husband carved out his madness, I promised I would help him."

She looked back to Andy, who was hanging on her every word. He had already made up his mind that if his grandmother had a vault of such stories he would be back again to hear them. These tales, undoubtedly embellished but no less powerful because of it, were like some of the stories he read in his brother's *Weird Tales* magazines. Gramma West's stories were a lot scarier though, simply because their roots were buried in truth somewhere. Half the appeal for Andy was not knowing how much was real and how much was made up.

"I took him from the room, his workshop, and brought him upstairs to bed, where he slept fitfully for a few hours and awoke weeping. I sat vigil by his side watching the sleeping pills take effect and his hands carve figurines above his chest. My own tears were silent as I watched whatever sickness held him in its grasp using him like a puppet. At times he would wake screaming, howling unintelligible phrases at the ceiling. As he slept, his hands would carve, and sometimes his nails would peel the skin from his hands until I gently pried them apart and set them on his stomach.

"I watched him die, Andy. I watched the terror his mind inflicted on him act itself out in one final display of shrieked gibberish and wide-eyed panic until his heart gave out and he collapsed back onto the bed leaving his final breath hovering in the air above him."

She leaned closer to Andy and he swallowed.

"But that's not the worst of it, Andy. Not by a long shot. The worst of it was that, as I watched over his body that night, as I prayed and wept aloud at last, as I rocked myself back and forth and listened to the baby cry in the next room, I was fascinated. Fascinated by his hands, that they could continue to carve their images from the air even as he lay dead beneath them."

"Woah," Andy breathed. "Is that why you didn't want to show me the room? Because you kept the figurines, right?"

The old woman fixed him with a look of intense sadness and slowly shook her head.

The figurines...

As he looked at her, his eyes widened in horror. He remembered the faint scraping sound from inside the room, the feeling of being watched in the garden. *A thousand hungry eyes.*

Gramma sighed. "I'm afraid I kept a little more than that, Andy."

SYMBOLS

"Hey lady, any hope of getting some service? I'm starving over here."

It was the wrong thing to say and had the kid been a regular at Joe's Gas & Gulp, he might have known that. But he wasn't and everyone turned to look at him as Daisy spun around, stub of pencil tucked behind her right ear like a mildewed horn, half-full coffee pot sloshing dangerously close to spilling in her left hand.

Daisy had taken over Joe's after Joe himself got run over by a drunk driver back in 1984.

Everyone had been a mite shocked about it to tell you the truth. The takeover that is, not Joe's death (hell, we'd all seen *that* coming. Any man who gets wasted and goes wandering along the center line of the highway after dark is asking for disaster). It had seemed as if Daisy and Joe had detested the sight of one another, always bickering and cussing and bitching. So, when it was announced that Daisy McFarlane would be running the business from now on, people were understandably confused. But in time, people stopped wondering and continued to fill their seats at the dusty little diner about halfway down Brimstone Turnpike off Route 71.

(You're probably waiting for me to tell you some spooky story behind the name Brimstone Turnpike, right? Well sorry. I don't know anything about that and as far as I know, no one else does either and if they do, they're not telling.)

But whatever else had changed about the diner, Daisy remained just as scowl-faced and ill-tempered as always. It wasn't something that bothered us anymore; in fact we kind of just respected it as part of who she was. Like a rabid raccoon, no amount of kindness is going to change the fact that it's rabid. But you don't poke a stick at it either and that's what the kid at the counter with the dull eyes and bad teeth was doing now.

I was unfortunate enough to be seated downwind of the kid and good *Christ* he stank—kind of a mixture of roll-your-owns and rotten fish. He couldn't have been more than twenty and wore a soiled, dark green army jacket.

I knew by the expression on Daisy's face when she offered him more coffee and he waved her away without looking up from the tattered paperback he had in front of him on the counter that she was hoping he'd give her an excuse to spit fire.

And now he had.

I wiped my mouth with the corner of a napkin, angry in a sort of distracted way that my quiet meal of ham and cheese bagels was about to be spoiled by another of Daisy MacFarlane's needless outbursts. I was well used to them you understand, but that didn't mean I couldn't wonder why she insisted on doing it every week like clockwork, or be happy about it. Only a fire could clear a place faster than Daisy. I guessed it was as essential a part of her being as the thick greasy makeup she wore which was at least two shades lighter than the skin beneath it.

"Excuse me?" she said and settled her three hundred-and-something pounds against the counter. A thick, short-fingered hand plunked down beside my plate like an blushing starfish as she steadied herself, the heaving of her massive bosom making Betty Boop's black and white ass poke further into the air on her apron.

The kid looked bewildered for a second and looked to me for support, as we were the only two seated at the counter. Jed MacLean and a bunch of his men from a construction site over in Harperville were seated in the booth behind me. One of them sniggered.

A sidelong glance from Daisy silenced him.

The kid gave her an uneasy grin. "Christ, sorry. I'm hungry all right, that's all I meant. S'not easy sitting here with an empty stomach and waiting to be served while a guy's sizzling steaks and hamburger right in front of your nose."

The 'guy' was Ralphie Grimm (I know, I know but no story there either), probably the most capable short order cook in the Western hemisphere despite his missing two fingers.

(And there *is* a story there, but it changes every week.)

Poor Ralph had a face that could turn your hair gray if you saw him in partial shadow but I have yet to meet a nicer guy, which makes it all the more upsetting that he died that day. I can still see him flipping those burgers and whistling soundlessly, occasionally flashing a smile or a lewd wink over his shoulder at Daisy's trundling form.

Now however I saw his shoulders tense and the whistling stopped.

Daisy's jowls tightened, her thin violet lips curving into a wicked sneer. "A man hungry enough to forget his manners ain't half a man at all," she said in a tone of voice that suggested she was recalling a passage from the Bible.

Over our heads, the old fan rattled. Someone coughed. The griddle hissed.

"Jesus, lady…"

"*Lady?* My name is Daisy and I own this establishment, boy. If you'd looked carefully enough you'd have seen the tag on my uniform." She tugged at the little white rectangle on her bosom. "Day-*Zee.*"

The kid shrugged. "I don't like to peer too closely at ladies' breasts, Ma'am. Gets you in trouble in some places, y'know?"

Mirth bubbled in my throat and the fact that all of Jed McLean's men were now wheezing laughter into their hands made it all the harder to swallow.

But next to my plate, the starfish had reddened further and the mirth had vanished.

Christ kid, I thought, *don't make her go postal on you.*

"A wise-ass," Daisy growled, teeth clenched. "Maybe a turn on the griddle would put some manners into you."

The kid feigned shock. "Are you threatening me, Day-*Zee?*"

I ran a hand over my face and briefly considered telling the kid to shut his yap before Daisy rammed a saucepan into it. But I just sat there, trying to mind my own business and hoping Daisy wouldn't resort to—

"You little shit!"

—cussing.

"Now you listen here. Get back on whatever pile of junk you used to carry your skinny little hippy ass here and beat it before I beat *you* seven shades of purple."

She had shifted forward a step closer, her face positively swollen with rage. The starfish drew in on itself and was now clenched against Daisy's side, attached to an arm roughly the size of a small keg. The coffee pot was still gripped in her other hand and if nothing else, I prayed she'd put the damn thing down before the kid ended up wearing it.

"That's not very nice," the kid said, sounding genuinely hurt. I looked at him, his eyes now hidden beneath his long black fringe as he stared down at the book. "Besides, I walked here."

A flicker of uncertainty passed over Daisy's face like a ripple over a calm pond. She cackled dryly and looked at Jed's boys and then me, perhaps hoping we'd join in. We didn't.

"Walked? Son, no one walks in this heat. That road out there is called Brimstone Highway for a reason you know. What kind of a hopped-up lunatic are you anyway?"

Her gaze hardened and she stepped right up to the kid and snatched the paperback out from right under his nose. "I'm talking to you and as long as your ass is taking up valuable real estate in here, you'll listen." She wiggled it in the air like a playground bully and I saw the name of the book, or at least what the name looked like.

Silver symbols against a black background. No letters, just lines and shapes, and squiggles.

I didn't think much of it at the time. For all I knew the kid was a Muslim and liked to keep up on his religion. I'd never seen Muslim language but I imagined it looked pretty similar to the hieroglyphics on that cover. There was no picture, unless you count a big black crooked rectangle with a speck of amber light in the middle and I don't.

"Give it back," the kid said, his voice sinking a notch. "I'm just hungry, that's all."

Daisy raised her pencil thin eyebrows and gave the book a cursory glance. "What's this? Nazi shit, no doubt. You kids are all the same these days, one cult or another as if the world isn't messed up enough without you bringing more crap into it."

Finally I found my voice: "Daisy, just give the kid back his book would ya?"

She spoke without looking at me. "Mind your business Tom or

you'll be out on your ass too."

And with a casual flick of her wrist, she sent the book flying over her shoulder where it came to land atop the griddle, among Ralphie's sizzling steaks. Ralphie gave a surprised '*uh*' and gawped at the newest addition to his menu. "What the...?"

Daisy set the coffee pot down on the counter and leaned in close to the kid, her hands clamped onto the counter at either side of her. "And you stink kid. Anyone let you in on that little secret yet? You smell like road kill. And I'll tell you something else for nothing, this is *my* diner and everyone around here knows that. They also know not to mess with me. Wanna hazard a guess as to why that is?"

I expected a witty retort but the kid's eyes were growing darker by the minute, his lips thin and bloodless. I wouldn't have crossed him then, despite my having a good sixty pounds over him. He looked like he was about to go bananas. Whatever that face of his was saying, Daisy was encouraged by it. She was grinning from ear to ear, big coffee and nicotine-stained teeth gleaming dully, her face mere inches from the kid.

"Give me the book back," the boy replied tonelessly.

Ralphie had suddenly become interested in the little scene ever since the book had landed on his stovetop. When he heard the kid ask for the book, he winced and swept it off the griddle and onto the floor, where it lay in a smoldering heap, edges blackened and curled. Daisy, who ordinarily would have pissed petroleum at such a mutinous move, seemed oblivious to everything but the boy's pale face.

Ralphie looked at me. I shrugged.

"People who mess with Daisy McFarlane tend to wind up in hospital," Daisy was saying. "We tend to favor only polite folk in here and any fool who swaggers through that door thinking he can act just as he pleases because a *woman* is behind the counter finds out the hard way that this is nineteen-eighty seven and not the Dark Ages. If he acts the dick, he's likely to find himself leaving without one. Geddit?"

You had to admire Daisy. Only she could pull off a hackneyed gangster shtick and make it sound convincing. If I had been that kid, I'd have been soiling my shorts right about then.

But he wasn't.

Instead, he was staring blankly into her eyes as she spoke, waiting for her litany to end.

"Snot-nosed punk." Daisy straightened with a grunt and nodded in satisfaction. "Teach you to be more polite in future. Now get the hell out of my diner."

She turned to leave.

"My book," he said quietly. "I need it."

Daisy turned back, her face scrunching into a grimace. "What the hell is with you and that dumb book? I said get out of my diner. Don't make me throw you out."

Jed and his boys finished their meals, bored with a show they'd seen countless times before and left with muttered goodbyes and shuffling feet. They couldn't wait to get the hell out of there. It was close to a hundred degrees outside but wearing the heat was a damn sight better than wearing Daisy MacFarlane's tongue.

I knew how they felt but I wanted to see how this played out. I wasn't sure why but something about the kid didn't sit right with me and it wasn't just the dead eyes or the loose-fitting clothes.

Meanwhile, Ralphie had picked up the book and was wafting the burnt edges and blistered back cover with his hand as he walked toward Daisy. She moved aside with a disgusted grunt as he slid the book back in front of the kid. "There you go, kid. Not too badly messed up. I reckon the words'll still be there."

He offered a broad smile and nodded before turning to leave. The kid muttered something and Ralphie half-turned, the smile still on his crooked mouth. "What was that, son?"

The kid looked up and I noticed there were tears in his eyes as he caressed the charred cover of the book with his fingertips. "I said I'm sorry about what's going to happen to you. I don't mean for you to get hurt. It'll be a case of standing in the wrong place at the wrong time."

"Uh...son, I don't know what..."

Daisy's sudden outraged bellow almost sent me flying backwards off my chair. "That's a threat if I ever heard one! Tom, call Sheriff McGrath! We got us a little no-good criminal here. In *my* diner!"

I didn't move. I never had the chance and what happened next would haunt my dreams for the rest of my life.

The kid wiped his nose against the back of his sleeve and picked up the book. I remember wincing when he cracked it open, tiny pieces of melted binding scattering across the counter. Daisy was still shrieking and at one point she nudged my hand but I didn't hear what she said. Whatever I'd felt—or sensed or whatever the hell you want to call it—about this boy was going to show itself now. I was sure of it and God himself couldn't have moved me off that chair. I felt the hair prickle all over my body as if the air had suddenly filled with electricity.

The boy opened the book. The pages it seemed were intact though the edges were badly burnt. He raised the book up to his chin.

Daisy had had enough. She shambled forward, shoving Ralphie out of her way and with a muttered curse she reached a hand out to snatch the book from the boy's hands.

The kid blew across the pages like a librarian blowing dust from an old tome, except it wasn't dust that flew from the pages of the kid's strange book.

It was the words.

As Daisy, Ralphie and I stared transfixed by this most impossible of illusions, a strange circular symbol, tiny, black and round lifted off the page and floated out until it attached itself like a fake tattoo to Daisy's jiggling arm. At first she simply frowned and crooked her elbow to get a better view of the bizarre attachment. "Now how in the hell did you...?"

Then she shrieked as it began to burrow beneath her skin.

My immediate instinct was to run like hell. I'm sure I might even have tried had the kid not turned the book on me.

"And you," he said and I felt as if my guts had turned to ice crystals. "You are another casualty of the mistakes of others. They will only silence you, nothing more."

I shook my head so hard I heard my neck crack but I knew what was going to happen just as I had known there was something different, terribly different about the kid and his strange little paperback book.

It lay flat in his open palms in a V-shape, framing his chin as he pursed his lips and blew. The page fluttered and exhaled a quartet of tiny black exes with barbed edges. They came at me like angry wasps and then I made the last sound ever to pass between my lips. I screamed loud and hoarse. The perfect opening for the symbols to enter my head. They tickled and hurt the back of my throat as if I'd swallowed powdered glass and I retched. Silently.

The alarmed cry this invasion inspired never came. My mouth was open but nothing emerged except hot, panicked breath.

I got to my feet, both hands clawing at my throat, feeling the rippling beneath the skin there, horrified and terrified all at once but knowing I had been lucky.

Lucky that the kid had spared me from the fate he was meting out to Daisy.

She was tearing at her skin, flaps of it were hanging loosely from her face as she spun round and round like a lunatic as the kid blew more and more of the little black symbols at her.

They were ripping her apart from the inside and while I had been struck dumb, Daisy's guttural cries of agony made the floor tremble.

I staggered backward, my back colliding painfully with the booth where just moments before Jed MacLean and his crew had been chowing down on some of Ralphie's Prime Rib.

The end, when it happened, took only seconds and when they tell you in novels that time seemed to stretch into an eternity you'd better believe it. Those last few moments were long enough for a man to lose his faith and turn old and gray.

The kid snapped the book closed but by then there was nothing more he needed to do.

Daisy had clawed most of her makeup and the two-shades-lighter skin off with it and yet the little black symbols continued to slice and tear at the exposed flesh. There was a sudden ripping noise and a long pink thing wriggled from her mouth, slapping against the counter before sliding to the floor.

I moaned and in my head I heard it, even though I hadn't uttered a sound.

Daisy spun wildly as a small black S-shape scissored open her left eye sending a jet of milky fluid into the air. She stumbled backward and rammed into Ralphie, who had been standing pallid-faced and paralyzed with fear as his boss was torn to pieces by the kid's symbols. Ralphie gave a startled yelp as Daisy's massive bulk knocked him off balance. His arms pin wheeled crazily before he was sent ass over teakettle into the frying vat where his specialty chicken wings ($2.00 before six) were bubbling and roiling in the searing fat. His legs drummed frantically even as he was being fried in his own vat but Daisy's weight kept him where he was and soon the struggling stopped.

My stomach spasmed and I doubled over, unable to ignore the smell of cooking flesh and perversely glad the chicken had been in there to at least partially mask the horrid odor. I vomited copiously and heard Daisy's scream fade to a pathetic warbling before a loud thump indicated the symbols had completed their grisly task.

I allowed myself a frantic glance over the counter. Between the white clad V of Ralphie's outstretched legs I saw the top of Daisy's head, flayed but still twitching as the symbols freed themselves from their dead host and returned en masse like a cloud of gnats to the kid's book.

I put a hand on my quivering stomach and stared in terror at the kid.

He got to his feet and regarded me with what I can only describe as sympathy though his eyes were nothing more than black holes in his skull. The return of the symbols was mirrored in them.

"They make me do these things you know," he said in a curiously child-like voice. "It wasn't written like this. People need to learn."

He nodded at me as if this was supposed to be explanation enough and turned.

The tinkle of the bell announced his departure as, book in hand like the world's most unlikely bible salesman, he stepped out into the noon sunshine.

I was alone with the smell of death.

In a drunken stumble I ran to the phone, had dialed the number with a trembling finger before I remembered my new condition and hung up.

Sometime later, the bell rang again and I flinched, sure it was the kid come back to finish me off. But it was a trucker who, despite his bulk, turned and spent his lunch on the linoleum when he saw what was left of Daisy and Ralphie. His eyes found me, widened and he ran back to his truck.

The police arrived and tried to question me until they finally figured out I was in shock and carted me off to the hospital. If I could have spoken, I'd have told them there was nothing they could do for me.

* * *

That was one year ago today and though the nightmares have

94

stopped, the fear remains.

The only image that remains any way clear in my mind now is the sight of those exes swirling through the air—miniature ravens caught in a cyclone as they head toward me, finally finding the security of my screaming mouth…

For a year I've tried to put it behind me but any recovery is tempered by the knowledge that those symbols are still inside me. In that respect, Daisy and Ralphie were lucky. They got to die.

And now I've figured out that the only way to escape this ugly, alien feeling that crawls beneath my skin is to join them. So tonight I'm checking out. My father's old Police Chief's Special sits next to me as I write this.

But before I go I'm going to try an experiment.

I'm going to finish my whiskey and stare at the words I've written here.

And see if they move.

EDITOR'S CHOICE

"Morning sweetie," Lynn said, spinning on her heel to retrieve the purse hanging from the back of the chair opposite Malcolm.

"Mmm," he replied, brow furrowed, back hunched as he pored over the morning's mail.

"How do I look?" she asked, adopting a catwalk pose that was lost on him. He grunted but did not look up, eliciting an irritated sigh from her as she headed for the door. "Anything interesting?"

He snorted, his eyes glued to the page in his hand. "Nothing I want to hear, that's for damn sure. This magazine *Pirates of Reality* makes me feel like a dog chasing a bone tied to a speeding truck. I mean, what exactly are they looking for?"

She was waiting by the door, hand resting lightly on the latch, already sorry she'd asked. "Another rejection?"

"The first story was one of my best efforts and they told me it was too cynical. Can you believe that? Rejected for expressing my political opinion! And now..." he shook the letter, his lips thin and drained of color, "...and now *this*!"

Lynn shifted her stance and sighed. "I'm really sorry, honey but I have to go. I have that job interview today, remember?"

"You know my story *Benjamin Cooley: Detective of the South?* One of my best, right? Even you said that. You said it is was the best story I'd ever written and you have a diploma in English!"

"Degree."

"Whatever."

"I have to go," Lynn said and opened the door. "I'm sure it's just a case of them not recognizing good quality fiction. I'll be back in about two hours, okay?"

"Damn amateurs!" he continued, ignoring her. "Wouldn't know professional literature if it bit them on the ass!"

Lynn shook her head and walked out the door.

"Wait!" Malcolm called and she paused.

"What?"

His expression was one of total bewilderment. "Where are you going?"

Biting her lower lip, Lynn closed the door, leaving Malcolm alone with his disgust.

* * *

Dear Mr. Pepper,

Thank you for sending us your story 'Hanging On The Coattails of Gorillas'.
Unfortunately, after much thought we have decided not to accept this for inclusion in Boomhatch *magazine.*
While very amusing, I found the structure a little distracting.
You seem to favor fragments in your prose. While this is not necessarily a fault in itself, I do feel that your work needs discipline. The tale seems a little stilted, the dialogue terse and unbelievable.
It is clear that you have some original ideas and I firmly believe that with a little work, you will be quite a capable writer.
Thank you for thinking of Boomhatch.

Regards,

Mike. W. Canavan
Senior Editor
Boomhatch *Magazine*

* * *

With a howl of rage, Malcolm crumpled up the paper and flung it across the room.

Distracting! Fragments! Discipline! Stilted! Unbelievable? With a little work?

How dare they!

"Sons of bitches," Malcolm growled and stalked upstairs to his office.

The room had one window, right in front of the computer and at this time of day, a hazy corona around the monitor was all he could see of the sun. That suited him just fine. An atomic bomb dropped right in his back yard couldn't deter him from the task at hand.

Charlatans!

On either side of Malcolm, hardcover books stripped of their dust jackets were aligned perfectly, four shelves high and set on shelves that reached almost from wall to wall. They were his pride and joy, the words within the inspiration that drove him to write. The smell of them was enough to fuel his desire to tell the stories he knew the public wanted to read, regardless of what those uneducated hacks at *Boomhatch* and *Pirates of Reality* thought.

After a moment spent pondering, his fingertips hovering over the keys, he exhaled and began to type.

Soon he was lost, immersed in a world that fell short of his own ability to describe in common language, the occasional chirping of birds the only sound struggling to compete with the frantic clacking of keys and click of the spacebar. There was no reprieve, the lapse of time evident only in the lazy movement of the glowing orb high in the summer sky outside both his office and creative windows. The splash of sunlight became finger-like bars of shadow as he wrote, his mouth working soundlessly, reading what he wrote from the notebook in his brain before they appeared on the filtered screen before him.

This would be a masterpiece, driven by fury and frustration, a challenge to those so-called experts. Let them turn *this* down. They would live with the mistake forever after if they dared.

The daylight faded in synch with his energy and he found the cursor blinking impotently, waiting to be prompted back into action or set free. With a husky sigh and a stretch that made his back pop, he decided he had done enough for one day. He checked the word count (five thousand, not bad), saved the document under the provisional title "Editor's Choice," and with a self-satisfied smirk, shut down the computer.

"You done?"

Malcolm had been halfway out of his leather swivel chair when Lynn spoke. Her voice startled him and he turned, thumping his thigh against the knee space below his desk.

"Ah, blast it!" he hissed and began to massage his leg, pushing the chair away as he did so. "You scared the bejesus out of me, woman! Don't sneak up on me like that! Where have you been until now anyway? It's almost..." He shrugged back the sleeve of his shirt and peered at his watch. "...Six o' clock!"

He fixed her with a look that demanded answers. Calmly, she leant against the doorjamb, eyes narrowed, arms folded. "I came home at about two o' clock, Malcolm. I stood right where I'm standing now and asked if you wanted to go to lunch. You ignored me so I went by myself. I met up with Christina for coffee and stopped at the grocery store on my way home. Is that okay with you?"

The sarcasm in her tone went straight over his head and he nodded as if she had genuinely been seeking his approval. "I was in the zone, baby. You know better than to try talking to me when I'm at my creative peak. Any distractions when I'm in such a frenzy could be detrimental to the integrity of the piece I'm working on."

"I see," Lynn said, unimpressed.

"And this piece is a real winner. I can feel it in my bones, Lynn! It's the best stuff I've ever written. Something to shove up the noses of those talentless editors. This'll get my name known, raise my profile, and put me on the hot list! Mark my words, babe. This one is gonna put Pepper on the map!"

She looked at him for a moment as if unsure whether to scream at him or break down in tears. His expression of delirious enthusiasm faded. "What's the matter?"

"Nothing," she said and turned away.

He rushed after her and caught her elbow. "Wait, what is it? You upset about something?"

She shook her head and pulled away. "I'm fine. Just tired, that's all. The interview was a nightmare. I think I blew it."

Malcolm clucked his tongue and sighed sympathetically, even though he hadn't the faintest idea what she was blabbering on about. She started to walk away and he halted her. "Hey."

She turned. "What?"

"How about you throw on some dinner while I take a shower. I'm starving and I'm sure a bit of food in your belly will make you feel better too. What do you say?"

She stared at him for a moment before nodding. "Yeah."

Malcolm watched her descend the stairs and smiled. *Poor thing*, he thought, *she'd never make it as a writer.*

* * *

After dinner, Malcolm sat himself down in the den; a thick book on his lap while Lynn lay on the sofa watching a comedy show on television. She had changed from the elegant attire she'd worn to the interview into a t-shirt and sweatpants. Malcolm hated to see her without make-up and dressed like a street thug but his frequent attempts to change this frustrating habit of hers seemed futile so he put up with it. Her eyes were hooded and it wouldn't be long before sleep claimed her.

Good.

That way he wouldn't be distracted.

Flipping open the hefty tome, he traced the bold print with his finger until he came to a listing that piqued his interest.

"*Analysis Hall: Words for the Wise*," he read aloud.

"What?" Lynn asked, suddenly alert and looking at him. Though he appreciated her feigning interest as she had many times before, he knew she couldn't care less about his work. He offered her a wink and returned to the spot he had marked with a fingertip.

"Seeks fiction or non-fiction up to eight thousand words. Pays ten cents a word. Most genres. Circulation 11,000. My, my. Wouldn't that be sweet?"

Lynn sat up. "What's the..."

He hushed her with a raised hand. "Wait, Lynn. Give me a second. This is important."

She huffed indignantly and lay down again. "Fine."

"Response time, a week! I can scarcely believe it. Usually the pros take forever. I was waiting on Boomhatch for two months!" He rubbed his hands together and grinned. "This is it, Lynn my girl. This is the one. I'll finish 'Editor's Choice' tonight and have it off to the good folk at Analysis Hall in the morning. No crummy editors here, no sir! These people sound like the genuine article, don't you think?"

Lynn opened her mouth to reply.

"Yes indeedy! This is the one," Malcolm continued, giddy with excitement. "Just the springboard I need for my career! First *Analysis Hall* and then *Playboy*! Think of the money, Lynn! You can buy all the…well, whatever you want!"

Lynn shrugged. "Great."

He curled the corner of the page down to mark his place and shut the book with a slam that made her jump. "Oh, c'mon Lynn! Be a little bit enthusiastic at least, can't you? I'm doing this for both of us y'know. Sure, it may be small potatoes now but you wait. Give it a year and we'll be out of this crummy neighborhood and living the high life!"

He got to his feet and headed for the door.

"Wait," Lynn said, craning her head to see him. "Aren't you going to ask me about the interview?"

He splayed out his hands in a gesture of helplessness. "You told me you blew it. What else is there to know?"

When she didn't reply, he blew her a kiss and trotted upstairs to complete his masterpiece.

* * *

The following morning Lynn was in a foul mood and Malcolm thought it best to avoid her, figuring it was that time of the month in which nothing he could do would be appreciated.

He ignored her cold stare as he lovingly paper-clipped a cover note to his pristine white manuscript and slid it into an envelope.

The phone rang just as he was licking a stamp and he raised his eyebrows when his wife looked at him. With a grimace that made her almost remarkably hideous, she shoved her chair back and stalked off to answer it.

Malcolm rolled his eyes and applied the stamp. He had just uncapped the pen and was scribbling the address he had jotted down on a piece of paper onto the front of the envelope when Lynn whooped in delight. He straightened and watched her dance back into the kitchen, a different woman than the ogre who'd gone to answer the phone.

"What is it?" he asked, watching her jiggle with excitement as she swiped a piece of cold toast from the table and nibbled at it.

"Gohjob," she mumbled, her mouth full.

"You got the job? Why that's great honey!" he said and returned his attention to the envelope.

"I have to be there this morning for training. I'm taking over from some old guy who's been itching to retire for years. They said they liked my approach and thought I could introduce some new ideas and a fresh perspective into their company! Isn't that great?"

Malcolm nodded absently and held the envelope out in front of his face. After a moment of scrutiny, he turned to Lynn, stooped down and kissed her on the cheek. "That's outstanding. Could you pop this into the mailbox on your way out?"

Lynn's chewing slowed as she watched her husband mount the stairs, whistling an off-key rendition of 'We're in the Money' as he went back to his office.

* * *

The wait was unbearable.

For the next week, Malcolm kept a vigilant watch on the mailman. Day after day, he struggled to keep his excitement at bay as the guy with the blue shorts and light blue shirt popped a wad of mail into the box outside Malcolm's gate and every day it was the same.

Bills, subscriptions...junk.

With the continual disappointment came the urge to look up the number of *Analysis Hall* and call them up. He could pretend to be asking for confirmation that his manuscript had been received. Ultimately though, he didn't trust himself not to inundate them with questions, sabotaging his chances of acceptance.

Did you read it? What did you think? Well, when are you going to read it? But your guidelines said...

Definitely a bad idea.

Then exactly two weeks later and with Malcolm ready to storm the offices of *Analysis Hall*, the letter came.

It was on the table amid the usual pile of Lynn's beauty tips, free sample sachets of God-knew-what and women's magazines.

Lynn sat next to the heap, reading *Cosmopolitan* and sipping a cup of coffee.

Although encouraged by the fact that it was a letter and not an envelope—something he had grown accustomed to and which meant return of his manuscript—he was also irritated.

"Why didn't you tell me the letter had arrived?" he asked Lynn, who turned and gave him a casual glance.

"Good morning," she said sweetly and returned to her magazine. "I didn't know it was something important."

"What?" he cried suddenly, outraged that she could treat the subject with such indifference. "You should have been watching for it. Don't you listen to anything I say? I've only been going on about this for two weeks."

Lynn shrugged. "Forgot. Why don't you open it and see what it says before you go running your mouth of about it?"

He stared at her, mouth agape and snatched the letter off the table. Carefully sliding his finger beneath the sealed flap, he shook his head in disgust. "You could do well to show a bit of interest in your husband's affairs, woman. This is a new publication and the only one I know of that will have the talent and education to see the genius in my work. It may mean nothing to you, but it's damn important to me."

Lynn said nothing.

He removed the letter and opened it out with trembling hands.

As he began to read, the color drained from his face.

It read:

Dear Malcolm,

Thank you for submitting you work to Analysis Hall.

After carefully reading your story 'Editor's Choice' I'm afraid I will have to reject it.

The reason for this is mainly due to the fact that your writing is quite simply—awful. Although I did read the whole story despite nearly nodding off after the first paragraph of senseless drivel, I found nothing of value whatsoever in the piece and with that in mind I recommend that you (a) not submit to us again as we receive too many quality submissions to be distracted by such garbage and (b) seriously re-evaluate your ambition in life before the talent you are convinced you have leaves you a bitter and lonely old man with nothing to live for...

Malcolm looked up, his face deathly white. "Dear God in Heaven," he mumbled.

Lynn pushed back her chair and straightened the lapels of her business suit. "I'm off to work," she said, smiling.

"Wait, you have to read this…this…" he pleaded, feeling bile rise in his mouth. "You have to see what they *said* about me…I-I…"

"What *who* said?"

He looked dumbly at her as she paused before the open door, a flare of sunlight brightening the walls in the hallway and he realized he hadn't read far enough to see who the author of this travesty had been.

When he did, his eyes widened and he dropped like a gunnysack into the chair nearest him. "Oh…my."

Lynn looked over her shoulder at him, winked and was gone.

A shawl of misery draped itself over Malcolm's shoulders as he stared at the familiar signature three-quarters of the way down the page.

He willed it to change, to prove itself nothing more than an optical illusion. When it didn't, it finally occurred to him that maybe he should have asked his wife about her new job.

FROM HAMLIN TO HARPERVILLE

They're hammering on the door again. But how can I really be that afraid when I saw it coming?

They'll find a way in, eventually. Despite my precautions and lunatic attempts at carpentry (my father would be proud), they are growing in number. Eventually the sheer weight of them crowding against the house will cause those boarded windows to snap, allowing them to spill and tumble and crawl and clamber their way into my crumbling sanctuary.

Before it's over, I must record this for the benefit of whoever remains out there.

This is a warning.

My death will be the true beginning of the end.

* * *

He walked into the town square at midday on Monday morning. (I find it hard to believe that was only two days ago.)

Although strangers have a pretty good chance of being noticed in a town as small as Harperville, it was Max's sudden frenzied whimpering and barking that drew my attention to him.

I was standing outside Strickler's store, loading sacks of groceries into the back of my truck and thumping a fist against the glass of the cab to chasten Max into silence when I saw him.

He was standing in the center of the square, right next to the statue of Harlan Masterson—the town founder—who now presided over a scum-filled pond with an understandably depressed expression on his marble face.

The stranger wore a dark suit that only served to highlight his stark white features, his hair wild and fizzing around his narrow skull like black electricity.

He would have looked odd to anyone else, standing there with his hands behind his back, head cocked slightly while all around him people were going about their business warmed by the pleasant August sunshine. But to me he didn't look out of place at all.

The dog bared his teeth and growled. I finished putting away my groceries and sat into the truck. Massaging the animal's shaggy coat as I gunned the ignition, I found it hard to look away from the man by the statue.

After a moment of staring in a manner that would have been considered impolite in any society, I started home.

A quick glance in the rearview mirror revealed that the stranger wasn't moving from his place by the statue and before I took my eyes off his dwindling form, I thought I saw him bring something long and thin out from behind his back, something that gleamed in the sunlight. Something he put to his lips.

* * *

I live alone. There are many reasons why that has to be the case but none of them are pertinent to this account. Although I don't consider myself an unfriendly fellow, I think perhaps the sight of the many demons cavorting in my eyes is enough to deter any potential relationships I might have developed with my neighbors.

My house is small, quite literally a 'cracker box' but it is comfortable and clean. At least it used to be before it became necessary to smash up the furniture to use for barricades.

When I got home, I put away the groceries, still troubled by the sight of the pale-faced stranger. He might not have bothered me had he just been going about his business, or acting like a tourist but he had seemed distinctly out of place in the square and I don't mean in the sense that any stranger might seem out of place in a town where there are no secrets and everyone knows everyone else. If anything, he looked as if he had been imitating the statue next to him. And the thing he'd been holding…

I grabbed myself a beer from the six-pack I had purchased at the store and sat down at the kitchen table, wishing I had something else to preoccupy myself with when the doorbell rang.

I hesitated, debating whether or not to answer.

There is a half-mile stretch between my home and the Sandersons next door. It had been almost six months since they paid me a visit and that had been an awkward affair, all uncomfortable silences and plastic smiles. Apparently, they had decided it was time to get to know their reclusive neighbor but I doubted I'd ever see them again after that brief encounter. If it wasn't the Sandersons, then it would more than likely be someone selling something and I was in no mood to face fresh-faced salesman on that particular morning. But I decided to see who it was if for no other reason than to distract myself from the inexplicable dread that had wrapped itself around me like a wet blanket.

I opened the door and sighed.

Geoff Sanderson.

He looked excited, double chin flapping and face wrenched into an enthusiastic smile as he did a little two-step on my stoop, as if he needed to go to the bathroom.

"Geoff."

"Hi Ed, listen! You're not going to believe what's happening in town!"

He was waiting for me to ask him what was going on but I didn't. I'm not sure I could have even if I'd wanted to. My skin had grown cold and slivers of ice began to slide down between my shoulder blades. Whatever was happening, I had felt it coming and now Sanderson was doing a jig on my porch confirming it.

"Rats!" he yelped and studied my face for a reaction.

I stared blankly at him, wondering what he was talking about. Had that been an exclamation?

He sighed deeply, looking at me as if I were slow. "Rats, buddy! The whole town has been overrun by rats!"

"What?" I had a sick feeling in my stomach.

"Yeah! I just got off the phone with Carl Brandner at the bank. He's a good buddy of mine," he said in a confidential tone as if this was something he was proud of. "He said that about fifty million of the little fuckers just came flooding into the square. Isn't that wild?"

I frowned at him, wondering how he could find such excitement in something that was making me physically ill.

"Christ. Is anyone doing anything about it?"

He waved away my question and I felt like punching him in the face. "Wait, wait! That's not the best part." He licked his lips. "Right in the middle of this shitpile of rats there's…wait for it…there's a guy!"

I felt the blood drain from my face before he said it.

"Playing a fucking flute! Can you believe it?"

I couldn't and the look on my face must have said as much because the smile vanished off Sanderson's face as if he'd been slapped.

"Hey Ed, you okay?"

I stepped away from him and slammed the door. He continued to mumble through it for a few seconds more and then I heard a car door slam. He drove away, no doubt regretting having taken the time to share such prized information with the weirdo down the road.

I drained the beer in one gulp, irritated that I hadn't something stronger and began to pace.

They found me, I thought, struggling to stay calm.

Outside in the back yard, Max began to growl. The phone began to ring.

And the world went to hell.

* * *

A state of emergency was declared, the media descended on Harperville like vultures and the stench of death permeated the air as people began to succumb to the effects of the infestation.

The next morning, accompanied by the echo of shotgun blasts and distant screams, I tuned out the world behind my faded curtains and switched on the television.

A weary smile creased my lips as I read the banner CNN had chosen to tag their lead story:

BLACK DEATH 2002 – HARPERVILLE, OHIO

Images of half-chewed bodies and twitching disease-ridden victims flashed across the screen but barely registered. I had been sensible enough not to stop drinking since Sanderson delivered the news and now my head felt light as a feather.

I felt guiltily satisfied that my rotund neighbor, who had derived such morbid glee from the 'plague' was probably himself now portioned out into hundreds of piles of rat shit.

Occasionally something would thump down low against the side of the house but I was too drunk to let it frighten me. Besides, it wasn't like I hadn't seen this kind of thing before.

The alcohol wasn't strong enough to dampen my grief however at the loss of Max. The golden retriever had been my only real friend since leaving Garretsburg and the sight of his mutilated body, lying on its side and still chained to the doghouse, brought tears to my eyes.

Grief turned to rage, then guilt.

I think now if I owned a gun I wouldn't be recording this. I'd have swallowed the barrel and gone the easy route out of this nightmare.

The only consolation is that it will soon be over anyway.

* * *

He came at midnight.

I was jerked from a fitful slumber in the armchair by the sound of someone knocking on the door. Disorientated, I rubbed my eyes and wiped drool away from my chin with the sleeve of my shirt.

The television was still broadcasting the atrocities that continued to take place at the center of the town. Apparently old Harlan Masterson had tired of watching the pond and was now lying face down in the murk.

I tried to tell myself as I hoisted my aching body from the armchair that it was the authorities at the door, come to take me to safety but I knew it wasn't. There are no safe havens for people like me and it was only then I was coming to realize that.

When I opened the door and saw the stranger standing there, I felt only the smallest twinge of surprise. The light from the room failed to reach his eyes and I trembled as I stared deep into those cold orbs.

Around his feet the rats swarmed like a living carpet, all fangs, claws and hair.

His face was all angles and completely bloodless as he looked over my shoulder as if checking to see if I had company. I stepped back and let him enter, leaving the rats at the threshold climbing over each other and squealing. Obediently.

I shut the door.

"Nice place," he said in a voice that sounded deceptively human. He sat in my Lay-Z-Boy armchair and clicked back the lever that folded out the footrest. Clomping two thick black boots up, he turned to look at where I stood paralyzed by the front door.

"Take a seat," he said. It wasn't a suggestion and I felt an inner pang of disgust at how fast I obeyed his command. I lowered myself into the high backed armchair in front of the window.

He cast a glance at the television and his lips curved into a smile, admiring his handiwork.

"You were expecting me," he said then, the smile gone, those black eyes boring into my skull. I realized that if I chose not to respond, he could simply tear the answer from my mind.

I nodded slowly. "I had hoped..."

"Hope is not something you have the luxury of entertaining anymore, Piper."

My head snapped up at the mention of the name. It was something I had forgotten how to hear, something I had prayed I would never hear again. How foolish of me to think I could ever step out of the shadow painted for me by past masters.

"Don't call me that."

He raised an eyebrow. "Is it something you're ashamed of?"

His impossibly long, almost feminine fingers drummed a tattoo on the arm of the chair.

I locked mine together to keep them from trembling.

"Do you miss them?" he said, nodding at the front door. The rats screeched in response.

I shook my head, bile filling my mouth with the return of memory.

"Not even a little bit?"

"No."

"I find that hard to believe Piper. A legend such as yourself should be proud of his achievements."

I looked down at my hands. "I told you not to call me that."

He sighed and the drumming stopped. "Can you really sit there and pretend that you're the victim? That the atrocities you so willfully caused were forced upon you?"

I heard the creak of the chair as he sat up and dropped his boots to the floor.

"I did what I was supposed to do, but it's over now. I'm just as human as the people you're killing."

He scoffed. "I'm afraid you'll never be as human as them, Piper. Never. You may have hidden yourself away in this shell of yours and you may act and smell and shit like them, but you'll always be one of us."

I looked into his viscous eyes, watched as the darkness shifted like tar. "Why are you here?"

He produced from his pocket a seven-inch flute, the mouthpiece solid gold, the pipe burnished silver. He twirled it in his fingers and grinned. "Play," he said.

I swallowed. At the sight of the instrument, my lips began to burn and God help me, I wanted to take it, to play the tunes that had been the signature of my old life, the melodies that had carried me from village to village, from Hamlin to Harperville. A desperate longing swelled in my chest, a sudden powerful urge to shrug off the pretense of my new found existence and bring the flute to my mouth, to fill it with my breath, to rub my fingers over the holes in its proud body with sensual fingers, to return to the world I had forsaken. To kill again.

No. I remembered. The children. Buried across vast plains of nothingness, their innocence torn from their naïve young bodies as payment for the deceit of their parents.

I remembered and oh, how it ravaged my insides. All the lives taken, all the violence. Lured from their homes with the promise of being carried to Heaven on the notes of a song only to find their mouths filled with dirt, their fingers removed and sent in crimson parcels back to their families. It would continue, of course. Nothing on earth had the power to stop it, but I could retain hope of salvation by resisting the urge to return to that life, to plunge my fingers back into the bodies of the innocent, to tear them asunder. In the face of such evil, I still had the power to say—

"No."

"It will never leave you," he said, visibly infuriated by my refusal and it was then that I knew that he too would be forced to pay a price if he failed to bring me back. "You are a pitiful sight, Piper. You concern yourself with the implications of a return to your old life.

You fear the sight, smell and taste of the blood of children but yet you are willing to let me wipe out this town if you refuse. Do you think that will redeem you?"

I forced myself to look away from the flute, afraid that if I stared at it any longer then I would have it in my hands and to my mouth before I knew what I was doing.

"Do you think *anything* can redeem you?" he spat and something rippled beneath his skin. Beneath the anger, I could see the faintest trace of fear.

"What will they do to you if you go back alone?" I asked in as calm a tone as I could muster.

The muscles in his jaw tightened. This time, when he crouched forward I thought the creak came from his bones and not the chair as I had previously thought.

"It took you some time to adjust, didn't it?" he asked, ignoring the question.

"What are you talking about?"

He fluttered a hand at me. "This…disguise. This shitty little mortal life you prescribe to. It took you some time to get used to it, didn't it?"

The sinking feeling in my stomach told us both that I knew what he was referring to. I could feel soft fingers probing at my brain and I shook them off.

"How could it be any different?" I replied, knowing he had dealt his best card.

"I didn't say it did. But by human laws, murdering children is one of the most heinous crimes of all. You no longer have your status as Piper to use as an excuse. You no longer have the treachery of mortals to use as an excuse. As a supposed human, the act of murdering children and burying them in your back yard leaves you viable to the most horrendous form of punishment."

Dejected and sick, I lowered my head and shrugged. "I didn't know how to do anything else."

His tone lightened, his face adopting an ill-fitting look of compassion. "Of course you didn't and I think if you look long and hard into yourself, you'll realize that you still don't know how to do anything else. You should be proud of what you did in Garretsburg, not ashamed."

I couldn't disagree with him. My transition from Piper to mortal had not been a smooth one. Infiltrating myself into humanity had only brought me closer to the children and the smell of them, the taste of them. I was trusted more than any Piper had ever been trusted and that made the killing worse. I fled from Garretsburg with blood on my hands and grief—a strange and savage new emotion—tearing at my insides.

I had found peace in Harperville. Now even that had led to disaster.

On the news, a shaky handheld camera shot showed the town square in flames as someone decided that the only cure for the plague of vermin was to torch them, and themselves. I sighed.

"I have one advantage over you," I said quietly and he cocked an ear toward me, straining to hear.

"Which is...?"

I looked defiantly into those orbs of darkness, the same black pupil-less pools that hid behind my own contact lenses. "I can die."

Alien color blossomed beneath the dead skin of his cheeks and he rose to his feet, his coat billowing out behind him. His eyes were full of murderous black thunder flecked with the lightning of fear. It was clear that he was not accustomed to rejection.

I almost laughed. Poor spoiled piper.

"Is that your decision then? You won't come back?"

"I made that decision a long time before you showed up."

He stared at me for a while and then brandished the flute like a knife, the mouthpiece clenched in one pale fist and for a moment I thought he was going to stab me with it.

"Very well then, Piper. If you insist on that I will do you the honor of seeing you out in the traditional way."

He put the pipe to his lips and began to play. The eerie music was like Heaven to my ears.

It echoed sweetly in the air long after he was gone.

* * *

The boards I nailed over the window are loosening. It won't take them long now.

I figure there's not a lot of tape left in this thing anyway, so I'll finish soon.

I'd like to have had more time, to discover all the things

humankind takes for granted, but it is all too clear now that we can never walk among you. Not if you are to survive.

The rats have gone, led away by my brother, their bellies full with the souls of those lost.

All that remain now are the children, tearing, ripping, snarling outside my house, and looking for a way in.

I suppose there is a kind of justice to be found in the fact that those children I murdered have come back to escort me home. My brother piper's touch.

Consider this my farewell.

Until this ends I am going to relax in my chair, pop the tab on another beer and maybe watch a little television.

Just like one of you.

COLD SKIN

Janice felt the world begin to blur, her eyelids growing heavy. Just as she was about to give herself freely to the cotton hands of sleep, she was shoved roughly from behind.

"Jan, wake up!"

Startled, she looked around with red-rimmed eyes until she registered the look of concern on her husband's face.

With a sigh, she propped her head up with a hand on her chin and stared into her cup of coffee, the tendrils of steam growing thin as the liquid lost its heat.

"What's wrong with you?" Jeff asked, pulling back a chair and sitting heavily down across from her. Her eyes drifted lazily to his face.

"Tired."

"Yeah, I can see that. Didn't you sleep at all last night?"

She shook her head. "N'much."

"Bad dreams?"

"Dunno. Cold."

"You were cold?"

She shrugged. "*You* were cold."

She looked back into her coffee and struggled to blink the sand from her vision. She sensed her husband's confusion but at that moment had no energy to deal with it. Besides, he would soon be gone to work and it would no longer be her concern.

"That's odd. I don't remember being cold."

"You were asleep."

He snorted. "Why didn't you just move away from me?"

Another shrug. "Couldn't."

"Why couldn't you?"

"On my side."

"I was over on your side? You should have pushed me off!"

She was too exhausted to reply. Instead, she picked up the teaspoon and began to stir the coffee. His chair screeched against the tiles and her nerves as he got to his feet.

"I'm sorry Jan. I didn't mean to keep you awake. Maybe you should get some sleep instead of going to work. You look shattered."

She had already decided to take the day off to catch up on lost sleep and might have appreciated his suggesting it had she had the patience. But all she could manage was a brief emotionless smile as he kissed the top of her head and left.

She sat in the kitchen, alone with her thoughts and a cold cup of coffee until sleep reclaimed her and she slumped forward onto the tablecloth and into unconsciousness.

* * *

Lydia grimaced as she pulled the body into the bedroom.

She had thought the plastic wrapping would prevent him from bleeding all over the parquet floor but apparently she hadn't sealed it tight enough and now she had the added inconvenience of having to scrub the bastard's blood off the wood when she was done.

Cursing, she let go of the folds in the wrapping and allowed herself a satisfied grin at the sound of his head hitting the floor.

"Didn't see this coming, did you?"

She stared at him for a moment, his face an opaque blur through the material, but he wasn't talking.

That suited her just fine.

Taking a deep breath, she bent down and grabbed the plastic where she had bunched it up at the top of the wrapping. Absently hoping that she had managed to avoid getting blood on the new carpet in the hall, she dragged the gruesome package over to the side of the bed where again, she let go, relishing the sight and sound of his head cracking against the floorboards.

She leapt onto the unmade bed and let herself bounce up and

down for a moment, immersed in the scent of recent sex, the protestations of the bedsprings bringing pleasurable memories back to the forefront of her mind. She giggled like a child who has seen a boy naked for the first time and peered over the edge of the bed at the body on the floor.

Beneath his plastic shroud, he was naked.

Chewing on a nail, she decided that maybe the fun wasn't over after all.

* * *

Janice woke with a start, the side of her face wet.

Disorientation gave way to discomfort as she groaned and raised her head from the table.

A brief glance at the clock told her that she had been asleep for little more than forty minutes. Yawning and flicking coffee from her hand, she pushed back her chair and stretched.

The table was a mess. At some point she had knocked over her cup and the linen tablecloth was now a dirty brown color. She decided it was something that could be dealt with later. Her immediate concern was simple. Bed. Sleep.

Stiff-legged and sore, she made her way upstairs where the promise of a comfortable slumber awaited her.

* * *

"Mr. Carroll? Ms. Bernhardt would like to see you in her office immediately."

Jeff groaned and sat back in his chair, his eyes roving around the small office as if a solution to this latest inconvenience could be found written somewhere on the drab gray windowless walls.

"Mr. Carroll?"

"Yes, Harriet. Tell her I'll be there in a minute."

He released the button on the intercom, rubbed a hand over his face and sighed. Thoughts of his sleep-deprived wife crossed his mind but he forced them away. The day was bad enough without having an attack of ethics.

Shrugging on his jacket, he brushed back the sides of his hair with the palms of his hands and opened the drawer nearest him from which he produced a small bottle of breath freshener.

A quick spray and he was out the door, smiling.

* * *

Lydia ran her manicured nails through the tangles of hair on his chest and sighed. "You were never this considerate when you were alive," she purred, careful to avoid the gaping wound in his abdomen.

He said nothing.

* * *

"You wanted to see me?"

Ms. Bernhardt looked over the sheet of paper she had been reading when Jeff entered her office and removed her spectacles.

"Who authorized you to hire Sally Graham for the records department?" she asked, tonelessly.

He shrugged. "She was perfect for the job. I assumed you'd agree with me on it."

She rose, the seventh story view silhouetting her until she rounded her desk and approached him. "It would be hard to agree with you on something you haven't mentioned to me, Jeff."

He backed up a step as she neared him, a faint smile flickering on his face.

"Close the door," she commanded and he obeyed, pushing the button in the center of the brass knob that locked it.

In a second she was on him, forcing his back against the door, her lips mashed against his, tongue hungrily searching his mouth.

When they parted, she smiled at him. "You've been naughty again Mr. Carroll."

He groaned as her hand slid over the stiffness in his pants.

"You aren't really pissed about the Graham girl, are you?"

She dropped to her knees before him. "Who?"

* * *

Janice tossed uncomfortably, ensnared in the arms of a nightmare.

Occasionally, a whimper would escape her slightly parted lips. The sheets were damp with sweat as she turned onto her side, hand outstretched, fingers searching.

At last she found him and the dream began to barrel away down a long hazy corridor as she found solace in the fact, even in unconsciousness, that she was not alone.

Her fingertips came to rest on his arm and through the depths of sleep, a frown surfaced.

So cold.

* * *

Burying him would be the hardest part and she didn't mind admitting that it wasn't woman's work.

So for now, Lydia was content to rest. She was in no rush and she was positive that he didn't mind.

Her face resting against his naked thigh, she stroked the length of his flaccid manhood and licked her lips.

How simple they were when they were freed of their opinions.

* * *

The office was emptying; pouring out exhausted bodies while two equally spent employees lay intertwined on the floor of the executive director's office on the seventh floor.

Jeff rolled over and crooked an arm beneath his head. He was still wearing his shirt and tie, his pants lying in a heap behind her desk.

She got to her feet and searched for her panties, which she suspected were ripped beyond all hope of repair. Not that she minded. It was a small price to pay for the kind of attention Jeff was able to give her.

"So I suppose it's nearly that time again?" she mumbled, picking up the ruined panties and frowning at him.

"What time?"

"Time for you to go running back to your beloved wife?"

Jeff looked at her through hooded eyes as she stuffed her underwear into her purse. A sly smile spread across his face, causing her to pause when she noticed it. "What?"

He sighed dramatically. "My wife didn't sleep last night, so I'm thinking she might sleep through until morning."

"Really?"

He nodded. "I'm all yours."

* * *

Janice snored.

Every now and then she would brush against the body beside her and shiver, the cold skin almost enough to drag her back into consciousness.

Almost.

* * *

Eventually, she was sated and her mind turned towards the grueling task of interring her lover. Propping herself up on an elbow, she looked into his glassy eyes and imagined them staring forever upward at nothing but cold unyielding earth.

She smiled.

Sitting up, she reached over onto the nightstand and found her cigarettes.

Through plumes of blue smoke, she readied herself for the job ahead. It was true what they said. A woman's work was never done.

* * *

"Here we are." She led Jeff into the dark hallway of her apartment.

"Christ, it's huge. How much are they paying you these days?" Jeff said, in awe of her ultra-modern dwelling and wishing secretly that Janice would agree to let him move them to a more prosperous neighborhood, even if they really couldn't afford to. He believed if you acted like you had money to burn, then someone would grant you that ability eventually. It was all image nowadays.

"Trade secret," she teased and ushered him into the kitchen. "I'm going to get changed, why don't you put on the kettle."

"I doubt it'll fit me," Jeff quipped, grinning.

She made a face and continued upstairs. "Smartass."

* * *

Janice was frightened.

Still deep in sleep, something kept flashing through her subconscious that had the potential to drive her mad if it refused to rise to the center of her mind.

As she moaned, at first softly and then more forcefully, her nails dug deep into the flesh of her sleeping partner's arm.

As the dream retuned, she screamed out loud, unable to awake. Her nails dug deeper. And still there was no blood.

* * *

There was blood.

Jeff cursed as he looked at his shoulder in the mirror. In the reflection, his lover floated into view, her hair tousled, her beautiful body lit by the bulb above the glass.

"You scratched me."

"Ooops," she said, grinning mischievously.

Jeff wasn't impressed. He had managed to keep the affair a secret for almost six months now but there was no way he was going to be able to explain the four long scratch marks that ran from his shoulder to his elbow well enough to have Janice believe it.

"Christ."

Her expression hardened. "C'mon Jeff. It's not like she's going to inspect you when you get home. Wear a shirt to bed or something."

"I don't wear anything but shorts going to bed. If I suddenly go to bed with a shirt on, she'll suspect something."

"Say it got cold."

He spun around to face her. "I'd like to have the luxury of being so goddamn blasé about this, I really would but unfortunately I didn't marry an idiot. She'll figure it out and I'll be out on my ass."

The look on her face gave him pause and he found himself swallowing a lump that had suddenly formed in his throat.

"Ungrateful prick," she spat and stalked off into the bedroom. She slammed the door hard enough to make him jump and he sighed.

"What the hell am I going to do?" he asked his reflection.

It stared blankly back at him.

* * *

Janice awoke in darkness, her eyes moist.

Her breath rushed in and out of her lungs as if she had been smothering and she turned to see if Jeff was still there.

A touch of her finger against his flesh confirmed his presence.

She pulled the covers up around his neck in an attempt to stave off some of the chill infecting his skin.

"Poor baby," she whispered and turned over on her back.

As she drifted back to sleep, she remembered and her mouth opened into a soundless scream as soon as sleep rushed in to get her.

* * *

"Ashley, open the door."

He could hear her cursing and swearing in the bedroom but she refused to acknowledge him. Pressing his forehead against the door, he considered his options. Leaving her in a state of fury was definitely not a wise idea. A woman in her frame of mind was likely to do anything and that included calling Janice and spilling the beans on their little misadventures at the office.

Breaking down the door would only frighten her and God only knew what kind of a reaction that might provoke from her.

He decided to play it safe and sat down with his back to the door.

"Look I'm sorry. You know you mean more to me than that bitch I married."

It was a lie and it hurt him to say it, but he figured putting Janice down in front of Ashley might win her over.

He heard the sound of a drawer being opened and shut again to the accompaniment of the woman's growls.

"C'mon baby. I was upset, okay? I don't want what we have to end, that's all and these scratches…well, you're right; she probably won't notice them at all. Dizzy little bitch doesn't know what day of the week it is at the best of times."

In an instant, he was on the flat of his back, the door open.

She stood naked over him and he smiled foolishly. "I knew you'd…"

"It's over," she said flatly.

"What? C'mon baby, we can…"

The rest of the sentence and his tongue were both scythed from his mouth in one quick snap of her wrist.

* * *

She was sweating heavily by the time she'd dropped him in the hole and filled it in. The thought of a nice long bath made her skin tingle in anticipation as she dropped the shovel in the weeds that bordered her garden.

The first drops of rain pattered against her forehead and she raised her mud-streaked face to them, open-mouthed and smiling.

* * *

Janice was crying.

Thrashing through the subconscious depths of a dream populated by demons her body shuddered, wracked by spasms that mimicked the blows she was being dealt in her mind.

"Nooooo," she said softly.

She felt his hands on her then and almost instantly the dream began to lessen in intensity as he chased the unseen phantoms back down the black spiral tunnel that had birthed them.

"Honey," he whispered into her ear.

She smiled and let his fingers trace invisible lines on her thigh, shuddering not uncomfortably at the iciness of his touch.

They moved downward and she made a low guttural moan.

Her eyes drifted open.

* * *

Lydia sat like a hungry vulture at the edge of the grave she had made for him. Her face was twisted into a scowl as she watched the rain gathering in muddy puddles at the bottom of the narrow trench.

It was empty.

The sky grumbled above her head as she rose up, cursing.

At least she had the consolation of knowing that wherever he had gone, he wouldn't be gone long. He would return as always in time for their game, in time for her to kill him again.

She turned away from the grave and shuddered.

Even in death you couldn't trust them not to wander.

And then she saw the footprints leading from the grave to the wooden gate between her yard and the one next door.

Cheater, she thought, outraged.

She opened her mouth, her face twitching in rage and screamed.

* * *

As a final bubbling sigh escaped Jeff's mouth, Ashley dropped the knife and backed away from the door. Her fingers crept towards her face like albino spiders, eyes widening in shock and horror as the full extent of what she had done suddenly dawned on her.

In the doorway, Jeff's ravaged face moved and she scurried away.

"I'm sorry I'm sorry I'm sorry," she wailed as her lover's body suddenly rolled onto its side, a blood-soaked hand clutching at the carpet.

"B...itchhhhh," he gurgled and began to crawl his way toward her, one punctured eyeball swinging on the end of its optic nerve.

When she reached the bedroom wall, she dared to close her eyes in an attempt to vanquish the morbid hallucination suddenly gripping her.

The hallucination reached for her.

* * *

Janice tried to move away but he held her tightly in his arms.

She struggled to turn her head toward him, even though he was holding her from behind and it was dark.

His face slid over her shoulder.

She saw his eyes and screamed, somehow still able to hear the sibilant whisper that hissed from his lifeless mouth.

"Honey...

NOT WHILE I'M AROUND

Rachel stares at the phone, blood draining from her face. She winces at the shrill cry from the hunched beetle-like thing. It demands she answer.

Upstairs, Bill: "Honey? You going to get that?"

Yes, she replies and realizes she hasn't said it aloud. Then: "Yes, dear," and Bill shuffles away from the landing.

Outside the house, an autumn breeze moans with the agony of squeezing itself through the cracks and gaps in her home. Her hand moves to the phone, seemingly of its own accord for she certainly hasn't willed it to do so, could never...

The phone falls silent. Relief. Her shoulders drop, the sweat between her shoulder blades cooling. The wind sighs, disappointed, then just as quickly resumes its hollow cry as Rachel jerks back to reality, pricked by the realization that the phone has stopped shrieking not because the caller has given up but because her hand is holding the receiver almost an inch above the cradle.

No!

Now the air grows heavy, despite the humming from the shower upstairs as Bill makes preparations for the night ahead. A night Rachel now thinks may not unfold as planned.

From the earpiece, the wind imitates the dead and above her head, the light bulb hums. Fades.

"Rachel..."

"Honey?" Bill is struggling to be heard over the inner and outer elements, trapped beneath his own rainfall in the bathroom. "Honey? Did the lights flicker just now?"

Her hand hasn't moved. Can't. She knows who the speaker is, knows for sure who whispers even though it's been so long. Worse still, she knows she was right all along, despite the condescending contradictions from the doctors. The thought angers her, adding a shiver to her already quivering body. All those nights she almost told the truth but deigned to protect that son of a bitch and now here he is calling her after all this time.

"Rachel…"

Her teeth pinch the flesh on the inside of her mouth but she is indifferent to the pain and the salty taste that flows over her tongue. Her hand is frozen. Invisible tendrils of cold crawl over the fingers clenched around the receiver, pouring from the holes in the earpiece, softly brushing against her skin…

"I'm coming, Rachel…"

It occurs to her that she may have lost her mind. It wouldn't be the first time she's been accused of it and what better way to usher in madness than to give audience to its greatest creation?

The shower stops but the wind doesn't, making sounds like ghosts jostling for a view through the keyhole of the front door.

"I'm coming for Billy boy, Rachel. I'm coming for the guy who's doing my baby…"

A contented whistling drifts down the stairs and Rachel hisses: "You leave my husband alone, do you hear me? You just leave him alone!"

A chuckle: Wind-choked vortex on the stoop or a long dead lover?

"You know how it is, baby. You know how it's always been. How it always will be. He ain't allowed to touch you. Not while I'm around…"

Out go the lights. She flinches them back on. Bill curses and the sibilant hiss from the bathroom is quieted. The wind snickers beneath the door.

"Stay away." Pleading now. "Don't come here. Please."

The ensuing silence is unnatural, an ill-fitting costume for the night.

"But you want me to. You need me to."

A creak. Footsteps on the landing. Her husband grumbles into view, his face florid, glistening with moisture. He pauses on the top step, one thick-knuckled hand on the newel post, bushy eyebrows raised as he points at her hand, the one still holding the receiver above the phone.

She swallows and summons a wooden smile. "Wrong number."

"*Oh no, most definitely the* right *num—*"

Rachel slams down the phone, both of them jumping at the resultant *ping!*

"Honey?" Bill's face contorts with worry. "Everything okay?"

She doesn't answer but stares at a point somewhere over his head as he approaches. Then finally she speaks, and is surprised to find determination in her tone. "We need to talk."

She leads him into the living room.

"But the party…" he says, glancing at a pale band of skin on his wrist where his watch normally sits.

"It might be coming *here*," she says and closes the door.

* * *

Through a gap in the curtains, she can see the twinkling of a streetlamp two blocks away, but distance is blanketed by darkness and perhaps it is something less benign, maybe the gleam in the eye of someone peeking into the room.

She tugs the folds together and turning away from the window, avoids Bill's gaze. There is nothing to see in his face but the kind of spousal impatience that might stall her words, dent her courage and doom them both.

Bill is agitated, cocks his head and studies the clock faster than the second hand can count off a minute. Rachel stops before the fireplace, looks at him and feels what romance writers might call a 'tugging of the heartstrings' though these particular strings feel more like piano wire.

"Rachel, I really think we should get ready."

She shakes her head, her lips tight. "We'd never make it."

A frown. "What?"

"I've always tried to be as open as I can with you, Bill but I haven't told you certain things because I didn't think they were important. Now I know that was a mistake though I'm not sure what difference knowing would have made. He'd find us wherever we went."

Bill's eyes narrowed. "Who's 'he'?"

"Jeff. An old boyfriend of mine from high school."

For now, the wind has died down and that preternatural silence has turned the air to crystal. The sound of the clock ticking hangs in the corners of the small room—an ice pick chipping into the shadows gathered there.

"I loved him and I truly believe he loved me."

Bill, trying to look interested, nods for her to continue and checks the time.

"Until he raped me."

Her husband braces his hands on the arms of the chair as if he's about to rise, but doesn't. "My God, Rachel. I can't believe you didn't tell me that. How awful."

"More than once," she says, her voice hollow now, like the wind.

"Jesus. Did you report him?"

"Oh no. I couldn't do that. He'd have killed me."

Bill shakes his head, brings thick fingers over his mouth. "God."

"Eventually we broke up but he never stopped chasing me. *Never.*"

"Why are you telling me this now?"

Rachel looks directly into his worried eyes. "Because he's coming here. Tonight. That's who was on the phone."

Bill reacts as if she's thrown ice water into his face and suddenly he's on his feet and stomping toward the hall. "For Chrissakes Rachel. What the hell kind of mess have you dumped us in now?"

"Bill, you don't understand. Please wait!"

Ignoring her, he flings the door open; muttering and chewing his unease into digestible chunks, his robe fluttering in the breeze his haste has conjured. "I'm calling the cops. Jesus Christ, this is insane. You told me it was a wrong number. Why would you lie to me? And speaking of numbers, how did he get ours?"

There isn't room to argue, so Rachel does the only thing she can think of. She sidles past him and with a vicious tug, rips the phone line from the wall. Like a headless snake, the black cord swings pendulously in her hand. She turns back, a triumphant look plastered on her pallid face. Bill stares at her in abject horror.

"What...what did you do *that* for?"

"They won't be able to help us. Bullets or restraining orders won't work on the dead."

Bill drops the phone. It clunks to the floor, narrowly missing his bare feet. "I'm going to fetch Doctor Simmons. You're ill." The light flickers.

"No, listen to me. I couldn't call the police when he raped me because my father would have killed us both."

"What?"

"The man…the *thing* coming here tonight has killed everyone I've ever tried to get close to. I thought…I thought it was over when I killed *him*."

A sound begins in Bill's throat, a low whine; the inner vacuum perhaps that is sucking the vitality from his face. When his mouth opens at last, he begins to back away, his eyes colder than any autumn his wife has ever seen. "Please don't tell me you believe any of this because if you do I'm afraid I may be losing you."

"Please," she says and steps toward him but a flutter of angry hands stills her. "You have to understand. I loved him. We loved each other but I never meant for it to be like this. He was supposed to stay dead!" The light flickers again, hums an unfamiliar tune.

Bill's back slams against the front door, his eyes wide and glassy with pain. "Tell me this is some sick joke. Tell me you're making this up or…"

"Or what?" They both turn toward the source of a new voice; a voice like an overflowing storm drain or the laughter of children heard through the blades of a combine and Bill's eyes widen for he has heard the voice but is oblivious to the sight of the speaker stepping from the living room. He only hears the voice and knows it is not his.

But Rachel sees. Rachel watches nightmare, memory and fantasy weaving itself into a walking patchwork of shadow, the only focal point in this swimming darkness a razorblade grin from which cerulean light flickers. She is horrified for all the wrong reasons. Horrified because the sight of him excites her. And now she knows she has missed him.

"Who said that?" Bill croaks, pushing himself so hard against the door it groans beneath his weight. "Did you hear it?"

But Rachel will not, cannot answer. Inside her trembling body, something stirs.

She watches, fascinated, repulsed, aroused as the shadow drifts across the hallway and leans in close to her husband, who looks frantically around for the source of his crippling dread. "Oh Jesus, Rachel what's happening? Where's that s-smell coming from?"

The shadow whispers into his ear. "That darkness, Billy boy..." and Billy shrieks, a high-pitched explosive burst of utter horror that sends him sliding to the floor, urine soaking the front of his robe, a steaming river trickling from between his legs. He is blind to the specter in front of him and it is this very transparency that grants him a glimpse of something infinitely worse.

Rachel, her breath coming in ragged gasps, her eyes glassy and fixed on the whisperer, feels an irresistible urge to go to this seething semblance of memory. Though she is horrified, it tugs her close and she is no longer fully sure that she is struggling against it.

"That darkness," the invisible thing, the unseen horror towering over him hisses, "is her brother."

"Rachel, help me?" Billy whimpers and his hands twitch. He feels a cold pressure against his palm as his hand is forced to the floor.

Rachel almost floats across the carpet, tears trickling down her face even as a low sensual sigh pours from between her moist lips. Helpless, she moves toward the specter and watches her brother, her *lover* placing the heel of his boot atop her husband's hand. The shadow turns with the sound of snapping twigs and she sees him smile.

"Baby," he whispers and takes her with a force much stronger than the wind that is suddenly raging through the hallway. Her cry is short.

The lights are snuffed out.

SOMEONE TO CARVE THE PUMPKINS

"Is that her?"

Joe nodded. "Told you didn't I? A ghost. A real as you or me, just like I said."

Chuck frowned and hunkered down beside his younger brother. He felt ridiculous hiding behind the hedge like a kid running from bullies, but if the old lady really was a ghost then he didn't particularly want her dead eyes focusing on him.

"She doesn't look like a ghost to me."

Joe looked at him as if he'd just cussed their mother. "Are you crazy? 'Course she does."

"She just looks like a regular old lady to me. Besides, ghosts are meant to be scary. Why is she just sitting there instead of trying to scare people?"

Joe's watery blue eyes were wide as marbles as he nodded at the leafy wall. "She's haunting that house!"

Chuck raised himself up enough to peer over the hedge. His knees creaked in protest.

The full force of the cold October breeze made his eyes water. He blinked away stinging tears and looked across Maiden Street.

She was sitting on the porch of a house they had always thought long abandoned.

He found it a little strange that there were no pumpkins to detract from the oaken gloom of the old house. It was Halloween after all and even the weather was playing its part to establish a deliciously sinister mood; burnt-orange leaves skittered along the pavement like giggling children and misshapen orange heads with candles for brains dotted the decks and porches of every house along the street.

Every house except *hers.*

She sat on a rocking chair beside the torn screen door, knitting something that might have been a child's sweater but looked to Chuck like oatmeal hanging from wickedly sharp needles. Her pallid face was scrunched up in an expression of concentration or worry. Her clothes looked dirty and old, a black shawl draped over her bony shoulders. The longer he watched her, the more he convinced himself that Joe was wrong about her. She wasn't a ghost. If anything, she looked more like a witch.

"Where are the pumpkins?" he muttered.

Joe thumped a fist on the grass. "She doesn't *have* any pumpkins 'cause she doesn't *need* them. What would a ghost need a pumpkin for?"

"Maybe she doesn't believe in Halloween. People who don't believe in things don't usually celebrate them, do they?"

Joe, still crouched on the ground with his chubby fingers splayed between his legs like a catcher at a baseball game, chewed his lower lip.

"But she has to be a ghost, Chuck. I mean she sits on that porch day in, day out. Sometimes late at night you can hear them needles from all the way across town, click-clicking like nobody's business."

"You think she's a ghost because she likes to knit?"

The excitement on Joe's face faded a little and Chuck decided it couldn't do any harm to let his brother have his ghost.

"Okay, so she's a ghost and she's haunting our neighborhood and we're the only ones who know about it, right?"

"Right," Joe said with utter seriousness.

"Then we have to do something about it."

Uncertainty flickered in the vibrant blue of his brother's eyes. "What are you talking about? What can we do? We're just kids."

Chuck grinned inwardly. "I'm gonna go over and tell her she has no business knitting and scaring people if she's supposed to be dead."

Joe grabbed his brother's ankle. "No! She'll—" He shrugged and gesticulated with his grubby hands but the words wouldn't come.

"She'll what? If she really is a ghost then she can't do anything to me, right? All she can do is say 'Boo!'"

Joe tugged harder at his brother's jeans and Chuck pulled away from him.

"C'mon Joe! Why don't you come with me and we'll both tell her to go back to wherever her body is?"

Joe shook his head so hard and fast Chuck thought it would fly off. "I'm scared of her, Chuck. You should be too. It's not right to mess with ghosts."

Chuck felt a pang of pity for his brother and considered forgetting the whole thing, but his own curiosity compelled him to introduce himself to the old lady, if for no other reason than to ask why she didn't have any pumpkins out on Halloween.

"I'm just going to go say, 'hello'."

"Don't," Joe whispered.

"Aw c'mon. Don't you think ghosts have better things to do on Halloween besides sitting on old porches knitting?"

The sky over their heads was a cold gray, the wind moaning high above them as if caught in a snare of clouds.

Chuck sighed and tousled his brother's dusty blond hair. "Okay. If you stay here and be my lookout, I reckon I'll have nothing to worry about. You can holler if it looks like she's about to change into a monster or something."

Joe blanched. "Don't let her get you."

"I won't. You got my back?"

"Sure."

Chuck winked, straightened and stomped purposefully off toward the gap in the hedge a few feet away from his brother. He heard Joe muttering a silent prayer at his back and suppressed a grin. At the gap he paused and looked back. He could see Joe's eyes peeking over the hedge, one eyebrow raised as if asking if he had changed his mind. Chuck sucked air through his nose and stuck out his chest in a dramatic gesture for Joe's benefit.

Chuck looked across the road.

The old lady in the faded floral dress rocked slowly to and fro. The faint sound of clicking reached his ears,

He began to walk.

He knew he should be looking up and down the road to be sure there were no cars coming like they'd been taught but his eyes were fixed on the lady and the crumbling house.

The porch looked as if it could collapse at any given moment, finally succumbing to the voracious appetite of the weeds and switch-grass that grabbed at its latticed framework.

Next to the rocking chair an empty yellow egg carton flapped mutely in the breeze and Chuck guessed some kids had probably dumped it there after bombarding the house with its contents. The brownish scabs he saw on the mildewed siding confirmed his theory.

Rusted paint tins clustered in the corner of the porch and the steps leading up to where the old lady sat gently rocking were splintered and broken.

Not a ghost but not much of a housekeeper either.

Chuck had reached the center of the road and suddenly the old lady stopped and looked up at him.

And he knew he had made a mistake.

Joe was right. He was a silly kid with a head full of silly notions but for once he was *right.* He knew it in that moment without a shadow of a doubt.

It was as if he was standing before the open door of a freezer, his body wracked with a sudden inexplicable trembling. *Oh no.*

There was a sound like long nails dragging down a chalkboard and the world dimmed as if an enormous shadow had swept across the sky above his head.

He tried to move. Couldn't. And *she* was staring at him.

He was vaguely aware of the old lady getting to her feet. She made a curiously human gesture of gently laying her knitting down on the seat behind her. But she was far from human.

Joe's voice: *Don't let her get you.*

Chuck tried desperately to close his eyes before terror blurred his vision.

He felt an odd tingling sensation as thin white rivers of electricity arced from his fingertips and vanished into the ground at his feet. Tingling, no pain. Joe was yelling but from oh so far away now.

The old woman stared at him with a parody of sadness drawn on her wizened face.

I'm frozen in the middle of the road. I'm frozen because she put a spell on me and a car'll come along and kill me and—

The paralysis broke, sound rushing back into his ears, lancing his brain and he cried out, fell to his knees on the white line in the center of the road.

The line began to glow.

134

And still the old lady did not move.

"Chuck!" Joe screeched in a voice choked with panic and Chuck turned to look at his brother. Joe was miles away; nothing more than a speck seen through a revolving tunnel of thorns but one thing was clear as day. The witch was making him glow too. He appeared almost angelic, glowing from within like so many of those images he'd seen in the Good Book.

White sparks flickered around Joe's head like lightning bugs.

Chuck looked back at the old lady. Her eyes were a milky white and he was struck by what he read in them. Unbearable agony.

Her voice came to him like the dry rustle of dead leaves. "Chuck, come home."

He could sense the urgency in her, ethereal hands attempting to lock their fingers around his own. She wanted him.

Company for the dead.

"Nnnooo," he grunted through teeth that refused to open.

She wanted a boy, a soul, anyone.

Someone to carve the pumpkins.

He screamed and spun, the white line flashing, blinding, searing as Chuck and his soul ran toward the gap in the fence, to Joe who was screaming, screaming, eyes wide as his brother dove through the fence.

The gap swallowed them.

* * *

I have no memory of what it felt like to live by time. To have my days and nights governed by something beyond my control.

I stand on this old porch and watch, listening to the dying screams of terror the breeze will soon carry away. And I wait.

They will come again, I know. They always come back, just never all the way.

I hate that I am a stranger to them. It shreds my heart that death has erased the familiarity from their fragile little minds. Now, they fear me. What kind of a symbol have I become to them? I'm sure I'm better not knowing.

I sit back in my rocking chair, my toes holding me still as the breeze runs its fingers through my hair but no amount of sympathy can make it better. The breeze can only assist in drying my tears.

I go back to knitting and whisper a silent prayer to whoever listens that

Chuck will be brave again someday and find the courage to reach the steps. Close enough to see the love in my eyes.

The love I have kept for Chuck and Joe.

My darling children. Taken from me by a stranger and buried out there in some unknown place beneath the October sky.

Come home...

Come home to mother.

THE MAN WHO BREAKS THE BAD NEWS

"Samuel! Answer the door!" Linda shrieks and Sam levers himself out of the easy chair with a moan. The simplest of movements are beginning to feel too much like hard work these days and he longs for some peace, or at least a place where he can get some.

He opens the door and gives the well-dressed stranger a suspicious glance. In this neighborhood and with Sam's increasing financial concerns, a man in a suit can only be the bearer of bad tidings.

"What is it?" he asks the stranger, his suspicion exacerbated by the omnipresent toothy smile on the man's long ashen face.

"Good morning, Mr. Bradley. My name is Thomas Wilder. I wondered if I might have a word?"

Sam's knuckles whiten on the door. "What about?"

"About last Friday."

Sam raises an eyebrow and flips through a mental index. Friday? What happened three days ago to warrant the interest of this dapper visitor? Nothing, he decides, unless it was some meager traffic violation—perhaps changing lanes where he shouldn't or clipping a curb. But wouldn't that have summoned the police?

The man on the porch doesn't look much like a cop. In fact, if anything he looks more like a mortician, dressed in a black three-piece suit and blue silk tie. His silver hair is pasted down on both sides of his skull, adding to the skeletal image. Coral blue eyes glimmer with intelligence.

Definitely not a cop.

"I don't know what you're talking about, Thomas," Sam says indignantly, hoping that his use of the man's first name will be enough to offend him.

Surprisingly, Wilder's smile broadens. "I understand completely. Perhaps if I could come in we could discuss this further."

"I don't think that's such a great idea. My wife is in there."

Wilder raises an eyebrow.

"She's not feeling well," Sam splutters. "Besides, who are you anyway?"

Wilder fishes a black leather wallet from his inside pocket and Sam has the terrible feeling he's dealing with someone far more important than a cop.

F.B.I? C.I.A? *I.R.S? Uh-oh.*

Wilder flips open the wallet, exposing his identification. Sam's squints at the miniature rendition of the man's face, a grim smile beneath a stern black acronym. "U.S.S.R.D? What the hell is *that?* You Russian?"

The other man gives a patient sigh. "Mr. Bradley, let me put your mind at ease. I'm not here to arrest you or to issue any papers. You're not in trouble, but it is important that we speak immediately and iron out a few...um...details."

"What kind of details?"

Wilder's eyes narrow as if he has to summon great concentration to deliver his words. "About your death, sir."

"My death? What, like life insurance? If that's what you're here for..."

"No," Wilder interrupts. "About your death last Friday on Route 32."

Sam slams the door.

* * *

Sam opens the door. He isn't surprised to see Wilder still standing there, patience painted across his narrow features.

"What does U.S.S.R.D stand for? And before you get cocky, I'm only asking so I know what to tell the cops when they ask for specifics."

"United States Special Retrieval Division. And calling the police wouldn't do you any good. They are well aware of our operation and support it one hundred per cent."

Sam sneers. "I'm sure, well if it's all the same I think I'll try them anyway."

Wilder doesn't respond. Once again, Sam shuts him outside and hurries to the phone.

"Samuel? Who's at the door?" Linda roars from the kitchen, startling him.

"Some nut," he calls back and picks up the phone. He dials and waits patiently to be put through to the Harperville Police. Eventually a bored voice answers: "Sergeant Stapler speaking. How can I help you?"

"Sergeant Stapler. Hi, this is Sam Bradley on Oak Street."

"Uh-huh."

"Our kids go to the same school?"

"Right," Stapler says, sounding as if he has no idea who Sam is and doesn't much care. "How can I help you, Sam?"

"Well, there's a guy at my door harassing me. He's an old guy, dressed in black. Says he's from something called the United States Recuperation Department or something."

"Yes?"

Sam frowns. "He says I'm dead!"

There is a long pause, sufficient time to bring beads of perspiration to Sam's brow and then Stapler replies: "*Are* you dead?"

"Well, I...*what*?"

Stapler clears his throat. "If someone from the U.S.S.R.D is at your door then I suspect you might have expired, Sam. Sorry."

Sam feels his brain itch. "Has the whole bloody world gone nuts?"

"My advice is to cooperate fully with them. There'll be less hassle that way."

"But I..."

"Be sure to give my condolences to your wife."

"What?"

"You have a wife, right?"

"I...yes! But you don't understand! I..."

"Tough break, buddy."

"Hey, wait!" Sam says but finds himself pleading with a dead line.

* * *

"Is there somewhere we can go to talk?"

Sam stares at Wilder, envious of his unfettered patience. "What kind of scam is this?"

Wilder sighs. "Please, just come with me for a chat and I'll explain everything. It shouldn't take too long."

Sam steps outside, closes the door behind him. "It better not. My wife is making steaks."

Wilder nods and turns away, Sam plodding unsteadily along behind him.

* * *

Greta's Diner was a hot spot for local teens to hang out in back in the seventies. The passing of time and modern technology however have stolen the appeal of the place and now it caters only to those who don't care about its crumbling façade, peeling paint or ever-present smell of old shoes.

The raucous laughter of youth has long been driven from the air by the ghostly smoke from the pipes of old men, who sit and grumble to themselves while watching the world outside their haven moving much too fast for their liking.

Wilder takes a seat by the grimy window and looks out at the cracked concrete parking lot, deserted but for a rusted pea-green Volkswagen with a flat tire. With a grimace, Sam lowers himself into the seat on the opposite side of the Formica table and glances at Wilder. "So?"

Wilder raises a hand. "Would you like something to eat?"

"No, I told you Linda's making steaks."

"Right. Coffee?"

"Water."

Wilder seems content to wait on a waitress that isn't coming.

Meanwhile Sam's impatience is burning holes in the back of his eyes. "So?" he repeats, "what's the deal?"

"The deal is, Sam, you're dead. You died Friday at around midday or eleven fifty-one if you want specifics while stuck in traffic on Route 32. Do you remember anything about that?"

Sam doesn't want to think about it but feels an obligation to prove this madman wrong. When he casts his mind back, he sees himself sitting in his Oldsmobile, smoking a cigarette and swearing loudly at the driver of the Taurus who has cut him off. The heat is fierce and he is suddenly finding it difficult to breathe. The cigarette of course, isn't helping but it's the only thing keeping him relatively calm. He remembers honking his horn and...

"Hmm."

Wilder leans forward on his elbows. "Yes?"

"I had a pain in my chest. Nothing special, I get them all the time."

"Do you get them now?"

Sam hasn't realized it until now but...he *hasn't* suffered chest pains in a while.

"Do you even smoke now?"

Sam shrugs. "The chest pains were particularly bad that day. I thought it might be a heart attack and vowed to quit smoking if it turned out to be nothing. It was nothing so I didn't smoke again."

Wilder gives a slight sad shake of his head. "I'm afraid it wasn't nothing, Sam. It was a heart attack. A fatal one. The reason you don't smoke anymore is because the dead rarely feel the need."

Sam slams a hand down on the table. "Will you stop saying that! I'm not d——"

They both watch the small fingernail skidding into the center of the table between them. Sam's eyes widen, his gaze dropping to the little finger on his right hand.

His nail has come off, leaving a mottled indentation in its wake.

He stares at it a moment longer, mouth open, a moan sounding from somewhere deep in his throat. "That's not right," he says eventually and looks at Wilder, who doesn't seem at all surprised.

"It is if you've passed away," Wilder responds calmly. "You shouldn't let it alarm you too much. This condition, this *reanimation*, isn't unique to you. An explosion of this type of phenomenon has appeared all over the country in the past six months."

Sam looks back at his finger, at the ugly warped space where his nail once sat. "Phenomenon?"

Wilder looks over his shoulder and, satisfied that the old man near the counter is paying them no attention, he says in a low voice: "We call them 'walking dead'. People who've died but for some inexplicable reason get up and walk around as if nothing happened, seemingly oblivious to their own passing."

Sam scoffs. "That's crazy. I saw a movie like that. Zombies, staggering around a farmhouse, munching on human flesh. It made me sick. Are you trying to tell me that's what I am? A zombie?"

Wilder waves away the notion. "I assure you, Sam. You won't find yourself strangely enamored by human flesh and although I detest the use of the word 'zombie', it is probably the closest description of what you are. Not a monster, we don't think of cases like yours as being akin to demonic resurrection, rather a sickness or a virus that leaves it's victim in a state of confusion."

"But..." Sam continues to shake his head, waiting for the punchline so he can go home to Linda. "That's insane. I'm not dead. Dead people stay dead, don't they?"

"They used to," Wilder says in a grave tone. "Until that meteor crashed in New Mexico. Since then it's been as you so succinctly put it 'insane'. I wish I had an explanation to offer you as to why you're sitting here listening to a stranger telling you you're dead, but I don't."

Sam's eyes narrow. "You could be pulling some kind of con on me. How do I know you're not?"

Wilder surveys the room again. "Put out your hand."

"What for?"

"Please, just do it."

Reluctantly, Sam slides his wounded hand across the table until it's close to Wilder. Wilder reaches into his pocket and withdraws a small black cylinder.

"What's that for?"

He hears a click and a six-inch metal blade springs from the top of the cylinder. He flinches and prepares to pull away but Wilder clamps a hand on his wrist and in an instant brings the blade down like a guillotine, severing the tops of four of his fingers, only the thumb remaining intact. The fingertips hop and scatter across the Formica.

"Oh ssshhhit!" Sam moans and inhales enough breath to power the scream barreling up his throat.

Wilder raises a finger to his lips and Sam catches the scream behind his teeth.

The old folks at the head of the diner look in their direction, shrug and go back to complaining.

"Look," Wilder says and points at Sam's ruined fingers. "Do you see any blood?"

He's right. Sam watches them for a moment. No blood, just dry stumps. More significant still, he feels no pain. Nothing. Not even the slightest ache.

I'm in shock, he tells himself but knows it not to be true.

He looks at Wilder who is busy collecting the fingertips and wrapping them in a pristine white handkerchief. "I'm dead?"

Wilder nods. "I'm afraid so."

Sam's face droops and he begins to blubber, Wilder's hand suddenly appearing on his shoulder. "I'm here to help you Sam."

Sam looks up; eyes dry because there are no tears available. "This *sucks*."

* * *

"What happens now?"

They are standing outside Sam's house, Wilder looking the picture of dignity, Sam looking dejected, shoulders hunched and head low.

"A car will come for you at dawn. There's no need to pack, anything you might need will be provided for you at the clinic."

"Clinic?"

"Yes, consider it a rest home for the undead. You'll be taken care of there."

Sam frowns. "What will happen to me?"

"We'll monitor the progress of your...decomposition and do our best to compensate for it. You'll be made to feel at home."

"You mean I'll...rot?" Sam asks, his voice brittle.

Wilder nods solemnly. "As all dead folk do. The only consolation is you won't feel it. There will be no pain whatsoever and you'll be doing science a favor."

"How?"

"By studying your post mortem brain functions, we can try to determine the cause of this most peculiar phenomenon and perhaps attempt to find a cure."

"What do I tell Linda?"

Wilder looks at the house and back to Sam. "As little as possible. If you were to stay with her, she'd be forced to watch bits and pieces of you dropping off until you were nothing but a talking skeleton. That would be a hell of a lot more traumatic for her than your sudden 'disappearance' don't you think?"

"I guess."

"I guarantee it would."

Sam shuffles toward the steps leading to his front door. He stops, turns.

"What happens when the study is over?"

But Wilder is already walking away.

* * *

At the dinner table, Sam finds himself completely repelled by the sight of the bloody sirloin swimming in his plate and turning his potatoes a dark maroon. The longer he looks at it the less human he feels.

But I'm not human, am I? According to Wilder, I'm a zombie.

The thought makes his undead stomach turn.

As he scrapes his chair back from the table, Linda fixes him with a puzzled look. "Something wrong with the meat?"

"Uh…" Sam begins, struggling to think of a convincing excuse. "No, it looks delicious. I'm just not feeling very well this evening."

"What happened to your fingers?" she asks, pointing at his bandaged fist.

"I…"

"What have you been up to Samuel? You have that look in your eyes that tells me you've been up to something."

"Nothing. Some idiot at the diner slammed the door on my hand. It was an accident."

"What were you doing at the diner?"

"What?"

"You never go there anymore. Why today?"

"Just felt like it, that's all. Jesus, what's with the third degree? I can't go for a coffee anymore?"

"We have plenty of coffee here."

"So I wanted to get out of the house for a while, okay?"

She levels him with a gaze brimful of suspicion. "I see. So you go to a diner you haven't been to in years, hurt your hand and now you won't eat your dinner. Would you not be at least a little suspicious?"

Sam shrugs.

Linda clasps her hands beneath her chin. "Who was that man today?"

"What man?"

"The one you were talking to outside."

"Nobody."

"He certainly seemed to upset you."

Sam looks at her, incredulous. "You were listening?"

"I thought it might be important."

"It was nothing. Life insurance."

"I see." Linda says, but it is clear she doesn't buy into his stuttered explanation. She recommences her assault on the meat before her; filling her mouth with the almost raw sirloin, blood trickling from the corner of her mouth. Sam looks away in disgust.

"I'm off to Bingo in about a half hour. Want me to stick your dinner in the oven until you feel up to it?" she asks when she's finished.

A butterfly of panic flutters against Sam's chest. "Bingo? Tonight? Do you have to go? I thought..."

She gets up from the table. "Thought what?"

He shrugs, defeated and gets to his feet, wincing inwardly at the crack of his knees as he does so. "Nothing. I...maybe you can skip it just for tonight, eh? We'll have a quiet night at home."

"I never miss Bingo," Linda says, frowning.

"Well, one night wouldn't kill you would it?"

"Just what is wrong with you, Sam? You look like death warmed over. Is something the matter?"

Wilder's voice fills his head like Muzak on an elevator descending into the darkness: *If you were to stay with her, she'd be forced to watch bits and pieces of you dropping off until you were nothing but a talking skeleton. That would be a hell of a lot more traumatic for her than your sudden 'disappearance' don't you think?*

"No. Nothing wrong," he mutters and wrenches himself away from the table.

He shuffles into the dark living room, propelled forth by his wife's exasperated sigh, and thumbs on the television. The white noise fills his head like angry wasps.

With trembling hands he slides open the cabinet beneath the television and squints to make out the titles of the videos stacked atop one another in uneven piles. At last he finds the one he's looking for and, trying his best to ignore the gruesome pictures on the cover, he shoves the tape into the gaping maw of the VCR.

Swallowing dryly, he clicks the button on the remote and eases himself into a recliner. His bones feel like kindling as he struggles to get comfortable.

On the screen, in gloomy black and white, he watches a black car winding its way toward a graveyard and wonders if that's really where he should be. A graveyard.

Dead.

Buried.

Worm food.

He shudders, his chest tightening at the thought of that black car waiting outside his house in the morning like a patient vulture.

They're coming to get you Barb'raaaaaa.

He switches off the television and sighs, coughs, hacks up bits of brown papery matter. Winces at the sight of them coiled atop his bandaged hand.

He forces himself to swallow a knot of fear.

They can't hurt me, can they? I'm dead.

The thought offers him little comfort as he sits there alone, cloaked in shadow.

* * *

Dawn creeps silently through the world and Sam jerks himself from non-sleep with a stifled cry. The room glows with hazy orange light that might, under any other circumstances have seemed warm, comforting, but now looks like the reflected light of a funeral pyre.

Damn Wilder, he thinks miserably, *I should stay with Linda. God knows she's a tyrant at the best of times but...I still love her!* This rare admission makes him sure he has felt his rotten heart kick but it might have been nothing more than a memory.

He slowly, carefully gets to his feet to a chorus of snaps and cracks and walks stiff-legged into the kitchen. Thankfully, Linda is still sleeping. He remembers hearing her come home, the feel of her lips brushing against the taut dead skin on his forehead. Rather than wake him, she opted to leave him sleep in the living room and now he aches for her for the first time in years. The ache becomes an almost physical pain, sparking doubts in his mind about the validity of Wilder's claims. If he can feel sorrow, loss, love...doesn't that make him alive?

No. He looks at his bandaged hand, the discoloration on the gauze. He thinks about his severed fingers, discarded like nail clippings with not an ounce of pain. His nerves are dead, of that there can be no doubt and soon he will shed his skin like a snake, sloughing off his identity to become nothing more than a cadaver exposed for all the world to see and study. The thought frightens him. Just how long will he remain aware of what they are doing to him? Once his eyes shrivel in their sockets and he can see no more, how long will his emotions, his loneliness take to die? If he has to lie on a cold table knowing what they are doing to him despite being spared the sensations that come with their needles and hooks, he does not want to be capable of thought.

Will they take care of that too?

I can't do this.

And yet he knows he has to. There are no other options available for him now that he knows the truth. All he can do is accept his fate as it has been written and go blindly into the jaws of science. He can only hope that when he finally abandons this crumbling vessel that sags on his bones like an over-worn suit, something infinitely better awaits him on the other side of somewhere.

He trudges up the stairs, head low, spine crackling and makes his way toward the bedroom.

Easing open the door, he looks at Linda; her hands curled slightly as if to maintain their grasp on sleep, graying hair splayed out around her head in a steel corona, chest rising and falling...

Breathing.

Sam puts a frail hand over his own mouth and exhales. Perhaps a slight chill brushes his scabrous palm but nothing more. He swallows. "Linda..."

Breathing.

His eyes widen.

The sheets rise and fall in soft whispers...

A small sad smile pinches the skin of Sam's mouth.

* * *

The car is waiting just as Wilder promised; a swollen cockroach nestled against the curb with black eyes for windows that stare vapidly back at Sam as he descends the steps of his home with deliberate slowness. He is appalled at the lack of mobility that has suddenly overtaken his joints and muscles, almost as if rigor mortis has been waiting for just this moment to take hold of him.

It hurts, but only his pride.

The car window hums down and he looks up to see a familiar face smiling out at him. "Good morning Mr. Bradley!"

Sam nods and forces his leg down the last step. With a sigh of relief that emerges more like a croak, he approaches the car in a stoop, like a man balancing a stack of fine china on his head.

"You're looking splendid!" Wilder proclaims and Sam summons the memory of a smile. "Thank you. I wasn't expecting to see you here."

Wilder purses his lips. "Well I think we both know why my presence is necessary, don't we?" His eyes drop to the fresh bloodstains on Sam's hands.

The driver door clicks open and Sam is surprised to see a chauffeur coming around to his side of the car. With a polite nod, the young man opens the door for him. Wilder scoots over in his seat to make room. "Hop in!"

Sam's bones click like castanets as he maneuvers himself into the vehicle. Once he is as comfortable as he can get, he looks at Wilder. "I couldn't do it you know. I couldn't do it alone."

Wilder smiles. "I know. You'd be surprised how often that happens. That's why it was important that I be here. After all," he says with a wink. "I'm the man who breaks the bad news."

Sam stares for a moment. "How do you think she'll take it?" he asks but Wilder doesn't answer.

They both turn to look back at the house.

And wait.

LEFTOVERS

The problem was, Alfred surmised, not what he had chosen to eat today but rather the quantity of it that he had forced down his throat. Never one for gluttony, he found himself vaguely repulsed at the heavy feeling in his guts and the greasy feeling on his tongue.

Shaking his head, he hacked up a gob of phlegm that clung to the memory of undercooked meat and herbs and spat it into the fog. The air was damp and his footsteps sounded like rocks being dropped from a height.

Rosemary, he thought. *Yes, that's what it tastes like.* In the heavy fog, he could see little and the onset of twilight didn't make navigation any easier. As it was, he was moving through the thickening gloom with only the intermittent blobs of hazy yellow light from the streetlamps as a guide. The disorientation made him feel like a moth, being lured eternally onward.

"Or perhaps Basil," he said aloud and watched his breath vanish like a shifting ghost into the smoky air.

To his right, where he estimated the pier wall began, a shadowy shape slid past, tearing ragged strands of fog away with it. "Evening," muttered Alfred and turned back to concentrating on his own struggle. It occurred to him that whoever had passed by had not made a sound. This made him wonder if perhaps he appeared obnoxious to anyone who couldn't see him because of his loud approach. With a grim smile and a hand over his gurgling stomach, he carried on.

Thoughts of home preceded his jaunt like a will o' the wisp, a warm promise to carry him through the murk. He had traveled to town and overindulged—no, not overindulged, *stuffed*—himself and now he felt awful because it was almost certain that Christine would be preparing a special meal for him, a fine feat with all the trimmings, a no-holds-barred banquet for her beloved...and he would have to decline. Decline or be sick, and that would be so much worse, to have eaten her food only to thrust it back up all over the beautiful spread she would no doubt have arranged.

Perhaps he would be in luck and he would arrive home to find she had forgotten their anniversary. He sighed. How likely was *that*? His wife never forgot anything. No. She left the lapses of memory to her husband. His belly roiled at the thought of packing more food into a space he had already filled to bursting.

A distant clang of a buoy, carried on the sibilant hiss of the surf crashing against the slimy rocks. The almost tangible weight of the fog pressing heavily against his skin like the cold lingering kisses of thin-lipped ghosts. Light drained from the air as twilight descended and the silence was amplified, echoed by emptiness as Alfred sniffed the evening and grimaced at an unscheduled belch that sang of seasoned meat.

Something dark was crouching on the pier wall, hunched like a simian and weaving back and forth, searching for a break in the gray through which it might view the walker. Alfred watched it suspiciously, fancied he could see its eyes, paler even than the fog and then nodded. "I ate too much," he told the evening and sensed the watcher slide from the wall and back down to the beach where the breakers hushed all speakers.

Cobblestones slid beneath his feet, almost sending him flying and he grumbled, righted himself and thanked his lucky stars he had not lost his sense of direction. He continued onward, the ground strangely warped underfoot, and realized that the dark had swallowed the streetlamps, but thankfully by now he had a reasonable idea of where he was. With the sea to his right and the cobblestones beneath his feet, he knew he was still on the right path, and that on a clear night he would be able to see his house from here.

Thinking of home reminded him of the feast awaiting him. How would he explain? The guilt bubbling up inside him couldn't have been worse had he cheated on his wife. She took pride in her cooking and he made eating every last bite of it part of a practiced ritual they had shared for as long as they'd been together. Rejecting it would be rejecting her and he was not sure he could muster the callousness to do such a thing to his beloved. Would it really be so impossible for him to force it down? A wet lurch in his stomach was all the response he needed.

He couldn't. Simple as that. He would have to come clean and tell her the truth. The thought filled him with dread, more so when the road began to rise, taking him up a path that he knew from memory split like a two-headed serpent at the end. One route led to Hawk Point, where he and the kids went to watch the storms rolling in over the horizon; the other would bring him up a narrow path to their house atop Gresham Hill. He swallowed and continued on, flinching once when something wet brushed against his ankle. He kicked out at it. Missed. Heard a low sigh recede into the darkness through the hole it had made. Alfred frowned after it longer than necessary and knew he was milking the distraction. Anything to avoid the scene that must surely unfold at home.

The crunch of gravel was quick to replace the clack of cobblestone and he felt the unease surge inside him like the coiling fog at his heels. He felt peculiarly small as he ascended the stone steps chiseled out of the hill upon which his house sat brooding. He sensed the magnificence of the sea beyond the cliffs, heaving, swelling, hiding untold things beneath the waves, their eyes breaking the surface to watch his progress. And like the waves, the fog receded, slowly, almost unnoticeably until the crisp cool night hung around him like dark curtains suspended before freezer doors.

On the top step, inches from the salt and wind-battered front door of the house, the hands of despair wringed his stomach and he doubled over to watch, through watery eyes, the vomit pour from his mouth. It splattered on his shoes, coated the pavement in steaming red piles and he backed away, cleared his mouth of the foul taste of blood and summoned a weary grin. As unpleasant as the sensation was, he had made room. Not enough perhaps, but some. If need be, he could excuse himself to the bathroom and force himself to make more. The grin turned to a smile. That was the answer. Christine would never know.

He pushed the door with the heel of his hand and followed its wooden yawn into the hallway. "Anybody home!" he called, knowing there would be no sudden rush to greet him. His family was all about surprises. He had taught them that. Sneaking around the corner, the smell of fresh-cooked meat assailed his senses and, to his surprise he found his mouth watering. This was no pre-vomit bile...No. He was *hungry!* He could scarcely believe his luck as he turned the corner into the kitchen and stopped. His jaw dropped. "Oh sweetie," he said, tears rushing up his throat.

She had outdone herself this time.

The finest cuts of meat were laid out before his place at the head of the table, the candles prepared around the room making the feast look like something from one of those swanky cooking shows he often watched on television. His eyes were not adequately trained to appreciate the spread all at once and he fell to his knees, overwhelmed and breathless, eyes brimming with tears.

To think, he had been struggling to come up with excuses to avoid this.

He crawled on all fours to the table and raised himself up, his heart hammering in his chest, saliva leaking from the corner of his mouth. "Christine...I don't know what to say..." It had been so long since they'd all been together for a meal, but now things were right again, even if he had done a lot of the work himself. He would never say that of course. It might upset the perfect mood. And he wanted nothing to upset this meal. Not when everything was so perfect.

He looked down the table to where Rosemary and Basil sat. The children stared silently back and he was almost overcome with love.

So perfect.

At last.

"I love you," he told Christine as he took her hand, brought it to his lips.

And began to eat.

THE DEFENSELESS

Gina stood by the window, eyes indistinguishable from the rain-tattooed glass for both were shadowed and both were wet. She stood and she waited. Waited for an answer to an impossible question: *Why me?* There would be no answers proffered and of this she was very much aware for she had led a life keeping the secrets of others with just the briefest glimpses of happiness in between and had grown to live with disappointment.

As Kyle had disappointed her. She had thought him strong, brave, so different from the others he could only be the part of her she was missing, could only be the part that made her whole, could only be *hers*. But again, she was forsaken, left to pine more for her lack of sense than her penchant for selecting erroneous suitors. And it was raining. Of course it was, because it never stopped raining in Harperville. She was sick of the sight of it trickling down her bedroom window and yet it held her gaze, almost hypnotizing her. Would it matter if the clouds lifted, for what was there to see up there that she hadn't seen a thousand times before? Nothing but an uncaring sky thrown like a smothering quilt across a city of indifference, with her nothing but a mote lost in the folds.

Damn you Kyle, you selfish son of a bitch! How could you do this to me?

But for this much at least, there was an answer, and it whispered across the darkened plains of her mind, barely stirring the reeds of her resistance: *Because sooner or later everyone does. You are a planet without gravity orbiting a cold dead sun. There is nothing to hold anyone to you and no brightness to look toward. You are nothing. You are empty. You are alone.*

She shook her head, only slightly and this was as much of a denial as she could muster. There was, after all, nothing she could say in her defense. Whatever caricature of herself she had been until now, the rain and the misery had finally washed away the pretense, leaving her raw and exposed to the needling of her callous conscience. She could not pretend her life had meaning anymore. Not when the hub of her existence had left nothing behind him but a melodramatic suicide note and an empty vessel to grieve for his passing. A shell, devoid of anything but self-pity and self-loathing for the violation she had let herself fall victim to for so many years.

She pressed her forehead against the glass, her hair bunching up into an auburn wave frozen against the magnesium glow of the streetlight shining through the window. The glass was cold but she did not mind. The ship in her mind sailed a colder ocean, casting out a net made of broken dreams and dragging up the memory of his face. Kyle. So understanding, so familiar with the razorblade edges of her world. So willing to walk through the black flame of her pain with her. So willing to listen. And now dead. Gone. Lost to his own weakness.

Her eyes focused, snagged on an incongruous shade in the gloom below the streetlight, blurred by the streaks of rain but most definitely a figure. A man. Head tilted upward, he appeared to be watching her and for the briefest moment, a cerulean spark of hope coruscated across the barren field of her dismay. But no...Kyle was dead and the only ghosts she believed in were those of happiness, when they lingered tauntingly beyond the reach of those who'd lost them. She watched, unmoving as a smear of darkness separated from the shadow beneath the light and waved.

Surely she was dreaming, for such a gesture implied a familiarity she did not have with anyone but the dead now. Curiosity bade her open the window and she did with a measure of caution, wincing at the immediate assault of the rain through the narrow wedge of night she had admitted. Peering into the nest of shadows gathered like lazy snakes beneath the streetlight, she saw that it was indeed a man and he was waving at her. But it was not Kyle. She chided herself for entertaining such absurd and impossible notions but did not close the window, now more curious than ever to see who was hailing her.

"What do you want?" she called, leaning over the sill just enough to allow a straight line of wetness to paint itself across her T-shirt.

Ordinarily, she might have worried about her father hearing her, but he had returned from the Twisted Oak Tavern hours ago and she knew nothing short of a tornado would wake him from the saturation of his drunk.

The figure responded, a muffled burst of words that were scrambled by the wind.

"What?" Gina cried.

She saw the figure cup his hands around his mouth and this time she heard the words: "Are you Gina Lewis?"

Answer. Don't answer. Yes or no. How wise was it to reply to a question like that from a shadowy figure basking in the darkness? After brief consideration, she decided that with nothing left to lose in her pitiful excuse for a life, a reply couldn't hurt. "Yes. Who are you?"

"My name is Dan Newman. I got a letter from your boyfriend. He told me to come find you."

* * *

Gina was used to climbing down the trellis next to her window, had mastered it in fact as a necessary escape route from the terrors that frequently invaded her bedroom. But she had never climbed it in such ferocious weather and now she was beginning to worry, the wind biting at the exposed skin of her wrists and ankles, whipping her hair into her eyes and struggling to pull the trellis from the wall, forcing her to lock her fingers on the thin wooden ledges as rain pelted her face.

Below, Newman had moved away from the streetlight, was now almost directly below her, his face a long pale smudge in the murk of wind and darkness. "Are you okay?" she thought he said and called a "Yes" even as she cursed and lowered herself another rung on the trellis. It was crazy. *She* was crazy to be sneaking from her bedroom at this time of night to meet a man who could be a killer for all she knew…or cared. And of course that was it. What could a murderer take from her that she hadn't already lost? Her father had taken her innocence, her soul, and Kyle had taken her hopes and dreams with him into the earth. No. There was nothing this guy could take from her now.

Her foot slipped from the rung and her nails scratched painfully against the wall as she righted herself and gasped into the rain.

Newman had moved closer. She took a deep breath and steeled herself against the relentless hammering of the storm. Soon, she was close enough to jump and Newman moved away to allow her room to do so. She landed on the soggy earth with a grunt and straightened herself, pulling the wet hair from her eyes and regarding Newman with undisguised suspicion.

"How did you know Kyle?" she asked and he raised a finger to his lips. From what she could see of him, he appeared handsome, if a little gaunt and wiry.

"Not here," he said and reached a long-fingered hand out to her.

She hovered, then grasped it and allowed herself to be led through the wet streets.

"Where are we going?" she called once and "to Devlin Woods. Out of the rain. I have something to show you," he called back.

She almost stalled at that, felt her resistance tug a little of the speed from their passage, but then relented. *Nothing left to hurt me,* she told herself and followed Newman away from her dark and silent house on Barker Lane, through the rain-swept streets of Harperville and up into the dark phalanx of trees that was the outer ring of Devlin Woods.

* * *

Devlin Woods was and had been for as long as Gina could remember, a miasma. But amid the gnarled trees and tangled vines was a place she had once called her sanctuary. A small, battered shack, little more than sheets of corrugated metal held together by steel wire and topped with a few layers of ragged tarpaulin, sat in a far corner of the woods. It was hidden from prying eyes by a veritable wall of brambles, upon which raspberries were rumored to grow, though no one had actually ever seen any.

It was here she had found peace. It was here she had found Kyle. And lost him to himself. Without him, the shack was nothing more than a shell, haphazardly thrown together, a shelter against the rain and little else. Gina could remember when she had thought it a fortress.

She stopped at the bramble wall and tried to corral the uncontrollable shivering that wracked her body. She was bitterly cold, water trickling down her back, freezing the skin. "Why are we here?"

she said, suddenly angry with Newman for presuming to have her trust and refusing to offer her any explanation thus far. "What do you want from me?"

Newman seemed startled by her attitude. He raised a hand to placate her. "Easy, I promise you it will all make sense soon. We do need to get out of this rain though or we'll catch our deaths."

She huffed her disapproval, ignored the hand he held out to her and walked ahead of him, the carpet of pine and fir needles squelching beneath her feet. The black mass of brambles was taller than both of them, and in the filtered light from the city below it looked like a wave frozen in the act of breaking, spiked tendrils clambering for release within an all-consuming whole. Gina, feeling suddenly and inexplicably hemmed in, skirted the network of vicious thorns and hurried toward where memory directed her.

The shack was like an oasis in the hostile night, feeble amber light flickering through the cracks in the structure as the wind struggled to extinguish a candle someone had left lit inside. A rectangular stretch of heavy fabric had been nailed above the doorway, a small chunk of wood laid against the bottom to keep the wind from tearing it off and it was here that Gina found herself, moving the wood and quickly ducking inside. A steady squishing at her back told her Newman was following.

Inside, she was surprised to see four thick towels stacked on top of a folding chair. A bundle of newspapers lay to one side of them casting a thick block of shadow, courtesy of a large hurricane lamp balanced precariously atop a small drawerless cabinet shoved against the wall behind them. It was not particularly warm, but it was dry despite the impatient drumming of the rain on the tarpaulin above her head. Newman bustled in and promptly turned his back to her as he folded the makeshift door at the bottom and set a short but heavy piece of wood on top of it. Satisfied that it would hold, he exhaled and straightened as much as the low ceiling would allow.

In the light of the hurricane lamp, Gina saw she'd been wrong in thinking him handsome. He might have been once, she realized, but now his cheeks were sunken as if he were biting the inside of his cheeks, shadows nestled comfortably in the hollows. His eyes were bright, feverish but in an unhealthy way, almost manic in their intensity. His thin jaw worked soundlessly as he watched her taking a seat on the stack of newspapers. To her relief, she saw no desire in those eyes and that let her relax a little. She scooped up a towel and slowly began to dry her hair.

"The towels were a nice touch," she told him. "Not quite the Holiday Inn but appreciated all the same."

"It's the least I can do for dragging you up here on such a terrible night."

"Are you going to tell me *why* you dragged me up here on this terrible night?"

"Yes," he said and surprised her further by reaching behind the folding chair and producing a red thermos, which he shook before him with a wry grin. "Coffee?"

"You're kidding. What next? Is there a hairdryer behind that chair somewhere?"

He chuckled. "This is the extent of the luxury I'm afraid."

She offered him a smile, slowly letting her guard down. "Then I'll take a coffee. Scaldingly hot sounds good right about now."

"You got it." He unscrewed the cap of the thermos, used it as a cup and filled it almost to the top with piping hot coffee. She accepted it gratefully, nodding her thanks and taking a tentative sip, just enough to scorch her tongue. Another, longer drink and she could feel it running down inside her like hot wax, settling comfortably in her stomach. She draped the towel over her shoulders and looked back to Newman. "So?"

He half-heartedly ran a towel over the thick black hair plastered to his scalp and sighed before he finally met her gaze. "I'm sorry about Kyle."

"Yeah, so am I," she answered tonelessly, then quickly added. "You said he gave you a letter?"

"Yeah. I found it in my mailbox last Friday. The day after he—" He swallowed. "The day after."

"How did you know him?"

Newman shifted his seat so that he was no longer casting flinching shadows over her. "We were good friends a few years back, until his parents moved away from Akron and came here."

Gina took another hearty swallow of her coffee, savoring the warmth. A burst of wind made the walls rattle and she jumped, almost spilling her drink. The flame in the hurricane lamp fluttered in protest. "Do you still live in Akron?" she breathed, a hand against her chest.

Newman nodded. "Born and raised."

"I didn't see you at the funeral."

He gave her an apologetic shrug and dropped the towel, a bead of water still clinging to his earlobe. "No. I didn't go. I can't hack funerals."

"Me neither, but it would have been wrong for me not to go."

If he was offended by the accusation in her tone, it didn't show and she quickly chastised herself for being needlessly rude. After all, how Newman dealt with his grief was none of her business. "What did the letter say?"

He sniffed, withdrew a ragged envelope from the inside pocket of his leather jacket and handed it to her. Bracing the half-full thermos lid between her knees, she took the letter and quickly opened it. While she read, Newman produced a cigarette from the same pocket in which he'd kept Kyle's letter, sat back and lit it, his exhalations slow and deliberate.

* * *

Dear Danny Boy:

I bet you're surprised as hell to hear from me after all this time and for that I apologize. I should have kept in touch but in truth, you were much better off not knowing the person I became, the hopeless soul the world made of me. They say the path we travel on is set and until last night when God himself visited me, I believed in that. Now I know different. As you shall too. We have suffered for too long, my friend.

Tonight I die, but in death I bring a gift to the underdog, to all our brethren who have tasted the boots of our oppressors. Tonight I bleed a tide that turns for all of us.

Find her. Find my disciple. Her name is Gina Lewis. She lives at 12 Barker Lane. Go there Thursday night and bring her to Our Place, the shack in Devlin Woods and show her what you've discovered, show her the meaning of the list I've written here, the Freedom List. Make her believe in herself again. Make her believe in us, in The Defenseless. Show her the light that burns inside all our kind and set her free…

I'll miss you old friend, but do not mourn. Instead, bask in the glory of your new life.

Always,

Kyle Winter

P.S. Here are the names of the first seven. They will be followed by seven more until the world begins to recognize us for who we are:

Marion Haines
Judith Weinstein
Josh Berkeley
Graham Lieder
Frank Streck
Alice Peterson
Peter Teller

* * *

"I don't understand this," Gina said and looked up at Newman. "Was he really that far gone? I mean, who are these people?"

Newman stood up and went to the doorway to jettison his cigarette. "I thought the same thing," he said. "When I learned that he'd really gone and killed himself, I thought, at least his madness made it that much easier for him. But over the next couple of days, I started thinking about the note." Stooping, he drew close to Gina. "Can you stand up for a moment?"

"Why?"

"I need to show you what made me change my mind about Kyle."

She looked down between her legs at the bundle of newspapers she'd been sitting on. Her wet jeans had darkened the top copy but she could see enough to recognize it as the local rag: *The Harperville Gazette*. She stood up and moved to stand next to Newman, who immediately hunkered down and produced a short-handled penknife from his coat.

"That's one hell of a pocket you got there," Gina said, moving back a step although she didn't really feel threatened. Not yet, at least.

Newman made a sound that might have been an airless chuckle and sliced open the thin red cord holding the newspapers together. He pushed aside the dampened copy and handed her the next one without looking back.

"Tell me what you see," he said and continued fishing through the papers.

At first she saw nothing, her eyes flitting over the headlines but finding nothing to grab her attention, and she was about to tell him so when her eyes caught on a small column near the bottom of the page.

"God," she said and heard Newman mutter his agreement.

The headline read:

WOMAN SOUGHT IN MURDER INVESTIGATION

But this was not what caused the hair to prickle on the back of Gina's neck. It was the first two lines of the story itself: *Alice Peterson (38), is wanted for questioning by the police after the authorities discovered the body of her husband, Bill Peterson (41) at their home in Gatesburg, Harperville last Monday morning. The victim had been stabbed to death.*

"She's one of the names in Kyle's letter, isn't she?"

"Yes," Newman replied, rising to face her. "And if you're thinking he might have had some information about this prior to writing the note, look at the date."

Gina did. "Today."

"Yes. Kyle died last Friday. Alice Peterson killed her husband three days later. He couldn't have known about it."

Gina thought about this and struggled to shake off the dread that crawled up her spine like a living thing. "Wait. Maybe he knew her. Maybe she got a letter too. Maybe…Maybe he *told* her to kill her husband."

"Does that sound like Kyle to you?"

"I don't know. I'd like to think not, but it's a bit too much of a coincidence isn't it?"

Newman shrugged. "If it is…" He handed her another two newspapers. "Then, these must be too."

She looked from his empty eyes to the papers:

MAN KILLED IN HUNTING ACCIDENT

"The victim was Arnold Streck. Shot by his own son, Frank."

Gina swallowed, remembering the name from the list and feeling increasingly detached from the insanity in which she suddenly found herself. She flipped to the next paper, eyes scanning until Newman's finger indicated a small box near the bottom of the front page:

LOCAL SCHOOLTEACHER DIES IN FIRE AT HOME

"Susan Teller. She is survived by her husband, Peter. And guess what?"

Gina nodded. "He's on Kyle's list."

"Yes."

She let the papers slip from her hands. "But why? Why are these people murdering their loved ones? Was Kyle psychic or something?" She sat down heavily on the remaining newspapers and sighed in exasperation. "This is making my head hurt."

Newman returned to his seat and lit another cigarette.

"Believe me, I was as surprised as you when I traced the names from the list to all these headlines." He made a sweeping gesture over the scattered papers. "It didn't seem possible. Surely no one could have that kind of influence over total strangers."

"Unless they weren't strangers," Gina said. "Unless he knew them all somehow but—Jesus, I *loved* him. I knew him better than anyone. He wasn't capable of this kind of madness!"

"Does that letter sound like it was written by someone you know?"

She looked up at him, his eyes glistening pools of oil in the lamplight. "What else did you find out? There must be more, unless you brought me here just to tell me my dead boyfriend was a cult leader?"

For a moment Newman was silent, the wind battering the hut like an angry animal, the hurricane lamp trembling and then: "Those who died were not the true victims. The true victims were the people who killed them."

Gina frowned. "I don't understand."

"I think you do. That list, according to Kyle is the Freedom List, the names of the first to be set free under some kind of power he believed his death unleashed. The question I asked myself was what these people needed to be set free *from*. So I started digging. And I found out that Alice Peterson was an abused wife, constantly living in fear of her husband, who a year prior to his death put his wife in the hospital after throwing her down the stairs at their home. She broke both her legs, her shoulder and nose and ruptured her spleen. The doctors suspected everything but her legs had been broken *before* her fall but of course she denied that."

"Then there's Frank Streck, a sixteen-year-old boy whose father had a habit of bringing little kids home and locking them in the basement, where the old man could play with them to his heart's content. Then, when he was done, Arnold Streck would make his son drag the bodies out to the old covered well at the far end of their property and heave them in."

Gina put a trembling hand to her mouth. "Jesus." She thought for a moment. "But how do you know all this? How come the police don't know about it if you do?"

Newman nodded. "I'll explain in a moment. But do you see the pattern? The seven names on Kyle's list were all people who were abused, trodden upon, beaten in one way or another. They were victims, and Kyle believed his death was the catalyst in changing their lives. He believed by dying, he would be imparting a gift to them. The gift of freedom, of being able to take back what had been stolen from them. He wanted to help the defenseless regain their power."

"But how did he know? If these people were strangers, then how could he know what they were going to do before they did it? There must have been some contact between them!"

"Unless he wasn't crazy," Newman said ominously. "Unless he really *did* see God, or *a* god or something that gave him the power he wrote about in his letter to me. It sounds incredible, of course, but when you think about it, would *you* turn away such a gift?"

"Of course I would," Gina answered, too quickly and saw Newman raise an eyebrow. "It's wrong."

"Is that what you really believe?"

"Don't you?"

It was clear to her now however, that he didn't. That he had brought her up here to try and convince her that Kyle had been on to something and that the only option left for her would be to buy into it. Her whole body shuddered and she was not entirely able to convince herself it was just the cold anymore.

Newman leaned forward in his chair. "We are victims too, Gina."

She struggled for the words to counter his statement but could find none. This in turn ignited a frustration in her chest that brought hot tears to her eyes.

"Your father likes to touch you," Newman said and her head snapped up.

"What the fuck do you know about it?"

A sad smile creased his lips. "Ever since the death of your mother, he takes solace in you, both mentally and physically. When you cry, he calls it grief. When you scream, he calls it passion. Such self-deceit keeps him sane while you crumble before him. I know, Gina. Kyle knew and it brought him here, to search for a God who could take away your pain, his pain and the agony suffered every day by countless others who walk crippled in the shadows of their tormentors."

The tears were coming freely now and Newman was a twitching mass of darkness and light when Gina looked up. "How? How did you know?"

"The same way Kyle knew about those seven people. The same way I knew about what drove them to kill their torturers and the same way I know who the next seven are."

He was on his knees now, his hands on hers. She convulsed with hitching sobs and shook her head. "He doesn't mean to do it."

"I know." His voice was soothing, brushing the gooseflesh from her skin with invisible fingers of warmth. "But he will have to answer for his sins just the same. God has said it to be so. Just as I have put my own mother in the grave for her malevolence toward me, you must do the same."

"No. I could never—" A fresh bout of tears burned her throat and she fell silent, Newman filling the space in the air between them with his newly-adopted sermon-like tones.

"You must. There is no 'yes' or 'no' here. It has been decided. You are no longer one of The Defenseless, not with the power, the *gift* Kyle has given you. You are on a new path, one with direction and it must be followed. The meek are taking back the earth. You are one of us now, Gina and you need never be afraid again."

"But the others…They'll be caught for what they've done." She blinked away the tears and saw that Newman was smiling.

"No they won't. You know how invisible we are in this world. The stink of anguish drips from our pores, driving people away until we become nothing more remarkable than an icy breeze on a summer's day. No one could ever see us. Kyle's gift uses that, cloaks us further. Take Alice for example. When nosy neighbors discovered her husband's body and the cops came, they immediately sent out a warrant for arrest. A search was conducted. Can you imagine how surprised they'd be if they'd learned she was there in that house watching them, even as they milled around? She was right there in front of them. Invisible, Gina. Embracing the gift makes you so."

"I still don't understand how you know so much about them."

He raised a thin strip of notepaper before her face and she had to lean forward in the hazy light to make out what was written on it. The handwriting was not Kyle's. It was a list and it started with her name.

"Because they found me. Just as I found you."

* * *

"You were right," Newman told her, his black eyes glistening in the light drifting through the hall window. "I thought he'd have woken up by now."

Like criminals, they had climbed the trellis and come through Gina's open window. From there they had crept across the hall and up to the door of her father's room, Newman wincing at the noxious stink that permeated the air in the upper level of the house.

Now they looked across the bed at one another, Gina's hair soaked once again and dripping on the bare floorboards with a metronomic tapping, as she shivered and looked down at her father. His naked, hairy arm was flung over his face as if to ward off the meager light penetrating his window, leaving only his broad expanse of forehead visible, dark tufts of tousled hair rising like nailed snakes from his head. Seeing him looking so vulnerable, she felt the slightest twinge of love, the wake of a better memory too quick to catch before it vanished and she sighed.

"Was it easy for you?"

Newman didn't answer and it took her a moment to realize that he must have assumed the question was directed at her father because that's where she was looking when she said it. She looked up at him, saw him shrug.

"I imagine it would only be easy for a monster."

They were speaking in loud whispers but still Stan Lewis showed no sign of stirring. Gina nodded somberly. *A monster like my father*, she

165

thought as Newman handed her the brown cloth package he had taken from a box hidden beneath the rug floor of the shack. She took it, gasping at the unexpected weight and then drew it close so that it was no longer held out over her father's slumbering form. Slowly, she untied the cloth.

A gun. Though she wasn't well versed in firearms, she knew enough to know that the long barreled Colt she held in her hands would vaporize whatever part of the anatomy it was shot at. The metallic gleam of the weapon held her gaze, even as Newman spoke.

"To outsiders, it will be a tragedy. To us, it will be a victory. You'll be setting yourself free, Gina and as painful as what you have to do may be, it will be nothing compared to the torture you've borne until now. Do it, and be done with your misery."

The pity in his tone reached her and she looked away from the gun, and down to her father. Almost immediately they came again: the buried memories shifting in their graves, their cries muffled beneath tons of packed earth as they struggled to be heard, struggled for an audience, begging to remind her that there was a good man locked somewhere inside the ogre she knew as her father. But they were muted by the sheer, impossible weight of reality, of fresher memory, carried on a scarlet tide of fury to the forefront of her brain where stood the monster. She began to weep, for the loss of her innocence at the behest of a man who should by all rights have been guarding it. A man, whose photographs lined the halls and beamed at her from a shattered frame on her nightstand at his request. A man, who she could remember loving. The lingering threads of that emotion now snagged in her heart like barbed wire, sparking new rage with every breath she took. Her father, a man who invaded her while offering sweet promises on a savage wind of sickly breath, who tore down the walls of her happiness and locked her in a sepulcher of her own misery.

She pressed the gun to the exposed part of his forehead.

Newman's looked away. "God bless you," he murmured.

Her hand was trembling, the gun pressed so hard now against her father's head he must surely awaken. She bit her lip, cocked the hammer and stopped breathing as her father's arm slid ever so slowly away from his face, stopping when one eye peered in confusion at her over the crook of his elbow. Something was muttered. Her name. A fresh burst of panicked breath, from whom she could not tell.

Time had stopped. Newman turned back, no doubt to see why the blast of the gun had not yet come. She could feel his eyes on her, like carapaces set in human sockets. A moan. Her father was moaning, realizing her intent, feeling the icy cold promise of the gun barrel pressed against his head. His hands came away, floating over his chest like driftwood, his eyes wide and frightened, the whites positively glowing in the light from the window. "Gina?"

She almost faltered then as she watched him lick his lips, briefly recognized the man he had once been because it had been that long since she had seen him scared.

"You can't stay trapped forever," Newman whispered softly and her father's eyes moved in his direction, his head not moving at all.

"Gina? Who's with you? What—"

"But you must be quick," Newman said and once again looked away.

In a voice brittle with tears, Gina said: "He's my father."

She thought she saw Newman nod, but in the poor light it was hard to be sure.

"We'll be your new family, Gina. We'll never hurt you. I promise," he said.

All three were silent for a prolonged moment, save for Gina's sniffling and the panting from the man in the bed. Her finger tightened on the trigger.

"Gina, honey doll..." her father said and a sudden, vivid memory flashed behind her eyes at the sound of his voice...

She is overwhelmed by the agony, paralyzed by the fear as he towers over her, smothering her with the scent of sex and blood and sweat and whiskey. He is thrusting, but it is as if he is stabbing her with the most wicked of blades, scissoring her open from groin to sternum and finally she can scream. She begs him to stop, tells him how it hurts, so bad, and his response is to slap her across the face. She is quiet then, watching as he labors in the gloom, a crooked smile on his moist lips as he whispers: "Ssssh, honey doll. Daddy loves you."

Gina pulled the trigger, the sudden explosion of light and noise enough to elicit a startled cry from her as the recoil sent her staggering back against the wall, Newman's pale oval face imprinted on her retinas.

"Good girl," he said breathlessly, the sound seeming to come from miles away.

She straightened, winded, and looked down at her father.

The position he'd been laying in had changed only slightly but his head had shifted to accommodate for the forced removal of everything above his cheekbones, liquidized in a spray of blood and gray matter that had spurted up the headboard and almost halfway up the wall behind it. Already it was starting to reverse its course, trickling back down from whence it came and Gina felt her stomach lurch.

"Oh God!" She dropped to her knees and bent double, one hand clenched on her stomach, bile seeping into her mouth.

Newman came around the bed and dropped to his haunches behind her. "Do you feel it?"

She spat sourness from her mouth, her ears throbbing painfully. "What?"

"I said do you feel it?"

"Feel what?"

"The power! Do you feel it flooding your veins? Do you feel the hope returning, the restoration of your dreams and wildest fantasies lighting up your insides?"

"I feel sick," she said and pushed him away as she struggled to her feet, remembering to avoid the bed and the gore that now adorned it.

A moment spared for the world to stop spinning and she turned away from the remains of her father. Her insides were not alight and nothing flooded her veins except for stark horror and repulsion for herself and what she had just done.

Newman grinned. "My sister," he said and held his arms out to her, the smile quickly turning to one of uncertainty at the sound of the clicking of the hammer. "What are you doing?"

"I could have lived with myself before this, as bad as things were. Now I can't and that makes you the only person I can blame other than myself. That's the nature of my unhappiness. Blame anyone but me."

Newman scoffed. "What are talking about?"

"You never told me how you knew about those people. What drove them to do the things they did."

His eyes glimmering in the blue light from the window, Newman splayed his hands out before him in a gesture of helplessness. "Yes. I did. I told you—"

"About a higher power. A force. I know," she interrupted. "Forget all that bullshit because from the moment you started in on that voodoo I knew there was something wrong with you."

"What do you want me to say then, if you won't listen to the truth?"

"I'm perfectly prepared to listen to the truth, but so far it hasn't been offered."

He made to step forward and she stiffened, the hand holding the gun whitening and Newman backed off, hands raised.

"So tell me," she continued, struggling to keep her voice even and calm.

"Tell you what?"

"Tell me how you knew about that woman. How you knew what her husband was doing to her before she killed him or—or how you knew about the kid and the bodies in the well. Tell me how you knew everything about people you never met."

When he spoke, all trace of cordiality had drained from his voice. Now he sounded tired, weary of her histrionics. "I told you. They came to me."

Gina forced a laugh. "Bullshit. You want to know what I think?"

"Absolutely."

"I think *you* went to *them*. I think you watched them until the time was right for you to show up outside *their* bedroom windows. I think you fed on their misery, told them their dead had sent you as an emissary to drag them from the mire of self-pity and helplessness."

Newman chuckled dryly. "Right."

"And then…after you watched them murder their tormentors, you killed *them* and made it look as if they'd fled the scene of the crime."

"That's quite a story. May I have the gun now?"

"You're kidding right?" Gina grinned, but her whole body tensed. "What would my headline have been, huh? 'Suicidal Teen Murders Father And Self'? Is that how this was supposed to play out?"

"Gina, give me the gun. I don't want to hurt you."

She couldn't tell from his voice if that was meant as a simple statement or a threat. She swallowed, perspiration trickling down her cheeks.

"Why are you doing this?" she asked him and backed up a step. He accordingly, took a step forward.

"Doing what?" he said. "Saving you from yourself?"

He stabbed an index finger at the body on the bed. "Saving you from this fucking pervert? You really don't get it do you? You really aren't tuned to the right frequency at all." He took another step forward. Gina watched the gun trembling in her hands, sweat making the trigger slick beneath her fingertip.

"Don't."

"Put the gun down and stop being ridiculous. You know why I came here."

"No. I don't."

"Gina, I'm warning you. You have no idea of the forces surrounding us." Another step forward.

"I said don't." Her palms were so moist she had to struggle to keep her grip on the handle. Newman stopped in the shaft of light slanting through the window, his eyes opaque, his expression somber.

"You're one of the Defenseless, Gina. You can't turn on us."

And with that he rushed forward, head low, fists aimed at her chest. She screamed, her finger reflexively jerking on the trigger and she was suddenly deaf in a very bright world.

* * *

Dear Kyle:

Although I know you'll never read this, you'll understand why I had to write it. Newman is dead. You do understand why I had to kill him, don't you? Of course you do. You always understood me. And daddy's dead now too. Funnily enough, I don't feel any different. I don't feel as if the nightmare is over or that the darkness had been scrubbed from my insides. I feel exactly the same. All that death for nothing.

Did he kill you too, Kyle? I never did get a chance to ask him and I wish I knew. Then maybe I'd be glad I killed him.

There's one bullet left in here and to be honest, it looks awful tempting; like a train ticket to your station. I have some time to think about whether or not I'm ready take that journey.

My head hurts. Newman must have knocked me unconscious but I couldn't have been out for long because I don't hear any sirens.

There is just a single word in my head now, repeating itself over and over again in whispers that aren't mine. Whispers that say: "Judgment." Who are they? Was Newman telling the truth? Did you really see a god? I'm so confused.

I have the gun loaded and close to me, just in case. I'm so scared, Kyle. I can almost believe Newman's story about people like us being invisible when I shut my eyes.
I'm starting to fade.

I love you,

Gina

HAUNTING GROUND

He's here.

I'm certain of it, but what good is certainty when you're surrounded by cynics?

Imbeciles! All the money they put into those machines, sensors, traps and telekinetic contraptions and he slipped in as easily as the night breeze, right under their noses, right into the house.

Right into my room.

No alarms have gone off. I know Richard will be furious when he finds out, but it's his own fault. I'm his wife, a woman and not a scientist or a clairvoyant like that preposterous old hag Mayfield, so he was lax with the machinery in my room, compelled to save the most expensive and significant devices for the places where the ghosts were expected. I can bet you Mayfield's room is wired like New York while I bask in the draft and the scrutiny of the very thing they're trying to catch. As if you could ever predict the haunt of a ghost. Idiots.

I can hardly wait to see the expression on Richard's face when I tell him of my encounter. He'll grit his teeth and give me that look like he suspects I summoned the ghost myself just to spite him and his efforts. And who knows, maybe I did? As sad as it is to admit it, I'm sure the ghost of Margus Kane has more life in death than my husband has now. He's certainly better looking. I see him now, reaching toward the candles by the dresser, making them flicker in the wind from his fingertips. He's little more than a flickering thing himself. How thrilling. A real-life ghost in my room! Not that it's the first time I've seen one mind you, but it is certainly the first time I've had one all to myself. And certainly the first time I've felt this excited and...dare I say it?...aroused by the presence of one.

I'll continue to scratch out these words in my diary while the revenant takes a seat on the footstool across from me, on the far side of the room, next to the dresser Richard has told me not to use. *It's a Louis XV Provincial Armoire, not a bloody storage closet*, he tells me. *This is not our house. This is our laboratory for the next six weeks and everything in here is worth far more than we could ever afford to replace should you have one of your 'accidents'."* Yes, he's a real prince among men, but right now neither my husband nor his studies matter. The ghost has come to see me. No. Perhaps 'see' isn't the right word, because he hasn't really come to *see* me, he has come to *watch* me. I can tell by the slight cock of his head, angled just so he can take in my slight form as I scribble away in my precious little book and pretend I'm not watching him back. But of course it would be impossible for me not to watch him, for while he may be nothing but a lingering memory committed to dust and forever beyond the reach of my hopes and fantasies, he remains a thing of beauty, a sentient thing with bound desires that make his presence so necessary. He is a ghost of frustration, a chained box of passions and tonight I am to be his audience as he tells me his secrets without ever saying a word.

The stroke of my pen grows light as I struggle to focus on the thoughts that just a moment before came so freely. My excitement is rising and in the corner of my eye the revenant shifts in his seat. I am struck with the sudden urge to cry out to my husband, to force him to watch as the object of his only desire confronts me, but I know I won't. That would be giving him something, allowing him to be part of this unique moment in which the line between life and death is forgotten, momentarily erased and anything may happen.

Margus Kane stands and the candle flames bow in reverence. The gray cast of his somewhat translucent skin is offset by the shadows filling the room. The light ceases an inch before his eyes, chastened by an unfamiliar darkness.

Margus Kane, lover, warrior, prince and murderer, moves toward my bed. I am surprised to see he steps rather lightly across the room. I expected to see him glide, or perhaps vanish only to appear next to me, a cool hand laid upon mine. He approaches and my breath quickens, hot against my lips. He is dressed is some kind of uniform but as my knowledge of Washington's history is woefully inept, I will leave the deductions to Richard, who can glean the specifics from my blissful account in the morning. All I do know is that the portraits of Kane in my husband's tome of this state's malevolent leaders are wrong. This being before me, though no doubt altered by the events that led to his passing, and of course the passing itself, looks nothing like the illustrated antagonist in *Washington Infamy: The Evergreen State's Black History*. He looks like a boy trapped in an older man's body, his frame skeletal, and he carries himself as though wounded, one arm cradling the other. He is a pitiful sight and I feel unthreatened by his presence. I am, however, curious as to what he intends to do with me. The manner in which he sidles up to my bed suggests he has secrets to divulge or a tale of woe to impart, secrets of which he is deeply ashamed.

I gather myself into a sitting position, my back pressed firmly against the headboard. This bed is a four-poster Irish something-or-other, according to Richard. Basically another antique I am marring with my presence, but now it is my sanctuary, the warmth protecting me from the chill air that rolls in waves from the approaching specter. For the first time I detect the faint smell of roses and a surge of excitement rises in my chest as Kane's ghost comes to a halt mere inches from my trembling body. He is close enough to touch but I continue to write, my handwriting spiky like an EKG reading. I am alternating feverish glances from the revenant to my diary, eager to commit this spectacular occurrence to the page, spurred by the knowledge that in all his years buried in parapsychology, my husband has never come this close to a ghost. Despite all the expensive media-hyped field trips to the world's most haunted sites—The Borley Rectory, Belasco House, The Tower of London, The Whaley House, Raynham Hall, even Amityville— Richard has left disappointed each time, consoled only by sheets of readouts and blurry photographs, the kind that could only excite a man who believes in something but has yet to see it with his own eyes.

Like I am seeing it now.

The temperature of the room has dropped, almost without my noticing and now it matches the cold that flows from Margus Kane. He is standing motionless next to me, staring with those endlessly hollow eyes, still cradling his arm and now the anticipation sends my breath clouding out through my teeth in shuddered hisses.

I am warmed inside by a terrible gloating.

Poor Richard, selfish and oblivious to anything alive and it is his long suffering wife who ends up with front row seats to a most magical event, the kind of transpiration that could make his career and see the fulfillment of all his dreams. An obedient wife would summon him but I am, and always have been, far from obedient. Instead, he may have this journal and know what his ignorance has led him to miss.

Kane is leaning closer now and his breath is rushing against my cheek. I'm sure I can feel the skin freezing there, but oh God how amazing this all is! While my husband, that spoiled brat Charley Jackson, and that charlatan Mayfield sleep soundly in their beds, dreaming of being woken by some phenomenon to give credence to their endless speculations, here I am with the most notorious ghost of them all close enough to touch! I'm not sure my heart can take it! But it must and I must be the one who sees, the one who reports back from the frontlines...

Kane whispers into my ear and his breath is so foul I unthinkingly turn away and as a result, lose his words to the otherworldly breeze that is now sweeping around the foot of the bed. Shadows stretch across the walls as invisible mouths extinguish all but one of the three candles. It is truly a sinister mood that permeates the room now and I shiver in delight. Though I have to squint to see what I am writing in this new gloom, I am committed to getting this all down. These words represent a reality I am wary of losing should I immerse myself too deep in this incredible situation. The words are my anchor. Besides, even in the periphery of my vision, Kane's countenance has grown a little too frightening for me to behold, thanks to the gloom and the sudden resurgence in memory of old childhood fears. And then he whispers again and the pen jolts in my hand at the sudden burst of cold against my ear. But...I'm uncertain now. Was it truly the cold or the content of that singular whisper that made me start, that allowed a sliver of inner ice to slide over my heart and forced the hair on the nape of my delicate neck to stand to attention? It was not the fact that this revenant knew my name for as Richard has said many times—we cannot know their capabilities until we fully know *them*.

It suddenly strikes me as peculiar—though it should have occurred to me well before this moment—that perhaps my latent friend's intentions are not as benevolent as my excitement has led me to believe. It is an unwelcome shadow of doubt that cloaks itself over me, competing with Kane's projected darkness to thrill me in an altogether new and unpleasant way. My writing has slowed now, a direct contrast to my frantic breathing and the room seems suddenly still. The ghost has whispered my name. No threat should be inferred by this alone and only a squeamish, nervous woman would. No. It was the whisper itself. The subdued voice that powered the word. The voice was familiar and now the ghost is moving again although he hasn't left his place by the bed.

Shifting.

I am recalling the argument that led me to this room, to this forbidden bed down the hall from the room I am supposed to share with Richard. An 'approved' room. It was an exchange in low growled tones in which only my own weaknesses were aired lest the pretentious Mayfield or the spoiled financier of this excursion, Jackson, should overhear. The argument was brief and as always, ended with a promise of silence for many days to come. But it is Richard's last words that are flowing from my brain and down to my fingers now, ready to be written for posterity so that those who read this will finally know a truth I should have seen coming and call me a fool for missing it.

There is another forbidden room. One Mayfield warned us was positively dripping with negative energy. The playroom—a lavish miniature theater, big enough to seat an audience of one hundred, although for decades it has only held dust. Behind the stage, hung on small brass hooks along one wall are costumes. There are magician's garbs, animal skins...and army uniforms from various eras of violence. It was here Richard stalked off to when I told him I wanted a divorce, that I wanted nothing more to do with his fraudulent quests. It was here he sought solace rather than face my threats.

The theater. According to Mayfield the most dangerous room in the house.

Costumes.

Oh Richard, no...

And now I'm afraid to look up because the exaggerated slowness of his movements only draws out the dread and whatever power this house has lent him, he is using it to thicken the darkness. Dear Lord, I am lost! He is changing, dropping the charade and leaning close once more and there is nothing wrong with his arm. It is reaching and Dear Diary, Dear *God*, he has fooled me for the last time but if he loves me, if he ever loved me there might still be hope that I can reach beyond the

THEY KNOW

"How valiant the heart is, and how clever, for so often does it use the mind as a shield against the dragons."

— Nocturnity

* * *

The phone rings just as the weeping stops. He stares at the glass and the amber panacea within, shutting out the trilling with minimal effort. There is nothing to hear. Just as there was nothing to hear the last time he answered the phone. Nothing but damnable winter breathing on the line and the faintest whisper, whispering the impossible: "They know."

Just the wind.

And the ticking from the walls of the deathwatch winding down.

* * *

Snow.

Jake Dodds was so very tired of it.

It seemed winter had crept in while he was sleeping, draping drop cloths over the town of Miriam's Cove and hushing itself with guilty whispers while it awaited his reaction to the desertion of color.

It was everywhere, layered on the ground, hunched over the hedgerows in the garden, bowing the branches of the trees in the yard, shotgun blasts of it on the sides of cars and windows, fired by children driven by manic excitement. It was on the roofs, the sills, the shoulders of people ducking to avoid the sharp wind that send it flurrying into their grimacing faces.

Everywhere.

And it didn't seem as if it would ever stop. It didn't seem as if the underlying vibrant green luster of life would ever return. Even the sun had been reduced to a foggy white cyst beneath the pale skin of the sky.

He was starting to feel as if the whole goddamn season with its twinkling lights and carols, dazzling storefronts and endless slew of commercials advertising mind-numbing electric toys, was to blame for the snow. People expected snow for Christmas and maybe the collective power of that expectation was enough to make it so. Whatever the reason, he didn't like it one bit. Christmas was a time for sitting around the fire eating marshmallows and fruit cake, for decorating the tree with loved ones and maybe indulging in a snifter of brandy before bed, for gifts that meant something and for the excited chatter of children when they discovered the bounty beneath the tree.

But now, six days before Christmas, sitting by his window and staring out at an almost monochrome world, Jake realized that all that was gone, not only in the minds of the masses, but from his own life too.

A distinct awareness of family values and a fondness for the ritualistic aspect of the season had not been enough to keep his wife alive or his children from growing up and scattering themselves around the world. Leaving him alone with the white and an empty house to watch it from.

Clearing the condensation away with a swipe of his hand, he scowled at the silent fall of snow as children giggled and flung handfuls of the stuff at each other.

In his garden stood a long-suffering walnut tree, a beard of white nestled in its crotch almost like mimicry of the season's patron saint.

Jake thought he knew what it felt like to be that tree – immobile, rooted to the ground, trapped and powerless to do anything but stand by and watch the passage of time, unable to run away from the grief, the sorrow and all the dark things that sharpened the edges of life.

He shook his head, sliding the cover over the well from which such melodrama sprung and allowed himself the faintest hint of a smile as a tall, wiry figure in a brown suit and overcoat appeared, ducked his head against the snow and turned the corner into Jake's driveway.

A visitor was just what he needed now and visitors were seldom welcomer than Lenny Quick.

Jake groaned at the ache in his bones as he rose from the seat by the window, and he took a moment to steady himself before making his way to the front door.

"God's dandruff," Lenny said, snapping his hat against the palm of his hand. He inspected the hallway as if he'd never seen it before (though he had been here at least once every week for the last thirty years – with the exception of that time in early '90 when pneumonia had kept him in a hospital bed) before he turned to watch Jake shutting the soft white world outside.

"No end to it, is there?" Jake said, smiling now. Ever since Julia's death, he had felt as if the walls were closing in around him, that somewhere beyond the rose-patterned wallpaper, a clock was ticking. He heard it at night, faint but most definitely there. *Tick-tick-tick*, the winding down of his own deathwatch. Company helped silence that sound and made the ghosts nothing but tricks of light and shadow.

Lenny shivered and brushed the snow from his shoulders. "It's supposed to get a lot worse too if the weatherman is to be believed." He hung his hat atop his coat on the mahogany tree in the hall. "Saw on the news Maine's gettin' hammered, New York, same. Gonna be a bad one no matter what way you look at it. Surprised *we* haven't gotten more than this already, to tell the truth." He led the way into the living room, as if drawn by the heat. "People have been saying since the summer we're heading for the worst winter in years. Hasn't happened yet though so I reckon the bad stuff must be getting close."

Jake followed him into the living room.

A cheerful fire blazed in the fireplace, occasionally spitting sparks the fireguard caught. With Lenny here, the fire and indeed the room, looked almost cozy. Alone, the flames drew the spirit from a man and made the room seem hollow and dark.

Lenny took a seat without waiting to be asked. They had known each other too long to stand on formality. Jake moved to the sideboard beneath the window, upon which gleaming bottles stood like soldiers with immaculate uniforms, most of them empty. He tried to avoid looking at the bleached white world outside. "Usual?"

Lenny nodded and leaned forward to show his hands to the fire. "That'd be just fine. I think I'm freezing from the inside out today."

Jake poured him a brandy, a whiskey for himself.

"Thanks," Lenny said, accepting his drink. He watched Jake grimace as he lowered himself into the seat opposite. "Knees still bothering you?"

Jake nodded. "Morning, noon and night. Mornings worst of all."

"You should let a doctor take a look before you end up crawling."

"I'd *rather* crawl than see a doctor."

"Well it isn't going to get any better if you don't go see someone."

"Like who?"

"Like...I don't know, a bone man or something. Doctor Palmer would be a start."

"Nah. It'll ease up once the cold is gone."

"You sure about that?"

Jake sighed. "No. I'm not, but unless you went deaf thirty or so years ago, you should know damn well how I feel about doctors."

"Sure I do," Lenny said with a shrug, "but is a family tradition of hating doctors for no reason going to make your life any easier if this cold spell turns out to be here for the long haul?"

"We don't hate them for no reason."

Lenny smiled. "You're avoiding the question."

"I was hoping it would convince you not to pursue it."

"Have it your way, but I have a twinge of arthritis in my fingers and I have to tell you, if it hit my knees so bad I could hardly walk, I'd be spread out before Palmer like a virgin on prom night."

Jake winced. "I could have died happy without ever picturing that. Thanks."

Lenny laughed, a deep rumbling baritone and slapped his thigh. Jake grinned, but it was short-lived. Lenny wiped his eyes and when he looked up, his expression was grave.

"What is it?" Jake asked, unnerved by the intensity of his friend's stare.

Lenny waited a beat, then sipped from his glass, swishing the brandy around his mouth before he spoke. "You mentioned dying," he said, looking down into his drink. "I was wondering if you remembered the last time we talked about it. What you told me, I mean."

"Vaguely," Jake replied, too quickly, averting his eyes from

Lenny's probing glare, a move he knew belied his words.

He remembered most of it and it shamed him. The snow had thickened, draining what little light had been caught dancing in the evening sky and for the gloom, he was suddenly thankful. In the firelight, the flush of color the lie had summoned to his face would go unnoticed.

It had happened two nights ago.

He staggers into the bedroom with a wail of grief and almost chokes on the breath he sucks in to power another. The shadows quickly move away from him, sliding along the walls and slipping beneath the carpet. The room ripples and sways in his tear-blurred vision, his gut full of whiskey, heart full of grief and dread. Sobbing, he drops to his knees beside the bed, repeating her name like a sacred mantra, as if it could ever be enough to raise her.

Beneath the bed — so cold, so terribly cold without her — *lies a shoebox and his fingers find it fast, first feeling the sides, the lid, then clutching and dragging it out into the dull light spilling in from the hallway. Urgently, he rips the lid from the box, wipes away tears and grabs the Colt .45 in his fumbling, trembling hands.*

"I hate the damn thing. Get rid of it," his wife had said the day he'd brought it home.

"It's for protection, honey. Just for protection."

"I don't like it. Bring it back. What if it goes off by mistake?"

"It won't. These things don't go off unless you mean them to."

Like I mean it to now, *he thinks, and clicks back the safety. Clll-ick! He can feel the shadows around him, pressing down on him, watches held to their ears, listening. Counting off the seconds to oblivion.*

In lieu of the gunshot comes a scream, a horrible guttural scream and the gun falls heavily to the floor, still wearing a bead of perspiration from his temple. He runs, runs to the phone and misdials four times before he finally hears the voice he so desperately needs to hear.

"You were pretty upset," Lenny said, looking strangely embarrassed himself, a look Jake did not see very often. "You scared the life out of me I don't mind telling you."

"Yeah," was all Jake could think to say.

"You were going to do it too, weren't you?"

"I guess I was."

Silence then, and in it Jake half-expected to hear a ticking. What came instead was a rattling, as the wind drove snow against the window.

"We've been friends for a long time," Lenny said, casting a half-hearted glance at the window. "Been through a lot together. I wish I was the type of guy who could advise you on things like this but I'm not qualified. Maybe if I'd watched more *Oprah* or that moronic *Doctor Phil* guy I'd be able to sort out all of that confusion and fear you've got gnawing away at you, but I can't." He jiggled his glass and watched the brandy lap against the sides. "I know you're lonely and hurt and scared and I keep trying to think up ways to fix that but the truth is…you've always been stronger than me, y'know? You were the one who helped me sort out my problems over the years. You were the one I turned to when my head threatened to explode with all the pressure. You were my surrogate big brother, the one I called on to slay the dragons, even if I'd never have admitted it. Too proud, you see. Now that you need help, I'm not so sure I'm any good to you."

Jake offered him a tired smile. "You've already been good to me. I can't remember everything about that call the other night, but I do know by the time I hung up I was more terrified of that gun than anything else. If I hadn't called you…"

He left the sentence die in the air between them and nodded. "You're a good man, Lenny," he said softly and drained his glass.

Lenny leaned back from the fire, the right side of his face fading in the deepening gloom. "Nah," he said, waving away the compliment. "I was just worried my local brandy pimp'd go outta business. Where'd I be then?"

Gratitude hovered at the back of Jake's tongue but he knew vocalizing it would embarrass Lenny so instead he raised his empty glass in the air and grinned. "To madmen, pimps and alcoholics," he said.

Lenny chuckled and touched his glass to Jake's. "I'll drink to that."

They both laughed until the wind thundered against the side of the house hard enough to make them both jump.

"So how are you feeling now?" Lenny asked.

"I have good and bad days. If the snow would let up or better still, vanish entirely then I wouldn't be able to count this as one of the bad ones. Goddamn snow drives me crazy."

Lenny frowned. "Why? It never bothered you before."

"I don't know. This year is different. I know it's ridiculous, but I'm a little afraid of it. Even back when the weatherman first said it was heading our way I felt apprehensive, as if he'd said a plague was coming."

"I think I'd rather the snow," said Lenny.

"I wish I could explain it. It just feels wrong, you know? I mean, I look out that window there just like I do every other year and I see the same damn thing I always see in winter – snow and lots of it. But for some reason this year it looks less like a bunch of ice crystals and more like some kind of mold, as if the world is going stale."

Lenny stared impassively, but Jake was suddenly aware how crazy he sounded and rose from his chair before Lenny could call him on it.

"Another?" he asked and Lenny handed him his glass.

As he refilled their drinks, he glanced out the window. The sky was darkening, slashes of silver glowing above the horizon. And still the snow fell, whipped by the wind into transparent white horses that galloped beneath the streetlights. Jake shivered.

It's growing, he thought. *That's what I was trying to tell Lenny. It looks as if it's growing, like a scab. And the street is the wound.*

He returned with the drinks and set his whiskey on the mantel while he fed the flames wood from a cast iron basket.

"Can I tell you what I think?" Lenny said.

"Sure."

"I think you need to start getting out of the house more. I'll bet you can count on one hand the amount of times you've been outside since Julia passed on."

Jake said nothing. Lenny gave a satisfied grunt.

"See? That's worse than solitary confinement. A man with the kind of worries you've got could drive himself stir crazy looking at these same four walls day in day out, especially with all the memories around here. And the snow thing? Sorry to have to tell you but I think it isn't so much the snow as the whole outside world that's got you spooked. You've become so wrapped up in your own little shell of suffering and anger – and I'm not belittling or begrudging you that; God knows Julia was one of the sweetest damn women I've ever known – that you can't bear to look beyond that window just in case it might offer you a view of a place out*side* the pain."

Jake raised his eyebrows. Lenny grinned.

"Well I'll be damned," he said, "Maybe I was wrong. *Oprah* watch out!"

"You could be right," Jake said, but he didn't think so. "But how does knowing what the problem is help any?" He rubbed a hand over his face. "I miss her, y'know?" he said quietly. "All the goddamn time. Sometimes so much I can't breathe. And at night…at night is the worst of all, when I'm asleep and I run my hand over the memory of her skin and wake to an empty bed and cold sheets. Sometimes the pain feels too real to be grief, Lenny. One night I woke up convinced I was having a heart attack. I almost called you then too."

The fire hissed and the flames caught, restoring the warm amber glow to the room.

"You should have called me," Lenny told him. "That's what I'm there for, just like you're here to fill me with cheap brandy." He smiled but it quickly faded. "I didn't mean it to sound like I have all the answers either. I don't. I can't even imagine what this has been like for you. But I hate seeing you like this, stuck in a house alone with nothing to do but remember." He straightened in his chair and let loose an exasperated sigh. "I guess I have some titanium balls telling you how to handle things, huh?"

Jake shook his head. "No. I appreciate it. Really. I'm just tired of being afraid, you know? Tired of waking up from a nightmare only to have the real nightmare crash down around me. I feel empty, Lenny. And alone. And pretty goddamn pathetic."

"Pathetic? Why? You think two months after you lose your wife you should be all smiles and organizing house parties? If I saw you doing something like that I'd have to take off my belt and whip the shit out of you. The way I see it is you're handling it as good as you know how. Another man would be lying in the ground beside his wife by now after taking the chickenshit way out."

"I came close though, didn't I?"

"Yes. You did." Lenny said. "But close is still a million miles away from done and you're still here talking about it. That's good enough for me."

Jake set his glass down and rubbed his hands together. "So what do I do?"

Lenny's face grew somber and he pointed a long gnarled index finger at Jake's glass. "Being a bit lighter on the devil juice might help you some. I'm your friend, Jake, but if calls like that one two nights ago start getting regular I'm buying an answering machine for Christmas."

Although Lenny chuckled to show he meant it as a joke, the point was clear. It scared Jake however to think what his nights might be like without the cushioning effect of alcohol. Then again, he realized, if drinking led him to that old shoebox beneath the bed again, the next cushion might be the one in his coffin.

"You need to start finding distractions," Lenny continued. "I'm not saying you jump into a whole routine but you could start setting aside days to go for walks. Go catch a movie every now and then. Come with me to Bingo some Friday night; see if we can't beat the pants off those Harperville hags. Hell, even stopping by to see me and the wife would be a start."

"I know, you're right, but most of those things you mentioned only remind me of who's missing from the picture."

Lenny leaned forward, his elbows resting on his knees, his hooked nose mere inches from Jake. "It'll get easier," he said and laid a hand on Jake's shoulder. "But you have to start somewhere before you smother yourself." He stared hard into Jake's eyes, as if trying to discern something written there. "Do you understand?"

The phone rang then and Lenny sat back in his chair. "Joanne, most likely," he said and Jake nodded as he rose, pain flaring in his knees.

"Will I tell her you're here?" he asked as he made his way out into the hall.

"Might as well," Lenny said. "She can sense it anyway."

"Still reading tealeaves?"

"Earl Grey, morning noon and night."

Jake was smiling as he picked up the phone. "Hello?"

The voice on the other end of the line was gruff, even over the static the weather wrought.

"Mr. Dodds?"

"Yes?"

"This is Sheriff Baxter."

Jake swallowed and felt a chill thrum through him, even though a distant voice inside him posed the question: *what's left for you to be afraid of?*

"Mr. Dodds?"

"Uh yeah, hi Sheriff. What can I do for you?"

"Is Lenny Quick there with you?"

The chill intensified. "Yes, why?"

"Good," Baxter said, ignoring the question. "Tell him to stay put until I get there."

"All right. But what's – " The realization that he was talking to nothing but static stopped him and he stared at the receiver for a moment before hanging up.

All sorts of nightmarish scenarios paraded through his mind as he slowly made his way back into the living room, where Lenny was gazing into the fire and humming to himself, but he pushed them away, blaming his own recent loss on the almost overwhelming dread that attempted to drape itself over his shoulders as he took his seat.

"Well?" Lenny asked a few moments later when his expectant look went unnoticed.

"It was uh…it was Sheriff Baxter. The line is buggered with all the snow. I couldn't hear him very well."

"Baxter? What did he want? Is he on to our little speakeasy here?"

Jake tried to think of a lie, or at the very least a semi-truth he could give Lenny to appease him, but the cryptic nature of Baxter's call left no room for anything but the truth.

"It was about you."

The joviality vanished from Lenny's face, replaced with an immediate look of concern that added twenty years to him. "What about me?"

"I don't know. He just asked if you were here. I told him you were and he said to tell you to stay put until he arrives."

"Why?"

"I told you, I don't know. That's all he said and then he hung up. I'm sure it's nothing. Maybe Joanne's car broke down and she's going to be late home or something."

Lenny slowly shook his head. "A sheriff wouldn't come looking for me just to tell me that. He could have told me that over the phone. No, something's happened."

"Aw c'mon, don't go thinking like that," Jake said. "Look out the window, there's nothing but white. Going to be all sorts of traffic problems tonight. I'm sure that's all it is. When you left, was Joanne heading somewhere?"

"Yeah," Lenny said, eyes glassy. "To the store, but that's only a

187

few blocks away. She wouldn't have taken the car."

"She might have, to be out of the cold."

"Jake, I see what you're trying to do, but she didn't drive. Whatever Baxter is coming here to tell me, it isn't about a goddamn break-down."

Jake couldn't argue further because he knew nothing he'd say would sound believable, even to himself. Lenny was right. When Sheriff Baxter made house calls, it was to ask questions or deliver bad news, and Jake felt certain his own tragedy had attuned him to bad tidings.

And his nerves were singing now.

Mind racing, he almost managed to block out the sound coming from the walls. But then his guard faltered and his heart skipped a beat, allowing that unmistakable ticking sound an undistracted audience.

Tick-tick-tick.

It ticks for thee.

No, he thought, braced by panic. *Maybe not. Maybe not me at all.*

Lenny rose, tugging Jake from his fearful musings and quieting the deathwatch in the walls.

"What are you doing?"

Lenny's nerves didn't seem to be faring much better. A faint trembling made the glass wobble as he finished his brandy in one gulp and started towards the hall.

"Lenny? What are you doing?" Jake repeated, rising to follow.

"Going home. If something has happened to Joanne, I'm not waiting on a cop to break the news. Might be too late by the time Baxter gets his fat ass through that snow anyway."

"Wait," Jake said and hurried after him into the dark hallway, his knees aflame with pain. In the few seconds it took to reach him, Leroy had already donned his coat and hat and was turning to the door.

"Damn it, wait!" Jake said again, and the near-hysteria in his voice made his friend pause, one hand on the knob.

"Something's happened," Lenny whispered, face grave.

I don't want to be here by myself, Jake almost blurted, immediately shamed by his selfishness. Instead he reached for his coat. "You wanted me to start getting out more," he said, "so if you're not going to wait, I'm coming with you."

He couldn't believe he had said it and only when it was out did he realize how truly small and unfriendly his world had become. In here was loneliness and despair, all measured by the ticking of the deathwatch. Out there was the snow, the loathsome blanket of putrescent mold beneath which Julia slept forever.

Lenny looked about to argue, then sagged and yanked open the front door.

The hostile night roared into their faces as they stepped out into the cold.

* * *

This is insane.

Jake bowed his head against the wet white kisses the sky drove into their faces. Already his skin felt numb and sore, his nose wet and dripping, knees raging with the agony of battling through the ankle-deep drifts that hunkered against the light like protective mothers.

The buildings on both sides of Brennan Street stood like monoliths, fringed with snow and twinkling with the ice that bejeweled them. In some, dim yellow light hugged the frosted windows; in others there was no light at all. Vehicles hunched against the curbs wore scaled skins of white. For such a change in the costume of the earth, noise was expected, but it was as if silence itself fell in shreds from the darkness above.

Lenny was a rail-thin silhouette against the gathering of lights at the head of Brennan Street, his stride purposeful, shoulders tight, hands jammed into his pockets, breath pluming.

Jake squinted, hobbling through the packed snow as fast as he could bear it, praying his knees wouldn't quit on him. The thought of ending up face down in that cold fluffy mold was enough to send shivers rippling through him. "Lenny, slow down," he called at one stage but his cry went either unheard or unheeded.

Lenny moved on, Jake struggling to keep up and wondering, as he guessed his friend was, what the hell Baxter had to report and what he'd do when he found they'd left the house rather than wait.

He prayed Joanne was all right, though a selfish part of him, a mindless, insensitive creature he kept locked away in the foulest recesses of his subconscious, yearned for her to be dead, so Lenny could share in his suffering. So he would no longer have to face the nights alone. Lenny's advice was good, but it welled from a shallow pond in which his friend had never washed, a source that sprung from sympathy, not empathy.

Only through his own loss could he understand Jake's and then, they could help each other through the dark.

Jesus, Jake thought, snapping back to himself, *what the hell is wrong with you?*

He'd been friends with Joanne almost as long as he'd known Lenny. She was a small, stout woman, full of well-meaning bluster but more than capable of adopting an evil temper if it suited her needs. In many ways, she was her husband's polar opposite and in this case at least, the old saying about attraction held true. Their love was as strong as Jake and Julia's had been, even if the Quick's method of maintaining their relationship was to feign indifference towards each other and to trade sarcastic barbs as much as possible.

Remembering that malevolent whisper from the back of Jake's mind brought a rush of guilt so strong it was almost debilitating and only a quick glance at the seething white mass engulfing his feet kept him moving.

Six blocks did a respectable impression of twelve before they reached Lenny's house – a small two-story stucco with sagging gutters and a crumbling chimney electric heating made redundant. A television aerial, lashed to the chimney, stood against the paler patches of wind-wracked sky like a stitch in discolored flesh.

Jake was somewhat surprised to see that Baxter's car was not parked outside. If he had already set out for Jake's house then they would have met him on the way here. The vehicle he had initially mistaken as the police cruiser as they approached proved to be Joanne's Toyota. From what he could see of it in the grainy light, it appeared undamaged.

Lenny, who had not spoken a word since they'd left Jake's house, suddenly stopped at the foot of the driveway and looked from Jake to the dark house brooding before them as if it was an alien thing, a cold and indifferent replacement for something he had loved. His face was unreadable.

"Something's going on. I don't like this one bit," he said, just loud enough for Jake to hear. "She always leaves a light on, even when she's out." He shook his head. *"Always."*

"Maybe she's gone to bed already."

Lenny stared at Jake for a moment before sidestepping a mound of dirty snow presumably left in the wake of a plow, though the street certainly didn't look as if anything but the wind had traveled it in the past few hours.

Heart thudding and unable to shake the feeling that there was something amiss out here, something other than Lenny's deserted house, Jake looked around, his breath emerging as ragged ghosts the wind tore away from him.

Quiet.

Perhaps that was it, he thought. Even for a night like this with apparently no end to the snowfall and the bitter cold, the streets were peculiarly empty. Miriam's Cove was a relatively small town but the people normally didn't forsake its streets until all hours of the morning. Where were the defiant drivers struggling to get home? Where were the emergency services, the police, the salt trucks? The absence of these mundane but expected sights unsettled him. It made him feel as if he and Lenny had missed the imparting of a monumental secret and now they were left alone in the world with the ghosts of their neighbors circling around them on white waves, waiting for them to realize their folly.

He shuddered and followed Lenny up the driveway where they had to squeeze between the Toyota and a clump of snow that resembled a misshapen hand with weeds sprouting from the knuckles. White eddies spun above their heads like tattered scarves blown from a clothesline. Lenny clumped to the door and when he raised his hand to the doorbell, it was trembling.

"Don't you have the key?" Jake asked.

"I wasn't intending on being out long enough to need one," Lenny said and poked the thin white plastic rectangle until 'Greensleeves' sounded within. It was a jingle Jake hated, but now it seemed horribly ominous because he knew deep inside there was no one in that house to hear it.

"Damn it!"

"Try again," Jake told him, at a loss for a better suggestion.

"She isn't deaf and she isn't there."

"Then where could she be?"

"Would I be standing out here like a fool if I knew?"

"Maybe she's at the police station. Maybe that's what Baxter wanted to tell you."

"Yeah, if he wasn't coming to tell me she's under a white sheet."
Under a white sheet. Jake swallowed. "Don't say that."
"Why? You saying you haven't thought it?"
"This isn't getting us anywhere, Lenny. Maybe we should – "
The street suddenly dimmed, as if something huge had flown overhead. As one, the streetlights winked out.
"What the hell?"
"Power's out," Lenny said and cursed as he launched a kick at the door. Startled, Jake wiped melting snow from his eyelashes and blinked into the dark. The mounds of white gradually began to emerge as if possessed of their own luminescence.
Even in the dark I can see it, Jake thought and shuddered. Though he was wearing a wool-lined overcoat, cold tendrils slithered up his legs and down his neck. He pulled the coat tight around him and lifted one foot, then the other, alternating stances to dissuade the cold and the feeling that the snow was trying to reach his skin.
"What now?" he asked, disturbed by the tremble in his voice.
Lenny was staring at the door, as if still expecting it to fly open.
"Lenny?"
"Maybe you're right," he replied. "Maybe the police station is where she went. We can't stand around in this all night, we'll freeze to death. At least if she isn't there, the cops will know the score. They can drive us back if we need it."
"Right," said Jake and they hurried down the driveway and back onto the street.
They had only gone a few feet, the snow blowing into their faces, when they saw lights up ahead, accompanied by a low growling.
"That a car?" Jake yelled over the wind and he thought he saw Lenny nod.
"Sure looks like it. C'mon."
Jake eventually managed to draw level with Lenny and they trudged on, heads lowered. More than once, Jake had to convince himself that his imagination was on overdrive and that any malevolence he felt at work around him was nothing but a reflection of his own sorrow and the result of weeks of self-imposed isolation. Imagination, nothing more. Had to be. Because rational men did not feel things moving in the snow around their feet.
"Snowplow!" Lenny exclaimed and Jake looked up, a hand tented over his eyes against the glare of the lights. The growling was louder

now and Jake saw that Lenny was right. A truck with a plow blade mounted on the front was slowly making its way toward them.

Jake felt a swell of relief. And then he noticed something odd. He tugged Lenny's elbow. "Why isn't the blade down?"

"What?"

"The plow blade. It's raised up. There must be almost a foot of snow out here. Why isn't he using the blade?"

Lenny turned back to look at the truck, then shrugged. "Maybe it's damaged. I don't know. Or maybe he's calling it a night."

Jake persisted. "That's Carl Stewart's truck. The guy always has these streets cleared before it gets too deep. For Chrissakes the town gave him an award for it a couple of years back, remember?"

"Yeah."

"So I don't get why he isn't using it now. And look at the way he's driving."

The truck's lights swept across their faces, washing the walls of the house to their right before returning to dazzle them once more.

Lenny moved in the direction of the truck. "You need to calm down a tad," he called over his shoulder. "It's snowing and snowing hard. Ol' Carl's tires are slipping that's all."

But for whatever reason, Jake didn't think so and was about to tell Lenny as much when the truck provided all the confirmation he needed.

The headlights dipped then crawled over the burgeoning plain of snow and fixed on them, turning Lenny into a black scarecrow amid a swarm of snowflakes. The old man tensed, his back hunching into a defensive posture. The truck came on, now less than twenty feet away, its engine roaring, steam billowing from beneath the hood, the upraised blade like a grim smile in the remnants of light it stole from the headlamps.

"Hey!" Lenny called then, waving his arms.

The truck kept coming, the suspension jerking as the vehicle bounced over hard-packed snowdrifts, the tires slipping and sliding.

"Hey, Carl!"

The beams found him again; the engine growled and whined.

Ten feet.

Jake shook his head and reached out a trembling hand to Lenny. "If he's seen us, he'll stop."

Lenny nodded, but continued to wave his arms with the fervor of a man who is not yet sure how much he has lost but is compelled to find out. In the headlights, Jake noted how very, very old he seemed.

Five feet and now the lights were as bright as the sun in their faces. On instinct, Jake lunged forward and grabbed a handful of Lenny's coat, tugging him back hard enough to send them both sprawling on their backs into the snow. The cold was immediate and fierce and Jake had to struggle not to panic at the feel of it pressing against his skin.

"What did you do *that* for?" Lenny yelled in his face, but sat up just in time to find out.

The truck hit a drift hard enough to make the front end rise, a lower corner of the blade scything through the snow. As Jake and Lenny watched, the truck showed a brief glimpse of its undercarriage before slamming back down, the plow blade twisting until it hung askew on the grille. The back end of the truck slid out, tugging the truck clear of the drift and sending it slipping backwards toward where the two men had stood watching mere moments before. Snow flew from both sides of the truck as it carved its way past where they sat gasping, spinning one last time on the frozen ground before it met the side of Mabel Brannigan's house and stopped with a bang that sent sparks racing up the wall.

"Jesus," Jake said, easing himself up. Steam from the melted snow and whatever damage had been done to the truck billowed from beneath its crumpled hood. Only one headlight worked now, its single eye blazing into the dark.

Lenny got up and brushed himself off, disbelief contorting his face. He looked about to say something, but instead dropped his gaze and studied the deep grooves the tires had left in the snow not three feet away.

Jake watched him for a moment, then shivered and started toward the truck.

"What are you doing?" Lenny called over the shriek of the wind.

"I want to check on Carl. See if he's okay."

"If he is, let me know. I want to give him what-for. Damn fool almost ran us down."

Jake reached the truck and resisted the urge to warm his hands over the heat flooding from beneath the warped hood. He was so cold now that all consideration for Lenny and his quest had frozen and shattered. He was going home, he decided, which was where he knew he belonged, ghosts of light and shadow be-damned. He would drink the memory of Julia's death and the ticking of that accursed deathwatch away, if only for a few hours, and if it led him to the box beneath the bed again, then so be it. Misery had been his lot for too long now and the ice on his bones only fed it.

Rubbing his hands together, he moved around to the driver side door and tugged on the handle. Something cracked but the door did not open. The glass was pebbled with ice and through it he could see the dim green glow of the instrument panel.

He looked back to where Lenny was still staring at the snow. "Lenny, I need your help. The door's stuck!"

Lenny looked up, but if he replied, his words were stolen by the wind.

"Lenny!"

No answer.

Great.

Jake turned back to the door.

And heard a dull thump as a horribly misshapen head flattened itself against the glass.

"Christ!" Jake jolted, his body immediately flushed with the welcome warmth of adrenaline as his hand clamped over his heart. The heat rapidly abated however, replaced by an inner cold that radiated outward.

The electric control for the window whined and slid down a crack, before stalling, ice grinding and snapping against the rim.

Jake composed himself and moved closer, his heart thumping so hard it almost hurt, his breath wheezing from his lungs.

Too much, he thought. *This is too much to handle. I need to get home.*

It had to be the frosting on the window that made the silhouette in the vehicle seem so out of proportion, for surely no one could survive with that much of their head missing. The green glow from the dashboard illuminated the slope of a bleached white cheek. Shuddering.

"Carl?" Jake called, pressing his hands to the glass and struggling to make out the man's features. "Carl, are you all right in there?"

The shadow bobbed, twitched, moved away from the glass, as if the man was stretching. Or in pain.

"Carl? Can you talk?"

The whisper that floated out from the cracked window made Jake move back a step as he frowned at the window and the flinching figure behind it.

"Yesssssss," it said.

Jake composed himself. He imagined Carl lying in there, bloodied and broken and in urgent need of attention. Now was not the time for fear no matter how unsettling the situation might be.

But God, it was so damn cold.

"Carl, can you move? Are you hurt?"

The figure jerked.

The reply: "They knowwwwww."

"What? I don't understand."

"Theyyyy knowwwwww."

"'They know' what?"

A gurgling sound that might have been a chuckle. Or a man choking on his own blood.

"Carl?"

Silence from inside the truck.

"Carl? Answer me. Can you open the door?"

No answer.

"Carl? Shit!" Jake slapped his palm against the window, knocking away more of the ice. He sighed a cloud of frustration and wiped a hand over his face. His touch was warm against the cold of his cheeks.

Inside the truck, tendrils of shadow rose.

Jake backed away. "Lenny?"

"Is he in one piece?"

Jake was relieved to hear his friend's voice because for just a moment a marrow-freezing panic had taken hold of him, filling him with certainty that when he turned around, Lenny would be gone.

"I don't know," he called back. "Maybe. I can't tell, but I can't get the door open either."

He turned to find Lenny shivering but moving toward him.

"Let's go find help," Jake said. "The door is stuck fast. The longer we spend trying to get him out ourselves, the more chance he stands of dying in there if he's hurt bad enough. Let's just keep going, make our way to the police station and get them to come back for him. It's too goddamn cold here anyway."

He couldn't keep the desperation from his voice and saw it reflected in Lenny's eyes, but no argument was proffered. The night was freezing fast and hard and they both knew they could die out here if the snow got so thick they lost their way.

They could send help. Assuming things didn't get so bad that they ended up being the ones in need of it.

A blast of wind-borne snow lashed into them, making Jake rock on his feet, the icy cold licking against his uncovered neck. "Shit!"

Lenny nodded, teeth clicking together as a shiver rippled through him. "Let's go."

* * *

They continued on into the storm, neither of them saying a word.

Jake had never seen the town so quiet, so deserted and he didn't like it. The absence of the streetlights made an alien landscape of Miriam's Cove, the hollow roar of the sea beyond Patterson's Point lost beneath the faint hissing as the snow fell in endless waves, white dunes heaping themselves high against the somber black buildings. The darkness weighed down upon them, a smothering thing.

They turned into what memory told them was Lewis Avenue, a narrow street which opened out onto Cove Central.

Jake could no longer feel his toes, and the cold was spreading. His coat felt like a sheet of plastic, the thickness of it rendered impotent by his fall in the snow.

When they entered Cove Central, it was as if they'd tripped a wire hidden in the snow. They stopped dead in their tracks, their eyes following the lamps around the thoroughfare as each one stuttered back on, flooding the area with harsh white light.

"That's something at least," Lenny said, nodding once in wearied satisfaction. "Maybe now we'll be able to see where we going."

"Yeah," Jake agreed. At the sight of the drifts piling high against the buildings and smothering the cars, he felt that knot of fear in his throat tighten. He had thought the snow hungry before, but now that he could fully appreciate the depth and the sheer *mass* of it, he amended that description. It was not hungry. It was *ravenous*. And no matter how implausible it was to think of snow as anything but innocent, to attribute such a natural thing with sentience, he knew there was something wrong with it. Something terrible *hiding* in it. And like bleeding swimmers in a shark-filled ocean, here the two of them stood, up to their shins in the stuff.

So let's engage this little madness for a moment shall we? a quieter, more reasonable voice in his head piped up, *and assume you're right. Why then, has it not already killed you?*

He didn't want to think about that. Couldn't, because aside from the fear and the inexplicable dread he was valiantly attempting to blame on the barbed wire coils of grief, he sensed something bigger at work here – something far more peculiar and unpleasant than unseen things in the snow. He felt *led.* Yes, that was it. He felt as if a hook had snagged in his soul and someone, some*thing* somewhere was slowly reeling him in.

The night had become a strange place, unfamiliar, unkind and filled with latent malice.

Carl Stewart was more than likely freezing to death, if not already dead from his injuries, lying there alone in the battered shell of his snowplow.

Joanne Quick was missing, or worse, a possibility that had to have settled itself on Lenny's shoulders, ageing him terribly as he struggled through the drifts to uncover a truth that might destroy his world.

The police station dominated the east end of the square, a narrow two story red brick building, unremarkable except for the cast iron black bars over the windows, making it look like it had been designed by an aged cowboy pining for the days of the old jails. Clumps of snow sat like sleeping cats in the gutters and atop the windowsills. Over the door, a brass sign marred by verdigris read: MIRIAM'S COVE SHERIFF'S DEPARTMENT.

Lenny paused at the foot of the wide stone steps leading up to the station. He frowned. Jake drew abreast of him and rested his hip against the low wall that bordered the steps, relieving some of the pressure from his aching joints but cementing the cold into his flesh.

Jake didn't have to ask why Lenny had stopped.

Even though the streetlights had come back on, the police station's windows were dark.

They stood together in silence for a moment, then Lenny sighed. "I can't figure it out. This is like a bad *Twilight Zone* episode or something. Looks like everybody's gone. Are we dreaming?"

Though he knew Lenny wasn't serious, but rather speaking from frustration and more than a little fear, a similar thought had occurred to Jake and, like Lenny, he had been unable to completely dismiss it as fancy. Dreams were not bound by natural law and wasn't that how things seemed in the town tonight? Jake wished it to be so, some inner part of him warmed by the idea of waking in his bed to find none of this had happened outside of his own feverish imaginings.

But the hope was weak.

The cold was real, too real to pin on a dream.

And let's face it buddy, even if it was a dream, the real world ain't so friggin' hot for you these days, is it?

"Maybe we should head back just in case Baxter's waiting at your house."

"Maybe," Jake said. "But I'm a little leery about following your suggestions after that last one about me getting out of the house." He grinned feebly and folded his arms. "Let's check out the station first. Maybe they'll at least have some still-warm coffee. If we can get in at all."

Lenny nodded and headed up the steps. Jake followed, wincing. He whispered a silent prayer that the door would be unlocked.

Just one break. Please. Just one.

Lenny slipped his fingers around the brass door handle, thumbed down the button and pulled. Ice crunched and tumbled from the crack in the doorjamb but the door did not move.

Jake sagged. "It's a goddamn night for locked doors, isn't it?"

Lenny didn't reply, but turned, a scowl on his face.

"Can you see inside?"

"What difference does it make?"

"Maybe they just locked the place up because of the storm?"

Lenny offered him a tired smile. "For a grieving man, you're sure quick with the sunshine."

"Call it desperation. I'm sick to death of this cold."

"Then maybe we should kick the doors down."

"Right, breaking and entering into a police station. That'll be one for the books. Assuming of course we had the strength in our legs to even try without crippling ourselves."

Lenny snorted and gestured out over the thoroughfare. "Doesn't look like there'd be many witnesses though, huh?"

"No. Guess not."

With a satisfied nod, Lenny turned back to the door. "Oh JESUS!"

Jake's scalp prickled and he took two paces back from the door, almost expecting it to explode outward with the same force that now held his heart in its hands. "What? What is it?"

Lenny was standing stock-still, arms by his sides, staring in through the rectangular glass panel on the left side of the door.

"Lenny?"

"I…I saw someone."

"Saw who?" Ignoring the fresh bursts of pain that coruscated across his knees at the suddenness of his movements and propelled by renewed hope, Jake rushed to join Lenny at the window. He almost screamed when he saw a white, hollow-eyed face leering back at him from the glass, but then it shrank and vanished only to reappear at the behest of Lenny's breath. Condensation, nothing more, but it had almost been enough to prompt those invisible hands into giving his heart a final squeeze. With a sigh, he squinted to see through the window.

Beyond the glass, the suffused light from the street allowed him a glimpse of a pale rectangular smudge which might have been the desk sergeant's computer. Like imitation moonlight, the silvery glow shining through the high windows sent fractured streaks across the tile-floor hallway. The hall ran toward the back of the building until darkness claimed it.

The station seemed as deserted as the rest of town, but in there, as out here, there were plenty of hiding places.

Lenny's tremulous breath rumbled in his ear.

Still scanning the hall, Jake asked: "What did you see?"

"A woman."

"Did you recognize her?"

"No."

"Well…why didn't you try and get her attention?"

He felt Lenny shrug. "The way she looked, I didn't *want* to get her attention."

"How did she look?"

"Dead," Lenny said simply. "Or damn close."

Lenny didn't answer, but his breathing had slowed. Jake guessed whatever had spooked him had already rationalized itself in his mind now that he'd said it aloud. But that still left the question of who *was* inside the station. Jake cupped his hands around his face, and tried one last time to see if he could detect movement from inside.

Lenny's breathing quickened almost immediately, thundering in

Jake's ear and heating the flesh there.

Inside the station, nothing moved.

"In all my years in this town I don't think I've ever seen the police station locked up, for any reason. So why now?"

No answer.

"It's bad but not bad enough to evacuate a building as solid as this one, don't you think?"

No answer.

We have to get home or we'll die out here, Jake thought as a wave of cold rushed up his back, making his teeth chatter.

"We better go back," he said.

Lenny's only response was his frightened breathing, now so loud that after a few moments Jake pushed away and rubbed a tickle from his ear. "Would y– " he began but stopped just as fast, one hand still clamped to the side of his head.

He noticed two things at once.

First, it was no longer snowing, but any joy he might have felt at that realization drained from him almost immediately.

Because Lenny was gone.

But he was just here! Right next to me. Breathing like a horse in my bloody ear!

His own breath shriveled before his face then, eyes widening as something dreadful occurred to him.

At least you think it was Lenny.

With a furtive glance around the town square from his vantage point atop the steps, Jake yelled Lenny's name, once, twice, then waited.

The town listened, but did not respond.

And after some inestimable time spent quivering and weeping uncontrollably, Jake did something he hadn't done in twelve years.

He ran.

* * *

Someone was whispering to him but he would not listen.

Instead he ran on, lurching forward in unsteady strides like a wounded deer, clutching his coat to his chest even though it was not open, as if doing so would keep his heart in his chest long enough for him to make it home.

Home. A million miles away now in this hostile frozen wasteland in which normality seemed to have been frozen too. Everywhere lay indistinct figures, smooth and glittering beneath their cold blankets, sometimes moving in the periphery of his vision, sometimes shuddering like yawning dogs, sometimes whispering to him in a language he did not understand, nor want to.

The cold rattled him as he lurched along, the snow accepting his booted feet, hampering his progress as he sank with each frantic step. The tears froze on his face, his lower lip quivering as he sobbed.

Home. All the demons he feared beyond the walls of his home, all the night things that whispered to him of his cowardice, all the sounds that made him feel crowded and yet hopelessly alone, that detestable ticking like tiny bones being tapped together, all of it he would suffer gladly now. Nothing could possibly be worse than this. Nothing, for it was not the snow and the things beneath it he feared anymore, but what they represented. Madness, pure and simple. Somewhere along the line – maybe when Julia died – his mind had split, crumbled, and betrayed him, sketching nightmares for him to have in his waking hours. Waiting until he was most vulnerable. Waiting until he was alone and cold and terrified. It was the simplest explanation and also the most horrible one.

And yet, the possibility offered hope.

For madness there was a cure.

For a reality turned nightmare, none.

He emerged from his own panicked thoughts to find he had reached Mabel Brannigan's house. Carl Stewart's truck was still there but Carl was not. A fresh skin of snow hugged the metal. The door of the pickup swung in the wind, the green glow from the dashboard oozing onto the empty seats. Beneath the door was a ragged hole, ringed with some kind of dark matter, and from the hole a two foot high mound of snow crossed the street in a zigzagging pattern.

Something had tunneled here.

The deposited snow ran like a barrier across the road but Jake crossed it in a hurry, and without incident, though the hair on his neck had stood on end as he drew one leg and then the other across it and hurried on, his breath warm around his face. Every inhalation felt as though he was drawing in sand and when he coughed, he thought his lungs would explode.

Then Lenny's house loomed, just as before.

With one difference.

The front door was open, granting him a view of nothing but absolute darkness within.

He considered venturing inside – at least he'd be out of the cold – but with all that had happened, he decided it was best to get home, to get safe. Then maybe, he'd come back, or call someone to…

Forget it. Keep moving. And he did, feeling as if someone had strapped still-burning coals around his knees.

There would be nothing to find in Lenny's house, he knew. Nothing he wished to find at least. Something was happening, whether instigated by his own bruised mind or not, he couldn't tell. People were vanishing, the town had changed and malevolent things lurked beneath the snow. Some tangle in his synapses had made Miriam's Cove a ghost town.

Alone.

He hurried on, ignoring the faintest suggestion of frenzied pale tendrils emerging from that oblong of dark that was Lenny's front door. If they were really there, then so be it, but nothing short of a broken neck would make him look in that direction. Not now, not when he was so close to home.

Fighting the white road, the all-consuming mold, the blanket beneath which the dead lay dreaming, a line from a poem he had read in his younger, healthier, *saner* days came whispering through the dark inside his head: "'*Fall, winter, fall; for he/Prompt hand and headpiece clever/Has woven a winter robe/And made of earth and sea/His overcoat for ever.*'" A.E. Housman, he recalled, mildly amused to find he had recited the stanza aloud. A poem he had read for students in his high school teaching days, days long gone, along with everything else, along with the history teacher he had met and fallen in love with there. Housman had known the deal, Jake knew, securing his suspicions of winter's wrath in the lines of a poem to escape ridicule and accusations of madness, accusations Jake couldn't hope to escape now that the projections of it had turned the whole world around him into a hollow white nightmare.

Keep going!

He did, hobbling, grimacing, hissing air through teeth cold as stone, squinting through eyes that saw as if through a film of ice.

And then, his street, silent as a tomb, buried in snow, twinkling in overwrought mimicry of something benign. His house, smoke ghost tearing itself from the chimney, light in the window. He stopped, fresh tears dripping down his cheeks, scarcely daring to believe it could be true. Light in the window. Warm amber light.

And in the driveway, Sheriff Baxter's police cruiser, gleaming. No sirens, no wailing. Quiet. Doors closed. No damage.

Jake nodded and cracked a smile from which inner heat seemed to flow. This was right. This was the way it was supposed to be. He knew what he would find in there. Warmth, safety, sanity, and Sheriff Baxter warming his hands by the fire, angry that Lenny and Jake hadn't waited for him. Joanne would be fine.

She tripped and hurt her ankle on the ice, Baxter would tell him. *Nothing critical. I sent Deputy Harlow to take her to the hospital. She's fine. Be out by morning. Now where the hell is her damn fool husband gone? Probably figured out that's where she'd be and walked over there.* Here Baxter would shake his head. *Bad idea for a man his age in this weather let me tell you.*

And Jake would smile, agree and offer the Sheriff a glass of something strong and the lawman would take it, because even lawmen were not impervious to this kind of cold. Then they would sit and wait in the warmth for word from Lenny.

Grinning now, Jake took a step toward his house.

And the lights went out.

No. Oh please...no!

In the snow around him something moved. No, not something. The snow *itself* was moving, slowly undulating like a sheet in the wind. Whispers, struggling to imitate the breeze but failing to sound even remotely natural, swept up from the rolling white, overlapping into a nonsensical chorus it hurt the mind to hear. Jake, despite his panic, remembered when he had heard it before, close to his ear and hidden in what he had mistakenly thought was Lenny's breathing.

Full insanity. Had to be. Such things simply did not, could not happen. There were laws that dictated it. And yet, all around him the snow erupted, tunnels tearing toward him, slick white tendrils bursting from the drifts and waving at him, opaque eyes unblinking in the darkness. The ground shuddered and his feet sank further, though this time it was not the snow that hugged his ankles. It was fingers, malleable slivers of ice that slid around the exposed skin there and held tight.

His bladder let go but he was only dimly aware of it, less aware when the urine froze halfway down.

The clouds of his breath caressed the facial features of things which had preferred to remain invisible as they circled him, but he could see them now. Grinning, their white eyes alight with fierce intelligence, with awareness...

They know, Carl Stewart had said, and it was clear now that they did. They knew everything. They knew he had tried to take his life in a drunken fit of suicidal hysteria. They knew the barrel had been in his mouth even after he'd called Lenny. They knew he had pulled the trigger and the gun had jammed.

But most of all, they knew about the cancer that had eaten his wife and the pillow that had stopped her breathing.

The churned up snow stopped mere inches from his feet as the tunnel digger ceased its labors.

They know...

Trembling turned to convulsing as if these things – whatever they were – had stripped him naked. The cold fed on him and he shrieked at it, at them, at everything that had brought him on this path, to this moment, to his certain death.

"Go away!" he screamed at them, his mind unable to cope with the sheer amount of movement that registered in his vision. Here, a hand only slightly smaller than Carl Stewart's truck, scarred and patterned with intricate loops and swirls, clutching at the sky with fish belly fingers, its wrist blue where it emerged from the snow. There, a dark figure, flinching as if beaten by unseen fists, its eyes elliptical slits stuffed with shards of glowing ice. To his left, a woman danced like a marionette with too few strings, her hair fashioned from the snow itself, clumps of it obscuring her face. She was naked, her body blue, breasts full, nipples black, legs studded with icicles that gleamed as she swung in the arms of an invisible partner. To his right, a glass scarecrow hissed and bowed in supplication. But not to Jake.

Whimpering, he watched as a hole formed at his feet, the snow pulled down by several pale hands scrabbling frantically.

"Please..."

But even as the words staggered over his trembling lips, he knew they would go unheard. They already knew all they needed to.

The hole widened. The hands vanished into the dark and then slowly, slowly, something started to emerge.

Jake pulled, desperately trying to tear himself free of the snow, but it was no use, the spikes of pain in his arthritic knees only served to remind him how old, how weak, how cold and how foolish he was. And how pointless it was to try and escape.

A face rose smiling from the hole, a gaunt weathered face with eyes like cold suns. The shock of recognition almost knocked Jake backward, a move that might have left him with two shattered ankles so tight was the grip of the snow hands.

"We knowwwwww," said Lenny, or the shell of what had once been his best friend. Jake fell to his knees and felt the resistance from the clutching snow, allowing him the fall but not his freedom.

Lenny still wore his coat, hands in pockets, hat askew on his head. If not for the eyes, the impression would have been flawless.

Jake lifted his head to look into the creature's face. "Why you?" he asked. "Why did they hurt you, Lenny?"

The Lenny-thing tilted its head. "We knowwwwww. And youuuu must knowwwwww tooooo."

Jake looked longingly towards his house. It was dark now, and unwelcoming, and he could hear the faintest of ticking sounds echoing from inside. The memory of Lenny's voice, spoken from fireside safety, spoken on the fringes of a nightmare, joined the deathwatch echo.

"You mentioned dying. I was wondering if you remembered the last time we talked about it. What you told me, I mean."

And now he did remember, more than he'd remembered before, as the cold shattered the walls of willing resistance.

He had called Lenny that night, had wept his sorrows into the phone. But that was not all. Amid the pleas and the desperation, there had also been a confession.

"Jake, calm down. I can't understand you."

"—her!"

"Talk into the phone. I can't—"

"I killed her, Lenny. I fucking killed her because I couldn't watch her dying in front of me and now I want to be with her. Help me!"

"Oh my God…"

Lenny knew. But being the loyal friend he had been forever, he had chosen to keep it a secret and that secret had killed him because these things, these creatures of guilt and punishment, had known too.

The thing in Lenny's clothes grinned, exposing a mouthful of icicle teeth.

Tick, tick, tick, the watch wound down, the same watch Julia had worn in her deathbed as she struggled feebly against the pillow, her hands trapped beside her face. The same watch he had used to count the seconds until her death, to count the beats of her heart.

Both had stopped running at the same time.

He swallowed and hugged himself. *This is how they mean to kill me,* he thought. *They'll keep me here, in the cold until it stops my heart.*

Silence.

Someone standing behind him reached a slim pale blue hand over his shoulder, grazing his cheek with its rough skin and clamping down hard enough to register pain over the numbing cold.

He turned shivering, teeth chattering so violently they must surely break. And his breath caught in his throat.

The woman standing there wore an ill-fitting expression of love that faded and changed to cold blue rage while he watched, stricken, paralyzed by utter, unbridled horror.

The hush deepened.

"I'm...s-s-sorry. I swear I am," he sobbed and sensed, rather than felt them all descend upon him as one hissing mass.

It began to snow.

* * *

Joanne Quick glanced at the clock above the fireplace and laced her fingers together to keep from drumming them on the arms of her rocking chair.

It was late, too late even for Lenny, who seemed to derive great pleasure from worrying her these days. First there was that night when the phone rang at some ungodly hour and Lenny returned to bed trembling after answering it, and now this.

Two o' clock in the morning and the snow was heavier now than before. The weather forecast predicted it would continue until well into noon before letting up.

Where are you, Lenny?

She glanced at the phone and thanked the Fates that she had called Sheriff Baxter before the lines had gone out. Baxter had agreed to call Jake Dodds' house and if Lenny were there, he'd go collect him, which sounded good to Joanne. She didn't want him walking even the relatively short distance from Jake's house in this weather. As the sheriff had said: *Bad idea for a man his age in this weather let me tell you.* Joanne couldn't have agreed more. She had nearly lost him to pneumonia once before and didn't want him fooling with his health again.

Restless, she rose and went into the kitchen, where her teacup stood alone on the table, a small brown teardrop resting on the rim.

She sat with a sigh, whispered a small prayer for Lenny's safe return and looked down at the clump of dark tealeaves gathered in the bottom of her cup.

She frowned at what she there, but a burst of wind against the front of the house startled her and she stood, a hand clutched to her chest.

Sounded like the devil himself trying to get in, she thought, waving the fright away with a fluttering hand. She moved into the hallway, almost expecting to see the front door had been blown open, but it hadn't.

She was about to turn away when movement through the beveled glass of the front door caught her attention. For a moment she stood, unmoving, uncertain. *Lenny?*

The front door rattled and a face loomed in the glass. She watched it bob, then quickly move away, and still she stayed frozen in place. A white face, too white to be anyone healthy. It had sent her senses, all six of them, into a frenzy.

After a few moments, her heartbeat slowed and she sighed. The face was gone, if that was what it had been at all. She supposed it could have been the snow.

Getting jumpy in my old age, she thought with a small smile and went back to reading her tealeaves. She passed her hand over the cup once, twice and again. And when she looked down the leaves had formed the crude figure of a man reaching toward the rim of the cup – a symbol she knew meant that she should expect a visitor, someone close. She smiled. Lenny would be home soon, the spirits had deemed it so. And they were never wrong. (Except about the lottery numbers, but she suspected there were rules about that kind of thing.)

And so she waited, listening to the wind settling in the rafters, the creak of the wood and the hush of the snow around the windows.

Sometime later, she dozed and dreamt of whispering snowmen

that obliterated into shrieking faces as she was abruptly dragged from her slumber by the ringing of the phone and a knock on the door.

AFTERWORD

Ravenous Ghosts was my first published book, and thus an important milestone in my writing career/adventure. It was for me an achievement, and one I had been dreaming of since I was a child. I had written a *book*, by golly, and not only that but someone had *paid* me real money for it (approximately $400, I believe, which was one half of the advance—I never received the other) and were now going to make it available for the world at large to read! Unfortunately, that last part didn't happen. To this day I don't know how many copies of the book the original publisher made available for sale before they went out of business, but it wasn't very many. As a result, over the years that slim little paperback increased in value on the secondary market in synch with my popularity. Once I bagged the Bram Stoker Award for *The Turtle Boy*, it was not uncommon to see copies of *Ravenous Ghosts* on eBay for a couple of hundred dollars, a staggering amount when you consider the original price tag was less than $20. A year or so after that, Delirium Books released a handsome hardcover limited edition of the book, but the limited part of that description means that even though the book was available again, only 150 or so people got to read it, and once those books ended up on eBay, their prices were no more palatable to the average reader like us than the first edition had been.

Almost a decade later, and digital publishing has made it much easier to put out-of-print books back in the hands of readers, where they belong. Almost all of my out-of-print titles are now out there again and finding a new audience as well as old readers who missed out on them when they first appeared.

And yet the emails keep coming in from folks who (like me), still do the majority of their reading via physical copies of books, asking if my out-of-print titles will ever again appear in print. And, because some of the books are not NY publisher friendly anymore (short story collections are particularly difficult to sell), I have taken it upon myself to rerelease them.

Which brings us to this, the third print incarnation of the collection that kickstarted it all. It's a rough and unwieldy beast, the style almost unrecognizable to me. My writing has changed considerably in the almost a decade since I wrote these stories. Back then, I was still trying to find my voice, still being heavily influenced by folks like Rod Serling, Stephen King, and Richard Matheson, and in a few of these stories, that's glaringly apparent, as is the lack of the necessary discipline I would only learn as time went on.

And yet, I'm still immensely proud of this book, and very much enjoyed rereading it. For me, it's a photo album, a memory box. Even though the twenty-something-year old who scratched out these stories still had a lot to learn (and this thirty-something-year old still does too), the passion for the craft is certainly visible in these tales. I even found myself creeped out by more than a few of them ("Familiar Faces", in particular, because I take a lot of road trips), and nodding along in appreciation of certain passages I would still employ today.

It is my sincere hope that you find yourself entertained and similarly creeped out by these stories. They're older, and dusty, and not without their flaws, but then, that pretty much describes the guy who wrote them. And like that guy, it's your support that keeps him alive. And for that, you have my thanks, as always.

— Kealan Patrick Burke
January 2013

ABOUT THE AUTHOR

Called "one of the most clever and original talents in contemporary horror" (BOOKLIST), Kealan Patrick Burke is the Bram Stoker Award-Winning author of five novels (MASTER OF THE MOORS, CURRENCY OF SOULS, THE LIVING, KIN, and NEMESIS), nine novellas (including the Timmy Quinn series), over a hundred short stories, and six collections. He edited the acclaimed anthologies: TAVERNS OF THE DEAD, QUIETLY NOW, BRIMSTONE TURNPIKE, and TALES FROM THE GOREZONE.

An Irish expatriate, he currently resides in Ohio. Visit him on the web at http://www.kealanpatrickburke.com or find him on Facebook at facebook.com/kealan.burke

Made in the USA
Las Vegas, NV
24 January 2021